# He Walked Among Us

PAUL FLEISCHMAN

He Walked Among Us

# He Walked Among Us

ISBN 9780786753901

Distributed by Argo Navis Author Services

# 1.

"The tide is out, the ocean's at peace. A deep turquoise, as flat as glass." Donna spoke in a lulling murmur. "You feel yourself shifting into a deeper relaxation."

Would more relaxation be a higher gear or a lower gear? Hugh's restless mind probed this point. From the CD player came the whisper of a wave retreating.

"Your feet burrow into the sand, like a child's."

He'd never liked sand between his toes. Fortunately, his pudgy body was stretched out on their bed, his wife sitting on his pajama-covered rump while her powerful palms steamrolled his back.

"A breeze passes gently over the sand." Instead of Donna's usual New Jersey-flavored bark, her voice sounded like an oracle's in a trance. "Then it riffles the leaves of the breadfruit trees."

Hugh's brows furrowed. Breadfruit trees? She's really getting into this.

"We hear a call, out over the water. We see birds."

Naturally, he thought. Lifetime Audubon Society member. Sierra Club. Taller than he was, big-boned, a hiker's long stride even when they'd walked down the aisle twenty-two years before. Should have seen problems coming right then.

"One of them dives. A greater crested tern."

Whatever. She was driving the fantasy. Probably needed the bird on her life list.

"They fly away. We're the only ones on the beach. It's quiet."

Quiet made Hugh nervous, having come from a highly flammable family, the youngest of five boys, each with his own cumulus of blond curls, all accustomed to shouting to be heard. His and Donna's teenaged daughters were both sleeping at friends' houses, leaving their Foggy Bottom townhouse strangely still. Donna moved up to his right shoulder.

"The only sound comes from the little waves."

More plot, Hugh thought.

"Just the waves."

The air-conditioning labored in the background. She kneaded him without speaking, his five o'clock shadow scraping against the sheet. Farther astern, Donna's kimono robe tickled his bare back. He looked over his shoulder at her. Below her black bangs, her eyes were closed. She'd come under her own spell. Not him. Then again, the White House's director of communications was supposed to have a hundred eyes like Argus and was paid to keep them open. Leaving his job at the office was as impossible as leaving his circulatory system behind. He'd failed to convince their marriage counselor of this. Her solution, self-authored, available for perusal in her office bathroom and for sale at her desk, was *Getting to Know You: Journeys for Couples*. It lay face down on the bed, open to Chapter Three, "Marriage in the Slow Lane." He wasn't sure how much more of the twenty-mile-an-hour life he could take.

He glanced at the clock. 11:08. While Donna's hands worked his lower back, he moved his head a millimeter at a time and brought the TV into focus over his right shoulder. He'd muted it when she'd entered with the book in one hand and the accompanying CD in the other; with her back to it and her mind in the ether, she seemed to have forgotten it was there. The screen showed a car ad. He searched blindly for the remote with his hand, threw his wife an appreciative moan, rejoiced at bumping into hard plastic with his fingers, and changed channels. A convenience store crime scene. His eyes felt the suction from the camera's sudden zoom onto bloodstains. He checked CNN. A commercial. He tried CBS. A bread line on P Street. An unwelcome sight for a president of either party, but more so for Hugh's Republican boss. He turned on captioning. An interview with a woman who'd stood in bread lines as a child in the thirties. A complaint from the young mother behind her that the bread being given out was stale. The male reporter opening a loaf and trying a bite. "[Chewing...]" Some difficulty swallowing. "Reporter: Maybe a little on the firm side." Great, thought Hugh. "[Crowd jeering.]" Cut, he instructed the cameraman. A man stepped into the scene. "Citizen: And what is it with all the pumpkin knickers?" Captioning wasn't acquainted with pumpernickel? "Why's the government sitting on tons of this [bleep]? I'll tell you why. 'Cause people hate it! That's why! I got caraway seeds coming [bleep] [bleep] [bleep]!" The man grabbed the reporter's loaf and threw it against the insignia of the Federal Emergency Rations Agency on the wall. "Reporter: Mixed reviews, I guess you'd say. Back to you, Tim and Tanya." Fear behind his fake smile. Hugh could almost hear the news van peeling out. "Tim: People speaking their mind. Democracy in action. Tanya: Great to see, isn't it?" Then a recipe on the screen for Pumpernickel Bread Pudding. "Tanya: Sounds pretty good." Hugh flinched. Only pretty good? C'mon, he fumed, sell it! "Tim: Just like my mother never made. "Tanya: Try it, you'll like it. Tim: You try it. [Chuckles.] Tanya: Oh, come on. Tim: Think I'll pass." Thanks for your support, asshole, thought Hugh.

"The sun is about to set," cooed Donna.

He checked NBC. Weather.

"The sand underneath you has the warmth and feel of another body."

He could see where this was going. Not the greatest timing. It was mid-July of the presidential election year of 2014. Speeches, ads, polls, the convention next month, fundraising, the ceaseless conveyor belt of bad news that he was somehow supposed to spin into gold. Election Erection Dysfunction. All his blood was tied up in his brain.

He zipped over to Fox, then ABC. Donna released her satin robe's tie.

"Slowly, the sun kisses the horizon."

Hugh felt her breasts touch down on his back. A wave broke, rushing toward him from all sides through the surround-sound speakers, bringing back his near-drowning in Lake Huron as a kid. Probably not the association their marriage counselor had in mind. He zigzagged between news channels to throw off the memory and braked at the sight of the president's wife. He was back with Tim and Tanya.

"...First Lady Bianca Shaw, searching the streets not for food, but clothing, at Bellezza, one of Washington's most exclusive purveyors of high fashion. Our own Kristy Cole was there."

Not right after the bread line story, thought Hugh.

Donna rested her cheek against his curls, then delivered a delicate kiss to his bald spot. "The sky begins reddening."

"Reporter: I sure was, Tanya."

Bianca was shown exiting onto the sidewalk, hemline high and neckline low, an auburn-haired James Bond femme fatale minus the foreign accent. Jewelry flashed from her neck and wrists like beacons.

Cut the bling, for Chrissakes! Don't you know there's a war on? And please, Hugh begged, no interview.

Donna intoned, "We feel ourselves catching fire from the sky. The heat begins rising through our bodies."

She bore down on his neck in a twisting motion, as if wringing it out. Hugh squinted, struggling to make out the captions.

"Reporter: I guess I'll ask what any woman would ask. Did you find anything?"

"First Lady: One thing, yes. A Carlo Fretti halter dress, silk, in topaz. And a bracelet to go with it."

"Reporter: Sounds like a success."

Please, prayed Hugh, don't ask what it cost.

"First Lady: I thought so."

"Reporter: How were the prices?"

Donna widened her legs, her knee lifting the pulled-back sheet, blocking Hugh's view of the First Lady's answer. His head instinctively popped up. His wife's eyes snapped open. She turned to see what he was looking at.

"Hugh!"

He unmuted the TV.

"...admit I was a little surprised. At first I thought maybe the prices were in lira."

"Turn that off!"

"I can't turn it off! It's my job to know this stuff!"

"How could you? I'm really trying! I'm making the effort! But you?"

He needed to hear the TV but sensed that shushing her might not be wise. He muted the set and thanked god for the captions' delay, sat up, and craned his neck around her, blind to the insult of choosing the news—and the local news, at that—over his wife's naked torso.

"First Lady: But we've had a good year. I don't think we'll have to pull Cassandra out of private school to pay for it."

"You bastard!" Tears streaming, Donna wrapped her robe around herself and fled the room. Hugh sat up and raised the volume.

"One last thing I'm sure everyone out there's wondering. Do your Secret Service agents go in the changing room with you?"

"No comment!" shouted Hugh.

"That would be a squeeze, since they're rather large." The First Lady gave a laugh.

Hugh's eyes protruded. "Holy—"

"But they do come in handy. Agent Boyce here has quite the touch with zippers."

Hugh stared at the African-American agent in the black suit beside her, the man struggling valiantly against smiling.

"I don't believe this!" A wave crashed on the CD. "Somebody shut this woman up!"

Donna, steely-eyed, reappeared in the doorway. "You got it."

She held one of Hugh's old bowling trophies by the gold figure's extended arm, wound up like the softball pitcher she'd been in high school, and let fly. The TV screen exploded. There was a gunshotlike pop, then the scent of combustion. She then picked up the fire extinguisher she'd brought, pulled the pin, and sent a hissing stream of powder at the machine she loathed, knocking over their trio of wedding photos on the dresser beside it as if at a shooting gallery.

She let up on the handle. Breathing heavily, she regarded her work. Glass glittered. White frost covered the TV, their last tube model. A hand clutching a bowling ball reaching surreally out of the realm within. Forehead slicked with sweat, her robe untied again, Donna glared at the machine she'd unknowingly married along with Hugh. She recalled the marriage counselor musing that bowling might be something that could bring them together.

She turned his way. "Any other requests?"

Fearfully, he shook his head no. The thought winged through his mind that a flat screen would save room on the dresser, then that it would be tax-deductible. She still held the extinguisher. Hugh felt like a roach staring at a can of Raid. His wife had once Maced a cat that had climbed the bird feeder. A wave came in, then receded.

"In the mood for a massage?" she said.

Hugh forced himself to nod.

"Good." She set the extinguisher on the dresser. "Me, too."

She let her robe fall, climbed up on the bed, and lay face down. "Make it a good one."

## 2

"She might as well have said 'Let 'em eat rayon'!"

Kayla, the First Lady's deputy chief of staff, backed up to avoid the spittle and poppy seeds flying out of Hugh's mouth.

"There's God knows how many millions of people out of work and she tells the country they've had a good year?"

Walking over from the East Wing, Kayla had known it would be bad. She'd never cared for Hugh's excitability or squishy body type. She lowered her eyes contritely. "I know."

"'I know' isn't good enough!"

"I know."

Hugh's eyes rolled in his head. Bianca's chief of staff was on vacation in Paris and the woman before him had no business filling in. She was too young for the job, thin as a slat, with a similarly starved resume, another of the First Lady's buddies from California who'd stepped out of the presidential moving van. He was fifty, going gray over his ears, and felt like her father. His eyes settled on the scaled tail of a tattoo emerging from under her sundress's neckline. Something was very wrong with this picture.

"I'm sorry," she said. She sat down. "Really sorry."

"Great, but that's not gonna help. Have you seen the news?" He peered past the curving swoosh of red hair into her tiny features, afraid to hear the answer to his question. "The garment workers are up in arms cause she buys foreign. The Police Officers Association is pissed for her slandering security providers and has just disendorsed us—a first. Pretty soon the only endorsement we'll have is the guys who club the seals for fur coats." Hugh's elbows were on his desk, his fingers raking his hair. "I'm telling you, Kayla, you gotta shorten her leash!"

It was only ten but his shirt was already dank with sweat, the West Wing's air-conditioning overmatched by the heat. He grabbed a remote, fired at his floor fan, saw one of his two TV screens go black, swore, fished out a different remote from his basket, and turned the fan up two notches.

"It's not easy," Kayla said. "You know what she's like."

"You're right, I do! She's like a bull who's goring us in the middle of an election! And if she does it again, she's gonna send us all home to the pathetic places we came from." Pasadena School of Cosmetology in Kayla's case, if he remembered correctly.

"OK, I hear you."

"And she's gotta hear you! Talk to her! Go over what reporters might ask. What she's gonna say. What she's not gonna say. What she's not gonna touch with a barge pole!"

Hugh reached his arms over his head, cracked his knuckles, still buzzed with undischarged tension, and paced the passage between desk and door. He stopped.

"Like the dressing room question! Jesus Christ! 'He's great with zippers'? And the man is Black! Did we need to rile up the South and reach out to adulterers, all with one line?"

"She's always been her own—"

"And that's gotta stop, too! She needs to get with the program!" He plopped back in his chair. "She could do us a favor and start shopping at Goodwill. And lose the plucked eyebrows and long fingernails. The country's hurting! People need Eleanor Roosevelt, not Cruella deVil."

"Who's that?"

"Never mind. What's she got scheduled today?"

Kayla's long nails clicked against her BlackBerry's keys.

"Pedicure. Family photo shoot. Then a magazine interview—"

"What magazine?"

"*Complexion Today.*"

"Cancel it! Wrong image."

"But she was—"

"I know she used to be a model! And we used to be in power if this keeps up! We need more than the former-model vote. Talk to Randy. I want her in women's shelters and soup kitchens. Got it?"

Kayla nodded and began thumb-typing.

"Hard labor!" Hugh glanced up at one of his TVs showing a drought-withered cornfield. "Gleaning for food banks. Dirt under her nails."

Kayla winced at the thought, typed "bring gloves," then highlighted the words.

"Job retraining," Hugh went on. "Hospitals. But strictly pediatric wards! No cheering up naked men! And no off-the-cuff questions! We're nine points down in Gallup, ten in Rasmussen." His eye was snagged by the crawl on one of his TVs. "And look at that—thirteen points down in Reuters! We've got all we can handle and she's stabbing us in the back. And then there's the daughter."

Kayla inhaled deeply at the mention. "I know." She checked her watch. "I'll get on it. Need to run."

"Hard labor!" Hugh called out after her. He closed his eyes, feeling his heart pounding and his bald spot expanding. He stood by his window, cooling himself with the sight of the shade under a tree on the White House lawn. It all should have been so easy. The Democrats and Republicans had traded stints on the throne, but the economy had taken no notice and had always kept growing. There'd been the blip in '08, but it had passed in a year, a moment of indigestion. With the past three presidents in their sixties, the Republicans had tapped Scott Shaw in 2010, a 38-year-old one-term governor from California, and had coasted in on a chorus of "Happy Days Are Here Again." And then they weren't. The economy had come down on the country like a circus tent, a second coming of the Great Depression that no one had seen coming, complete with hoboes and apple-sellers and middle-class families picking through landfills. The reelection that should have been a given had become a gauntlet. Not because of the Democrats, who'd long before borrowed the Republicans' allegiance to Big Business and given up defending the downtrodden, but by third-party candidate Joe Fiore, the Detroit congressman and former autoworker who was leading the race, the first nonmillionaire to grace the ticket in decades. With the two major parties seen as hopelessly insulated—the fois-gras-for-votes scandal that had enveloped the Democrats had been miserably timed—the country had embraced Fiore and his Your Party with a desperate, near-religious zeal.

Hugh watched two Secret Service agents cross the lawn, then realized that the tree he'd been staring at was a maple. That spring, metal taps for draining sap had begun appearing in maples on a few hardscrabble streets north of the Capitol, then in Langston Golf Course, then in the suburbs. People were hungry. Gangs had moved in, turf battles had become deadly, mobile sap boiling operations were still being uncovered in Rock Creek Park. What was the world coming to? And why couldn't the Shaw administration stop the slide?

The president entered Hugh's view, sauntering toward the tree. Hugh narrowed his eyes in study, trying to find the man's one-time appeal to the country. He was tall, seemingly a requirement for the job judging by the long string of six-footers before him. Was it all really biology, not politics, the nation looking for a male of the species who could father many children and protect them? Hugh watched Shaw lean a hand against the maple. He was still blond, without recourse to dye. Blondness was practically part of Shaw's platform, a wordless declaration of youth, vigor, optimism. What was left of the Beach Boys had performed at his inauguration, despite temperatures more conducive to hockey than surfing, followed by a blond female poet his staff had selected via Google Image Search. Shaw's hair was still full, parted on the left but with its disobedient lilt still in place, a child too endearing to discipline. His Blondness, His Blandness, say what people would, letting Shaw's hair crest his ears gave him a boyish appeal that had repeatedly raised his approval rating two to four points. His locks were now at their maximum allowable length.

Chuck Thorne strode across the lawn, mouth to his phone, the long-jawed strategist who'd guided Shaw to the White House. It hadn't taken much. Shaw was handsome, a quarterback at UCLA, his political campaigns funded by his family's banking fortune. He'd learned his lines well, first from his imperious stage-mother of a father during his run to the governorship, then from Thorne, a Reagan vet who'd been made White House chief of staff after the victory. Pinocchio wanted to be a real boy and Shaw showed occasional hints of the same. The Sacramento staff he'd fought to bring with him knew nothing of Washington. Thorne had brought in Hugh when Shaw's first communications director had flamed out. There'd been a lot of that the first year.

A photographer approached, burdened with bags like a tourist, trailed by the First Lady, assorted aides, and Cassandra, First Daughter. Hugh scanned his four-way split-screen TV, felt ready for a break from the snarling faces hurling words at him, and headed outside.

"Morning," Thorne greeted him, gravel-voiced, from behind aviator glasses. He was a head taller than Hugh, an ex-Marine with a silver crew cut, his spine still straight as a flag-staff. Though they'd worked together off and on for twenty years, standing beside him Hugh always felt returned to the short wise-cracking editor of the school paper he'd been in high school, called over by a coach.

"Another nice day," said Thorne.

Hugh snorted. "Nice? It's the thirty-eighth day in a row over ninety. Maybe, just maybe, we oughta rethink our climate stand."

"C'mon. Toughen up. Summer's supposed to be hot."

"Not like this." Hugh wondered if all the hot air his staff had pumped into the atmosphere was partly to blame. He mopped his round face with a handkerchief. "Another fifty years and it'll be like the surface of Venus."

"All people want to know is they can drive all they want. So that's what we tell 'em." Thorne, a true believer, was still in his coat. Hugh had rolled up his sleeves.

"And the customer's always right? Even if it's five hundred degrees?"

"Our policy is one hundred percent customer satisfaction."

Hugh felt no bump in his spirits from the bucking-up shoulder pat he received. "I'm not sure how many more times I can say 'inconclusive.' "

"Try 'not incontrovertible.' "

Hugh sighed. "I'll do that."

Aides blotted sweat from the First Family's faces. The bustling photographer, long-limbed as his tripod, labored to herd his subjects into view. Hugh swigged from the water bottle he'd brought, enjoying not feeling in charge.

"If President and Mrs. Shaw would move a little closer together."

The president was in khakis and a sport shirt, his Everyman out-fit. His sleeves were rolled back, suggesting imminent action: fixing a leaky faucet, solving the Palestinian question...Bianca stood beside him, shorn of jewelry except earrings, stone-faced in a simple belted white dress. Somebody clearly had talked to her, thought Hugh. He marveled again at her lack of common sense, then at her husband's performance on *Meet the Press* the week before, taking three tries to push his tongue up the hill of "Herzegovina." He reminded himself: no more working for political outsiders, especially young governors from western states. Too much assembly required.

"And now Cassandra, if you'd sit between them."

An aide had placed an ornate wrought-iron chair in front of the First Couple. Cassandra sat down, a sulky, zaftig sixteen-year-old whose dyed black hair, black eye makeup, black fingernails, and black dress gave a stronger scent of the Addams family than the Adams family.

"I was kind of getting used to the blue hair," whispered Hugh. "And the lip ring's gone. Things are looking up."

"Infection," said Thorne.

There was a god, thought Hugh. Now if only she'd lose the Goth look and twenty pounds before the mandatory family scene at the convention.

Peering through his viewfinder, the photographer noticed her left hand's third finger discreetly extended.

"Let's try your hands folded in your lap, please, Cassandra."

She sighed heavily and complied.

"Now for the smiles."

"If you'd give me something to smile about," she muttered.

"Try to be appropriate," snapped the First Lady.

"Try not to be related to me by blood."

The photographer backed away from his camera. Hugh closed his eyes. Not much of a poster for the Family First Initiative they'd been touting. He thought of the struggling family in South Dakota who'd won the Powerball the week before, nationally acclaimed until the drug use, mail theft, carjacking conviction, and videotaped incest came to light. First Families were just as risky. Somehow these people had entered the country's living room. Would they sit demurely or throw up on the coffee table? It was a reality show he could barely bear to watch.

"With your weight," said Bianca, "I doubt people will guess we're related, actually."

"That's okay, cause with your brains, I doubt people will guess you're human."

The president grasped his daughter's shoulder. "That's enough!"

She twisted out of his grip.

"You want me to smile? Then get government off of people's backs." She rubbed her shoulder where her father's hand had been. "That would make me smile, big time."

Thorne turned toward Hugh. "See her blog this morning?"

Hugh hadn't.

"Take a look."

He tried to enjoy the few minutes of blissful ignorance before he read it. "If we can just make it to November without her getting busted or pregnant."

"Melinda gave her a batch of that new Dutch contraceptive."

Hugh's eyebrows lifted. "The one we're opposed to? That we've tied up for years?"

"Sometimes you can't wait for the FDA."

The photographer returned his eye to his viewfinder. Out of her parents' sight, both Cassandra's middle fingers were now extended. The gesture brought a thin smile to her face. The photographer smiled as well. He'd take advantage and crop the photo at her forearms.

"Excellent," he said.

Thorne's phone rang. He turned his back to the others. "Yeah, Jim." A pause. "McGillick?"

Hugh saw Thorne's closely shaven cheeks quiver once. "Jesus Christ." Another pause. "Thanks for the good news."

## 3.

Thorne stared at the Remington painting of a buffalo hunt, the herd flowing before the mounted braves. He'd wanted to be an Indian when he was a kid in Kansas. He wished now he'd pursued that line of work and fantasized climbing over the gilt frame into the scene, vanishing from the West Wing conference he'd convened. Then a reggae ringtone erupted from a cellphone, yanking him into the current millennium. He turned.

"So here's the deal," he said. "Jim McGillick's turned up."

He stared at blank faces. Cora Zucker, of Zucker, Cardozo, Dalrymple, and Girard, media consultants for Yemen, the Soy Milk Producers Coalition, Boeing, and the Shaw campaign, reached for her water and wished it were whiskey, fearing whatever was about to come. She was sixty-six, beaky and lean, with a jarringly dyed persimmon bob and a desk sergeant's seen-it-all face, well-earned. She'd bounced back and forth between the West Wing and K Street and had been press secretary during Snowgate, the CIA-rigged avalanche in Peru that had buried a town of 8,000 but spared Hugo Chavez. That era seemed golden compared to the present. "So who's Jim McGillick?"

"The president's body double on a couple of Middle East trips," explained Thorne. "Then he had some drinking problems. Got booted out and dropped out of sight. Until now."

"And?" asked Hugh.

"Someone at Secret Service got a call this morning from one of the *New Yorker*'s fact checkers. McGillick's written a book and they're running an excerpt. And the excerpt's about Holly."

Thorne's audience of five again looked baffled. Barry Schraftstein, the hefty, megaphone-voiced campaign manager, saw Monica Lewinsky highlights on his retina. He'd always known there'd be payback for Linda Tripp.

"What don't I know?" he demanded. "Holly who?"

"The *hurricane*," snapped Thorne.

Jess, Cora's fresh-faced girl wonder and now partner, looked out from between matching veneers of light brown hair. "Sorry," she said. "I guess I don't—"

"Three years ago. When the president was on Marine One inspecting damage, it was really McGillick."

Hugh's jaw fell. "You're kidding."

"I wish the hell I were." Thorne looked enviously at the buffalo hunt.

"Why?" asked Cora. "How come he didn't go?"

And how come I didn't know? thought Hugh.

Thorne gathered strength, avoiding the others' eyes. "You know the drill. Flyover. Concerned facial expression. Talking to victims. Shaking dirty hands. Bad coffee at the high school gym." He sighed. "He'd just done the same gig in Colorado—wildfires. And two weeks before that, the earthquake in Alaska." He was among friends but out of habit labored to put the best face on the matter. "He was lobbying for the Defense of Hunting Act, he had the speech at the U.N. to get ready for, and that big Asian trip around the corner."

"And probably tickets to a Redskins game," Cora sniped.

"Probably right," said Barry. "That was the year they went—"

"The point is," Thorne interrupted, "he had other commitments. So he decided to take a pass." He swirled the ice cubes in his glass.

"Too many concerned expressions can give you wrinkles," said Cora.

"We issued the usual statements of heartfelt commiseration. Promises to help. All of that."

Disgusted, Hugh remembered working on them.

"But you can bet the relatives of the thirty-eight people who died, and every flooded-out homeowner in seven states, and everyone else in the country," continued Thorne, "is gonna howl that Shaw doesn't care about his people."

Trevor Hirakawa, chief of speechwriting, adjusted his gold wire-rims. A debater at Harvard and Oxford fifteen years before, with a whiff of Masterpiece Theatre in his delivery, he began sketching the opposition's attack. "Dishonest. Aloof. Neglecting his subjects."

"Actually, Trev, we call 'em 'citizens' here," said Barry. He held his own meaty head as if about to twist it off. Cora wished he weren't wearing one of the new shirts made popular by the rise in temperatures, sheer nearly to the point of see-through. She pried her eyes off his breasts, larger than her own.

"The father of the fucking country," he moaned, "a deadbeat dad. I'm supposed to sell that?"

"We could let his hair grow out another half-inch. Pass it off as a boyish prank."

"Any more hair and he looks like a drug-dealer," said Jess. "We focus-grouped it in thirteen states last week."

"I can see the cover of Newsweek now. 'Hocus POTUS.'"

"AWOL in our hour of need."

"So much for Kindhearted Conservatism."

"So much for the whole campaign!" boomed Barry.

Cora rewound her memory. "Weren't some of the victims children?"

"Twin girls. Six years old."

"I believe," recalled Trevor, "that I had him say he'd spotted their house."

There was a general pause, the bad news spreading like a bloodstain.

"Maybe McGillick's bluffing."

"He might just want a payoff."

"He's got it," said Thorne. "Nine hundred and eighty thousand from HarperCollins."

Barry reached instinctively for the cigarettes in his shirt pocket, then remembered where he was and what century he was in. "Block publication! Claim national security!"

"We'll try that, naturally. Not sure it'll work." Thorne ran his hand in electric trimmer fashion over his gray crew cut. "It's not a state secret that we use doubles."

"A week after the Afghanistan trip it was all over the Internet."

Cora thought back. "Remember, maybe twenty years ago? There was a double who did a *Rolling Stone* interview. Secret Service did some cutting but it still came out."

"The book's scheduled for October. Three weeks before the election."

"It's like being on the Titanic and seeing the iceberg."

Hugh looked at Trevor. "There goes all the work we did trying to give him a Lincolnesque feel. A brooding side. Can't put the country's pain out of his head." He thought of the 'Day in the Life' piece on Fox. The president opening his mail, answering a letter by hand like Lincoln replying to a Civil War widow. Staring out from the Truman Balcony, lost in thought and distress. The mention of bad dreams. Bianca's much-rehearsed lines expressing worry about him.

"A logistical problem? Scheduling foul-up?" Trevor bounced his fountain pen off his Brylcreemed black dome, then vetoed his own thought. "Too weak. And doesn't comport with the gravitas we've been trying to project."

"It's hopeless!" declared Barry. "The man's kaput!"

Thorne had done two tours in Vietnam and refused to give up the fight so quickly. Reagan had survived Oliver North. He'd seen it. It was his job to pull off the same for Scott Shaw. His mouth contorted while he thought.

"We'll claim McGillick's memory's shot from booze," he announced. "Brain like Swiss cheese." He turned toward Hugh. "We'll use an x-ray if we have to, from a medical textbook, to show what can happen. I'll get Patrick on it."

Hugh's blue eyes darted nervously. The bad feeling he was getting didn't come from the crab cakes he'd had for lunch in the White House Mess. "Just be really sure it's a human brain and not a chimpanzee's, or something else's. Cause you know somebody's going to check, and if Gil stands up at a press conference—"

"Chimps don't drink," said Barry.

Hugh felt his brain cramping. "Who cares! The point is we'll lose all credibility if—"

"What credibility?"

Thorne ignored them. "Maybe there's something more we can dig up on McGillick." He stood, thinking aloud while he circled the room, trying to fill all the holes in the dike. "For now, we'll use 'admitted alcoholic.' He did a stint in rehab. Maybe more than one."

"'Well-known imbiber,' " said Trevor experimentally.

"And 'raconteur,'" added Cora. "With a name like McGillick he's probably Irish."

"Good. He made it all up to get a publishing contract."

A blend of Scotland and Ireland himself, and a storyteller by profession, Hugh tried not to take offense.

Jess asked about the pilot.

"Died last year," said Thorne. "But the co-pilot's still around. Patrick's working on it."

"Maybe he'd like his own Lear jet?"

"Or let him fly Air Force One around the block."

"Memory implants?"

Thorne raised his arms for silence. "Okay! Okay! We can deal with it! That's not really why we're here, believe it or not."

Cora's eyes widened.

"There's more?" wailed Barry.

"McGillick's just part of a bigger problem we can't seem to deal with—the compassion problem." Thorne halted in front of a portrait of Jefferson, the presidential face filled with far-sighted wisdom. "And believe me, character's huge when there's a depression going on."

"Just ask Herbert Hoover."

"And Herbert Hoover's what we're looking like," Thorne went on. "Dancing at the country club with a bunch of tax-dodging CEOs while the country goes down the drain."

"And now, too damn lazy to glance out a helicopter window."

"Much less lift an actual sandbag."

Barry loosened the tie from around his thick neck. "And in the other corner you've got Fiore, missing that goddamn fingertip from working at Chrysler and with his big Italian family around him. God, they love him. And not just Italians and immigrants."

Jess opened a folder, dug down four pages, and scanned the latest numbers from Klaus Krober, the campaign's private pollster. "Hispanics, eighty-four percent. Grandparents, sixty-eight percent. Mothers, all ages, all income, sixty-five percent. We've got the Family First Initiative. He's got an actual family."

"With a plus-size wife who wears an apron and actually cooks."

"Frumpy's good," Barry said. "Women are tired of competing and losing."

"Then the First Lady's a lose-lose for us. Her looks and her lines."

"Somebody threw a brick through that dress shop window this morning."

Hugh thought back to Bianca's tax returns, released under duress, which had included $288,500 in clothing expenditures on Schedule A under "uniforms."

"Speaking of family," said Thorne, "Cassandra's come out for the Free Party in her blog. Government off our backs, that sort of thing."

"That's our platform."

"Was," pronounced Trevor wistfully. Due to Depression 2.0, as it was being called, the nation was begging government to get on their backs.

"She also," Thorne said, "claims Bianca's bulimic."

"Jesus Christ."

"Is our tent big enough for bulimics?"

"And does it have a toilet?"

"Frumpy's good," said Cora. "Dysfunctional isn't."

Silence.

"So what do we do?" Thorne scanned the room. "We're entering free-fall. We need something big and we need it now. Something way outside the box. Anything less won't be enough."

His eyes settled on Cora, petite but with an air of command. She stared back at him, stumped. There was no noise but the whirring of the floor fans.

Hugh cogitated, tongue hunting any remains from lunch. Then his head lifted. "A disease."

"Too far outside the box."

"We're desperate, remember? The country rallies round. Look at FDR. Polio, crutches, a wheelchair, four terms."

"C'mon."

Trevor tapped his pen against his head, sending a fact from his memory to his tongue. "Actually, the Reagan assassination attempt kept his numbers up for several years."

"Please don't let's go there."

"Did phlebitis help Nixon?"

"Too rare. People couldn't relate. Pain but no gain."

"Anemia," tossed out Barry. "You'd get women, plus Blacks, with the sickle cell thing, plus senior citizens—"

"Why not give the disease to Cassandra. Something serious. Kill two birds."

"C'mon, get serious," snapped Thorne.

Jess waited for the chatter to subside, then filled the vacuum. "If the problem's that the president comes off rich and removed, then the answer should be to reverse that image."

"Poor and engaged?"

"He gives away his possessions. Goes from Episcopalian to Buddhist."

Hugh turned toward Trevor, whose family had traveled in the other direction. "You could give him some tips."

"He doesn't do chopsticks. Remember the restaurant in New Hampshire?"

"You know what I mean," said Jess. "We have to show that he's one with the little guys. But we can't just say it. People know words lie."

"Thanks to us."

She kept following the thought. "But they will believe deeds. He needs to do something. Get down on their level, walk in their shoes. He needs to show that he's genuinely concerned."

"Great, but how?"

"If he was concerned, he'd be gray by now."

"He's gotta dye that hair! I'm telling you, it's a problem."

"Grecian Formula in reverse. A little grayer every day."

Politics was impossible, thought Cora. They pick a candidate for his youthful looks, and now he's under siege for not turning gray.

Jess turned toward Trevor and his background in European history. "Didn't Peter the Great travel incognito some place?"

He thought. "He did, yes. Through western Europe. To see the latest technological advancements. A fact-finding tour."

Jess consulted her calendar. "And the president's got a vacation coming up"

"A week in Malibu," Thorne confirmed. "Then a week of campaigning. He leaves August fourth."

Jess's green eyes darted. "What if..." There was a rabbitlike alertness to her. "What if he doesn't go?"

"Why not?" asked Thorne.

"Because he's deeply disturbed over the shape the country's in."

Hugh studied her—white blouse, perfect hair, tan skin—the kind of cute girl he'd never been able to attract in college.

"He's trapped inside the Beltway. He gets briefed, he sees the news, but that's not enough. He's dissatisfied with second-hand and third-hand reports... And so, against the counsel of his campaign manager—"

"I got a feeling you're right," said Barry.

"—and boldly defying the Secret Service, he cancels his vacation. Puts campaigning aside. And he crosses the country on his own fact-finding tour. Not in Air Force One, but riding Greyhound."

The rest of the group inhaled in unison.

"I'd go with polio," said Barry.

Jess waved her hand like a fourth grader with the answer. "Or better— he doesn't just look at the country, like a tourist. He works. Picking crops here, washing dishes there. Trying to find work. Actually living the lives of his people. And the only way he can pull that off and get at the truth he's determined to get at—is to go incognito. It's proof that he cares."

Cora attempted to digest the notion. She'd elevated Jess to partner for her energy and outside-the-box ideas, but a lot of them had to be discarded. This one was outside Earth's orbit.

"Wow," said Hugh. "I don't know. I mean I do know. It's wacko."

"There was a senator in Florida," said Trevor. "Bob Graham. He did something similar. I believe he called them 'workdays.' But he didn't go incognito."

"So why the disguise?" asked Thorne.

Jess held her cold glass against her cheek. "If he goes as himself, it'll look like a stunt, that's why. Pure PR."

"You think?"

She rolled her eyes and drank. "When you see a magician make an elephant disappear in Vegas, do you think just maybe the stage has been specially prepared?" She looked around the table. "People aren't dumb. They know a photo op when they see it. And believe me, Shaw sitting around the break room with a bunch of smiling workers, half of whom look like plants and the other half Secret Service—that's just not going to get us where we need to go. We need something stronger. Way stronger."

"Speaking of Secret Service—"

"And that's the beauty of this. You wouldn't need 'em."

"Are you crazy?"

"People want to kill the *president*," said Jess. "But if nobody knows he's the president, where's the risk? If you go the Bob Graham route, that's when you've got a Secret Service nightmare."

Barry stretched, the white wave of his belly washing over the table, then receding. "Could be too much identification with the commoners. The corporations wouldn't like it."

"It's not like he'd be passing out The Communist Manifesto," said Jess, sticking to her guns. "Our core message is still the country's institutions are sound. We'd just be tipping our hat to the little guy for two weeks. A course of antibiotics."

Hugh found the cure worse than the disease. Beyond that, he resented a newcomer to the inner circle grabbing the limelight. He looked at Thorne. "I was joking about diseases. But this is even weirder."

"Something like footwashing," said Cora, letting it percolate through her brain. "Identifying with the lowly. A spiritual quest."

"The churches would like it."

"Actually, the churches aren't so into the lowly," Hugh said.

"Widened the eye of the needle so they could drive their SUVs through."

"But it couldn't hurt," said Jess.

Trevor tapped his pen against his pad. "We might be able to use it to explain the hurricane incident." All faces turned his way. "The president wasn't on the helicopter because he was actually on the ground. Among his people."

"In disguise, so he could find out the truth," said Jess.

"Which the Secret Service kept hidden at the time."

"He does this a lot?" Hugh's voice was disbelieving.

"Frankly," said Barry, "I'd be a lot happier with that than the chimp-brain defense."

Thorne exhaled. He looked unconvinced.

"So fast-forward," said Jess. "Everyone thinks he's out by the pool in Malibu. But then he arrives—sweat-stained, humbled, enlightened. And we let the cat out of the bag at a live news conference in front of the whole country. It's the ultimate in reality TV."

"Walk and Awe."

"Write that down."

"Hold on," said Barry. "Why only film the end? Why not film the whole thing? Secret cameras catching him cleaning bathrooms, using an anvil—"

"An anvil?" asked Hugh.

"Then waiting for the bus at some windswept crossroads."

"A train in the distance, Johnny Cash on the soundtrack."

"I'd go with Aaron Copland."

"B. B. King."

"Then we edit it down," said Jess, "and show it at the convention. The whole country sees it on TV."

"Finally, a convention they'll watch."

"He could also keep a diary."

"Or we could keep it for him."

"Which we publish as a book—"

"*Poor White Like Me,*" Hugh suggested.

"*This Land is My Land.*"

"Arlo Guthrie might sue."

Jess's fingers skittered over her tablet's keyboard, then stopped. "*He Walked Among Us.*"

The president's chief of staff turned toward Cora, his ad-maker and message-massager on three decades of campaigns, most of them successes. "What do you think?"

"I think you asked for something outside the box and you got it." She looked back into Thorne's baggy eyes. "Hard to believe it's come to this, but maybe it has. We'd need to refine it. But it's worth a look."

The room fell silent.

"If it goes haywire, we're cooked," warned Hugh.

"True," said Thorne. "But we're already cooked."

"We'd have to get it past Secret Service," Cora said.

Thorne nodded. "And then there's the president."

# 4.

Birds rose at the crack, wingtips clicking. Mist lay in the hollows. It was shortly past sunrise.

"Nice," said Cora, admiring the president's drive. She wasn't a golfer and was awed by the distance the ball traveled. Her bare forearms bristled in the chill, a sensation pleasant and rare. Shaw teed up a second ball, this one orange, and produced another gunshotlike report. With the trees looming in the haze, they might have been explorers in the forest primeval but for the electric cart they stepped into, the Secret Service agents walking and riding behind them, and the impeccably mown fairways of Holly Hills Country Club.

"This is the place to be," said the president. "No congressional task force. No blue ribbon committee. No admirals. No press. Nobody."

He drove the cart, the only vehicle he was permitted to drive, steering as well around the topic of the two venture capitalists who'd planned to play with him for a fat campaign donation but who'd backed out. Cora would take advantage of their being alone.

"Paradise," she agreed with him. The goal was to put the president in the most receptive frame of mind possible. Shaw had slept well, as he always reported doing at Camp David. The First Lady and Cassandra had stayed behind in the White House, an uncoupling that always improved his mood. The Threat Assessment report had been practically salubrious. He was free of most of his gnat-cloud of a staff, engaged in a sport he loved, and since he was playing against himself, couldn't lose.

"Gotta remind myself not to overpronate my wrists," he said. He was a natural athlete, a two handicapper who was seen often on the White House putting green—too often for Cora's liking. The press seemed to run more photos of him sinking a put than signing a bill. His low handicap, like his lack of gray hair, was becoming a problem. A president should know less about wrist pronation.

They motored ahead to Shaw's shorter ball. He drew a six-iron from the bag with the presidential seal, sent the ball toward the fleck of a flag in the distance, and dropped it on the green with the ease of a piano teacher lowering a finger onto middle C. He did the same with his other ball, then sank both his birdie putts. They moved to the next tee.

"I'm glad I'm not playing against you," said Cora.

"Been rolling the rock pretty good lately. I'd be tough to beat."

Facing away from the president, Cora added nonchalantly, "A little different story in the polls."

"Yeah. Well..." He retrieved his water bottle from the cart. "People are hard to please."

"Yes they are," Cora agreed. "And they like to have a scapegoat. You played football. You know how it works. When things go sour, they fire the coach."

The president, in blue shorts and white polo shirt, sank down on the shaded bench behind the tee box. "I guess things are fairly sour."

"You could say that." Cora joined him on the bench, his wizened political caddy, full of lore, tricks, local knowledge, and national experience. "No bread riots yet, but we're getting close. And fairly or not, a lot of the country blames you."

In silence, the pair picked spears of grass off their shoes.

"There's some more news I ought to give you while you're sitting down," she said. She looked around to make sure the Secret Service agents were out of earshot. "Jim McGillick's turned up, and he's written a book."

"You're kidding." Shaw faced her, his blond eyebrows wriggling like caterpillars. "Fabulous." He snorted. "What other news you got? A meteor headed this way?"

"It's actually not that dire. Or it might not be, if we play our cards right."

"Yeah? What cards do we have?"

Cora described the proposed cross-country trip, her voice deliberate and comforting in the manner of an end-of-life counselor's.

"Whoa!" came the response. "Are you pulling my leg?"

Cora shook her head again.

"Jesus Christ."

"We're kind of backed into a corner, sir."

"Man. I guess so." Shaw drank. "It's that bad?"

"We're battling a number of negative perceptions. Klaus gave me some new numbers last night. Your favorables are down in the danger zone."

"And you don't think anybody's going to notice that I've dropped out of sight for a couple of weeks?"

"Twelve days. And actually, the timing couldn't be better." Cora heard in her overly buoyant tone her father's insurance-selling spiel. "Congress is on vacation all of August, so there's less focus on Washington. Less press around. The Olympics start in Seattle on the first. You open it, then everyone forgets about you. The media gets completely wrapped up in the parallel bars. Strange, but true. It's like the whole country goes into an air-conditioned theater to watch a movie and doesn't come out for two weeks. Those are the weeks you'd be gone."

"I guess people are as sick of politics as we are."

"No doubt." Cora fiddled with her visor, not wanting to rush him. "You were going to be on vacation anyway for—"

"And I was *going* to play a round with John Elway at Riviera."

Cora paused, searching for her hospice-worker's patience. "Actually, sir, both the vacationing and the golf have gotten to be a bit of an issue."

"Yeah, yeah, it's a rich man's game."

"Rich. White. Water-intensive." Drought-battered cities by the score were letting their fairways go brown. Los Angeles, Tucson, Des Moines, and most recently Atlanta had moved their burgeoning tent cities onto golf courses.

"Maybe we ought to try praying for rain again," said the president.

Cora wondered if he were kidding. The press had pilloried them for the event, held at NOAA headquarters in Silver Spring. Passages from Genesis and Leviticus had been recited in stirring voices. The Weather Channel, always grateful for material, had covered it live, then checked in with its team of reporters stationed beside corn fields, reservoirs, and cracked lake beds. The only measurable precipitation had fallen in Olympic National Park in Washington.

"The Baptist Convention is urging us not to. When it doesn't work, it makes them look—"

"So add a rabbi and a Muslim like I suggested. Spread the risk."

"But then what if it *does* work? Look at the takeaway. Allah is great. It's a problem."

"Worse than no water?"

"Much worse."

The president rolled his eyes. "So, to sum up, my takeaway is I ought to be playing stickball instead."

Cora smiled. "I don't think you—"

"First I had to give up hunting. No blood sports. Then people lost their jobs and we're *promoting* hunting to put food on the table. Then people buy guns and start blasting each other and it's 'Please Hunt Responsibly' and 'Support America's Slaughterhouses.' The NRA's heads must have been spinning. And now it's golf!"

Cora let him vent for three holes. On five the president sliced his drive for the third time in a row, threw down his club, and swore he'd get the IRS on Titleist's case. On the green, he backed off from his putt and yelled at one of the agents for talking too loudly into his wrist mic.

"They're just trying to protect you," Cora said.

"And I'm just tired of being protected! By them, you, everybody. Feeding me talking points. Fussing over my damn hair. Telling me what to think, where to stand, when to smile, how to pronounce 'welcome' in seventeen different languages. And now this trip, pretending to be Joe Blow—another big idea that's not really mine. The acting part should be a real breeze with all the practice I've had."

"If you've got a better idea, we're listening. Believe me."

The president strolled distractedly around the green. He returned to his ball, stared down, said nothing.

"No one's forcing you," Cora said. "All I'm doing is saying what surgeons say, that the consequences look life-threatening if you don't. The choice is yours."

"Wouldn't five days be enough?"

Cora prayed he wasn't trying to save the tee time at Riviera.

"Respectfully, no. It takes five days just to drive coast to coast, without stopping to live with the locals. The situation's serious. It needs a serious response. You've got to walk a full mile in the country's shoes. To the corner and back isn't gonna cut it."

Shaw swung his putter at an acorn on the green. "I can't believe this."

"I should also remind you of something else. That you're betting with a lot of other people's money." Cora faced the president eye to eye across ten feet of green. "You're the candidate of the Republican Party. The incumbent. No opposition in the primaries. You're the man. A national committee behind you, fundraisers, phone banks, letter stuffers, state committees, local committees, Republican Ladies Clubs in little towns you've never heard of. All those people are working for you. But that comes with responsibilities on your part. Like doing things *they* need you to do even if you don't want to. Taking one for the good of the team."

Shaw took a swipe at another acorn.

"So who'd run the Free World while I'm gone?"

"You'd be in daily contact with everybody, the vice president—"

"Is *he* behind this?"

For ballast, bearlike Gordy Coburn had been forced upon him as running mate four years before, a three-term senator from Ohio and a table-pounding member of the Armed Services and Judiciary committees, still under fifty yet able to navigate Washington's maze of mole tunnels by scent alone, and a man not without ambitions.

"Gordy knows nothing about it," Cora insisted. "And it's not like he'll drop the big one while you're gone." She turned toward the rearmost cart in their train, holding the president's constant companions: a doctor and an officer with a black overnight bag, nicknamed "the football," that contained the nation's nuclear attack plans. "You're still the quarterback. The football goes with you. No different from any other trip you take."

The arranged marriage with his vice president had always been strained. Coburn dominated meetings, made decisions that weren't his to make, and annually diverted the proposed routes of Shaw's State of the Union addresses. Before press conferences, when the president would be dangerously untethered from prepared speeches, Coburn had been known to test his fitness with pop questions beforehand and to suggest turns of phrase much as Shaw's own father had done. Two years in, like a divorcing couple, they'd dropped the traditional weekly lunch by mutual consent. Yet once again, they were yoked on the same ticket.

"All Gordy's going to get is a few extra briefings," said Cora.

Shaw's spirits improved. Why not let the self-important bastard go blind reading reports on fish-farming pollution, Peruvian reparations, phonics-based reading, AIDS in the hobo population, restructuring the tariff on Norwegian salmon... Maybe this was the vacation he needed.

"What about Secret Service?" he asked. "They couldn't be wild about the idea."

"Chuck went to sound them out yesterday."

"And?"

\* \* \*

"Impossible! Absolutely not!" The flushed hairless head of director Dewey Archibald vibrated, red eyebrows slanted upward in outrage. On the other side of his desk sat Chuck Thorne, feeling as if he were facing the Wizard of Oz. As presidential chief of staff, he was unused to being yelled at.

"Are you out of your mind? Who thought this up?"

The scarecrow, Thorne almost answered. "Not important. The point is—"

"The point is it's not happening!" Archibald's Tennessee accent grew stronger under stress. He'd come up through the Fraud Division and had been publicly embarrassed three weeks into his new job when someone on a White House tour had snuck two Mexican vampire bats past security and released them, both flapping upstairs into the First Family's quarters. He'd lived at threat level orange ever since, determined that no further humiliations should appear in his reign's Debit column.

"Our motto's 'Worthy of trust and confidence,' not 'Open to hare-brained campaign schemes.' "

Tall and slow-fused, Thorne ignored the remark. "The problem is, the president's realized that he spends so much time in the bubble that he's out of touch. He needs to get out. See what's really going on. Feel what the country's feeling."

"Because his political life depends on it?"

"That's a factor, I'll admit, but it's—"

"His political life's not my problem! My charge is protecting his physical life." Archibald reclined in his leather chair, the Service's seal above him seeming to second his words. Thorne gazed up at the gold sheriff badge, wondering if there was a camera in it. He inhaled and took another running start.

"It's not as harebrained—" He stopped, backtracking around that characterization. "It's exactly what you and he both need, actually."

"Is it really."

"Think about it. You've got the Olympics in Seattle going on at the same time. Like the Super Bowl only a thousand times worse." Thorne ignored Archibald's beg-to-differ expression and pushed on. "Teams from two hundred plus countries, ten thousand athletes, Munich always in the back of your mind, not to mention Atlanta. Eric Rudolph. Talk about ugly. Plus you've got the border with Canada right there, not only the roads but the damn ferries. An incredible drain on manpower, resources, dogs. Puget Sound's going to turn yellow from all the pee from all the thousands of bomb-sniffing dogs you'll need. And—" He held up his hand to forestall Archibald interrupting. "On top of that, you've got the party conventions right afterward. And right after that, the G-7's in Boston. And I almost forgot—the Mona Lisa's coming to New York and Dallas and San Francisco. Another couple million man-hours. Talk about a full plate. Meanwhile you've got so many people hurting for money and so much counterfeiting going on that sales of color printers are the only good news in retail. Did you see the *Time* article last week?" He already knew the answer. "The one about whether you're losing the battle?" Archibald gave no reply. "This morning I bought coffee and the cashier actually held my five-dollar bill up to the light! And the frosting on top of all this is that you've got the candidates campaigning—not two, but three, not to mention their wives and siblings and kids, all in different places, naturally. Rope lines, town halls, lunch counters, baseball games, rodeos, state fairs…And you know as well as I do what that means. Resources get bunched up in one place, they're thinner everyplace else. And what happens then? An embassy bombing. Poison gas in a subway. Maybe something worse. Why else have we had bank robberies everywhere the president campaigns? The local cops are busy helping with protection and the crooks know it. Cleveland, what was it, six different banks while he was at that prayer breakfast? Must have been praying for redistribution of wealth. Same in Tampa. It's wild out there. Banks are praying he goes somewhere else. A PR nightmare for law enforcement, obviously." Thorne glanced sadly up at the massive gold badge. "*My point being* that this trip isn't a curse. It's a cure. Balm of Gilead." He knew Archibald was a born-again. "It's making your life easier. A chance *not* to have to deal with Seattle and both conventions and the G-7 and Monopoly money and Leonardo da Vinci *and* the twenty-six different campaign stops we had planned for the week of August eleventh, each one of them a little Super Bowl all its own. It's a gift!"

Archibald, in cobalt shirt and black tie, hands tented on his chest, had decided to let this storm blow itself out. When it had, he offered an interval of silence for footnotes and afterthoughts. He then leaned forward in his chair and softly intoned, "I think we can handle it."

Thorne's lips tightened against each other.

"It's our job." Archibald's voice was eerily calm. "And we do it quite well."

Who couldn't with a billion-dollar budget, thought Thorne. He realized why he was actually feeling chilly—the Secret Service's air-conditioning system was the only one in Washington strong enough to best the heat.

"You do, indeed." Thorne cleared his throat. "Though there was the incident in Florida." He knew there was no need to specify Jacksonville, where a handshaker on the rope line had maneuvered a jelly doughnut between his palm and Shaw's, staining the president's red and causing his detail to throw him into his limousine, providing forty-three seconds of viewing pleasure to two billion Internet users. "And Detroit." The unemployed autoworker with the urine-filled water pistol. "Yale." Where the president's commencement address had been interrupted by a hijacking of the sound system, which began blasting Nafro's "You Haven't Done Nothin'." A bellringer of bad memories, Thorne let the reverberations clash against each other. Archibald made no reply.

"All those things happened in spite of survey trips, preadvances, advances, manhole covers welded, airspace closed, crowds magged, you name it. Why? Everyone knew the president would be there. And some people—a growing number of people—aren't too thrilled with him." Thorne leaned back, then gestured toward the south-facing window. "Now think back two weeks. Shaw did that impromptu at Burger King in Arlington. No dogs, no metal detectors, no snipers, no background checks. Uncontrolled access, men working under the street, airplanes overhead—and he was fine. Why? Because nobody was expecting him. Which is why you let him do impromptus. They're safe. And what we're proposing is even safer. Not only won't people be expecting him, but when he enters, they'll never even know it's him."

Archibald snorted distastefully.

"I'm giving you a gift, Dewey. You know what we're usually asking for. *More* visibility, *more* access to the public. But I'm asking for *less*. Just when you've got less. When you're stretched as thin as the Shroud of Turin. I'm taking those twenty-some campaign stops off your table. And that's not including the First Lady's seventeen events. Or his brother's. Any one of which could blow up in your face big time."

From his desk, a faded photo looked back at Archibald, of his wife standing in front of the ramshackle one-bedroom apartment they'd rented early in their marriage. It had been a grueling, Everestian climb to the top from the lowlands of the Memphis field office. He'd only made it to his present perch eighteen months before. He wasn't ready to head back down. But he also wasn't willing to put the president at risk.

"I don't know." He rubbed his bald dome, then jerked to his feet, strode over to his window, and looked down on H Street eight floors below. "But c'mon. We're not talking a few handshakes. He'd be spending whole days working with people we'd know nothing about. Strangers. Them."

Sandburg's *The People, Yes* would make a nice Christmas gift, Thorne thought. A career assessing threats had taken its toll. The man's eyes had the disquieting squint of a sharpshooter's.

"And what about food? Doctors? Communications?"

"Doctors?   He'll have Weiss by his side, as usual," Thorne promised. "Full communications, just like on any other trip. As for food, he's not going to have his stewards cooking for him in the employee break room, obviously. Or at some truck stop. He's going to have to eat like everyone else. We've got three hundred million people doing it every day, you and me included, and I don't think any of us see ourselves as daredevils. The American diet might not be the healthiest, but it takes longer than two weeks to kill."

Privately, Archibald acknowledged the trip's advantages. Then its great vulnerability rose up before him.

"And how is it that no one's going to recognize the most recognizable figure in the entire world?"

Thorne was ready. "First, we keep the group small, so nothing trips people's suspicions. The less conspicuous we are, the safer he is. No thirty-five car motorcade. No "Hail to the Chief." Absolutely barebones. No taking over whole hotels."

"Just a couple of rooms at Motel 6, I suppose," said Archibald.

"Not far off, actually. On top of that, he uses a fake name. And as far as the world's most recognizable face goes, rumor has it that you guys know a thing or two about disguises."

Archibald exhaled. "And what about having someone with him at all times? That's policy."

"We'll get an agent hired with him and keep 'em close. And you can have as many as you want farther back. We'll sneak in cameras so we can watch him. And he'll be wired, naturally. But that's all we should need. Bosses, coworkers, nobody else knows."

Archibald returned to his chair, sank back, and released an interminable sigh.

"It's the safest trip he'll ever take," said Thorne. "Relax. Just leave the driving to us."

Archibald replied with a joyless stare.

## 5

The Chinese restaurant's hostess gave Barry a menu stamped with a thumbprint of sweet and sour sauce, then used mime rather than English to indicate that he could sit anywhere he liked. It was noon but the place was nearly empty. Growing up Jewish, he still associated Chinese food with family Christmas dinners back in Toledo, memories at odds with today's searing heat. He glanced around, walked to the rear, and poked his nose through the bead curtain that screened the first of the private booths. The remains of a meal greeted him, like an art installation, complete with discarded fortunes and a cockroach nibbling from a serving spoon. In the fourth booth he found Hugh reading the *Post*.

"Jesus, how did you pick this place? *Washington on Seventy-Five Cents a Day?*" He sat his bulky body down, plunging unexpectedly far into the red banquette and putting himself closer to eye level with Hugh. "The place is a health hazard."

"Actually, it's perfect. It'll get my stomach ready for all the greasy spoons coming my way."

"They've got private rooms at better places than this dump."

"Where the walls have ears and the waiters are all blogging? Forget it. Not with Operation Commoner in Chief."

"Is that its name?"

"They're calling it Operation Compassion. I'm calling it crazy fucking campaign stunt-driving that's gonna get us all killed. But let's order first."

The menu was bilingual, heavily sauced with adjectives. A waitress materialized through the beads like a Star Trek character beaming up. Both men loudly declaimed a number from the menu.

"No cockroaches on mine," Barry called out after her. He moved his amber plastic cup of ice water around his big face, gray from decades of smoking but flushed with the heat. The doddering fan above them was too weak to lift his combover's black hairs.

"It's gonna be hot on the road," said Hugh. "I might as well get used to it."

"Speak for yourself. I don't need boot camp—I'm staying."

"True. I owe you. Lunch on me at Citronelle when I get back."

"So who else is going?"

"The few, the proud, the totally deluded. Jess, Trevor, me."

"Three speechwriters?  What happened to the lean surgical-strike team?"

"Three is lean. It takes that many of us to write Shaw's breakfast-table banter." Hugh drank from his ice water. "Lola's doing makeup. Victor's filming—"

"Mr. Personality?  Again?"

"I know, I know.  But the guy's a genius with a camera.  He's interrupting a shoot in Africa."

"Yeah?"

"Some puff piece for a dictator."

"Our own Leni Riefenstahl."

"The famous Agent Boyce is coming, too." Hugh crunched a chunk of ice from his water. "Shaw's putting him on his own detail.  Doesn't want Bianca alone with Mr. Zipper for two weeks."

"Smart move."

"Maybe the only smart part of the whole damn thing."

"All expenses paid and you're complaining."

"I should be.  And you, too.  It used to be you and me that Chuck turned to.  Now it's Cora." He drank from his ginger ale. "It's a robot rebellion.  The consultants used to be tools.  You told 'em to go make a commercial about something. But now they're doing the thinking and we're the tools. I'm the fucking White House director of communications and suddenly I'm working for that kindergartner Jess."

"Wunderkind envy." Barry smiled. "I remember when you were the golden boy. You've still got the hair. Most of it."

Hugh followed him mentally back to 1992, his ad that sank Cheever, the first House Speaker to lose reelection since the Civil War.

"Sibling rivalry's a bitch," said Barry.

"Tell me about it." Hugh thought of his four brothers. "So why aren't you mad? You don't feel squeezed out?"

"Sure. And not just by Cora. The whole campaign was giving me fits. Ulcer started bleeding again. But then something changed. My wife gave me a copy of *Stoicism for Dummies—*"

"Not this again!" The book had swept the country in the past year, with its depiction of inner sanctum in the midst of uncertain times. It was proof of how bad things had gotten, an embarrassment, especially for the two parties who'd created the mess. The message had been repackaged for teens, had hauled Marcus Aurelius' *Meditations* up the bestseller lists, launched fan-sites for Zeno and Seneca...

"I'm telling you, it's amazing!" Barry's voice had risen. "Just cause things are out of control, I don't have to be out of control!"

"You're sounding pretty out of control."

"Make fun all you like. The Stoic thing's working for me, but you're stuck in all these negative emotions."

"Seems pretty fitting. All our chips are on a number I don't like. Jess's little brainstorm has become my nightmare."

Their waitress brought egg rolls.

"Who knows?" said Barry. "Maybe she's on to something. She rebranded Grabowksi." The immigrant-bashing Colorado congressman who opened his own chain of taquerias when the Latino vote began turning elections. "She was three for three on senate campaigns last election. Got the RNC to bring the website out of the Paleozoic. Massacred Ahern in Kansas with those cellphone ads. Just the sound of the fetus's beating heart."

"I'm eating."

"All I'm saying is there's a reason she's caught Chuck's eye."

"She's twenty-six. She's a twerp."

"And in case you haven't noticed, it's the twerps who run things. It's their world. So what if they don't know how to use a dial phone?"

"They're all statistics," complained Hugh, "instead of gut instincts. Half of 'em don't really care about politics. It's just one more product. Might as well be marketing cereal."

"Give her credit. She came up with something new."

"Copying Peter the Great counts as new?"

Barry leaned in. "And where do new ideas usually come from? From the past!" He crunched down on a second egg roll. "Look at Fiore. Immigrant parents, urban, blue collar, street smarts, humor. Neither party's had anyone like him since vaudeville and LaGuardia. Suddenly they're wild for him, cause he's new."

"Next it'll be spats. We should get Shaw a pair."

"Maybe so."

"And maybe I should open a DeSoto dealership. Cause the whole plan's crazy and you know it. It's beyond rebranding. More like reincarnation. Shaw's barely worked a day in his life, unless you count shuffling papers at the family bank."

"So he'll put on some muscle. Better for photos, right? And forget 'rebranding.' We're 'faceting' him. Showing a side people hadn't seen but was actually always there."

"Where the hell did you pick up 'faceting'?"

"This morning on a lobbying blog."

"Yeah?"

"C'mon, Hugh—the twerps are coming! You gotta keep up."

\* \* \*

Cora sat on a bench in the atrium of the L Street building her consulting firm occupied. She held an iced coffee in one hand a copy of *Guns & Ammo* in the other.

"He'll need a new do."

Beside her, Jess ripped the foil off a yogurt. They were alone among the greenery but spoke softly just in case. "Buzz cut. And a dye job on what's left. Black."

Cora looked up from the photo of a SWAT team shown target shooting. "Wow. You don't want to mess around." She noticed Jess's foot bouncing nervously.

"It's like witness protection," said Jess. "We can't take a chance."

Cora pointed at a photo of a marksmanship instructor. "Same head as Shaw's. Doesn't look great with no hair." Cora had given press conferences into her sixties and was sharply attuned to appearances, undergoing two facelifts in the line of duty. "Accentuates the squareness."

"Too bad," said Jess. "National security. Shaw can drop by Salon Christophe after the trip."

Cora turned the page. "You think black hair will go with his skin?"

Jess considered. "Maybe you're right. Needs to look natural. Medium brown?"

"Better."

"And we can't forget his eyebrows." Jess looked up, thinking. "Do we wax his arms and legs? To get rid of the blond?"

"He doesn't have that much hair. It's fairly dark. We don't want him to look like an alien."

"Fine." She didn't want to forget anything important. With so little time before the trip, she was deathly afraid she would.

Cora flipped several pages. "Sideburns would be a nice touch."

"Definitely."

Cora indicated a Civil War reenactor with a luxurious set of mutton chops. "But he shouldn't stand out." She moved ahead to an ad showing a deer hunter with L-shaped sideburns.

"More like it," said Jess. "Dog-ear that page."

"Mustache?"

"I was thinking that, too." Jess pointed her spoon at the head of a man with a menacing Fu Manchu.

"We're going to give him a total identity crisis," Cora warned.

"Which is good. It'll keep him in character. Less likely to slip and forget that he's actually supposed to pay for his lunch. I'm afraid he's going to blow it."

"I hear you."

"On the other hand, we can't make him too much of a badass."

"His Secret Service code name's 'Roughneck.' "

"Yeah, but we have to get him hired." Jess chewed her lip at the thought, then pointed at the glaring Fu Manchu owner, his arsenal of submachine guns artfully arranged in a spokelike semicircle on the wall behind him. "Other than at the Mercenary Expo, I'd say this guy's a tough hire."

Cora flipped to the ads at the rear and stopped at a mustached shop-teacher type hawking walnut gunstocks. "There we go."

"Just enough to throw people off."

"He should probably wear glasses."

"Already thought of that," said Jess. "They can make 'em the same prescription as his contacts. And guess what I found out? His irises are brown. So he'll lose the blue eyes when he takes out the contacts."

"Even better. So what kind of frames?" Cora gave a giggle. "It's like playing with dolls."

"We need something out of date."

"Heavy and black like Kissinger's maybe."

"But he shouldn't look like Rip Van Winkle. Can't have everybody laughing when he walks in the room."

"It might do him a little good," said Cora, "after four years of "Hail to the Chief." The trip's not just PR—it's a reality check."

"Exactly. He needs to come back changed. People will sense it. Then *they'll* feel changed in how they think about him."

"And he can start stealing some of Fiore's thunder."

They skipped backward through the magazine, deciding on plastic frames for durability, brown for skin tone, oval for head shape.

"And then there's clothes," said Jess.

"Clothes unmake the man." Cora opened the issue of the *National Enquirer* she'd brought.

"Kmart's having a sale."

"I'll mention it to Bianca."

"Better explain the whole Blue Light Special thing."

Their fingers jabbed at boots, overalls, t-shirts, jeans, briefs, and belts.

Cora gazed upward. "That's going to be some Candid Camera moment when all those people realize they'd been belching in the break room next to the most powerful man in the world."

"Somebody's going to sue," predicted Jess. "Some union will claim he was spying on workers."

"Or someone whose butt you can glimpse in the background will howl about never signing a release."

Jess sighed heavily. "And let's not even mention all the security issues." She stopped talking while a pair of men passed through the atrium. When they'd left, she stood and made sure no one had entered through the east door and taken the bench tucked among the tree ferns.

"Trip's got you on edge?" Cora whispered.

Jess nodded.

"Good. You'd be a fool if it didn't."

"It's like anything else. You've got a problem, you come up with a solution, then the solution gives you a different batch of problems. And we're looking at a lot of 'em."

"True."

"And the whole thing's so rushed. We leave in eight days."

"Have to. It's the perfect slot."

Jess uncrossed and recrossed her legs, wagging her other foot. "I keep thinking maybe the whole idea's crazy and I oversold it. A problem with me."

Cora knew she came by it naturally. Her father was a mechanical engineer and inventor. Her mother wrote and spoke on self-esteem. She patted Jess's knee. "You were the only one who had any ideas that day. And it's not like we gave 'em a money-back guarantee. If it bombs, at least we tried, and Shaw was gonna lose anyway. If it works, it'll bump you up to a whole new level."

"Yeah. Right up there with the Watergate burglars."

"C'mon. There's nothing illegal going on. The president's inspecting his country. As he should. We're just facilitating."

Jess finished her yogurt. "And if the press or anybody else finds out—"

"It's gonna be air-tight. Hermetically sealed." Cora swirled her ice and chugged the end of her coffee. "Joe Klein's not riding this bus. Nobody on the trip can keep any kind of notes. Bianca will know, but not Cassandra. The vice president, top staff, the Secret Service, and that's it."

"I almost wish I hadn't thought it up."

"You said the same thing about the campaign for Krispy Kreme, and look how well that went."

A troubling turn of events for a tofu-eater like Jess. "Take my place?" She knew the answer was no. Cora had to keep on top of the whole campaign, not just this element.

"It's your baby and you're gonna be great," said Cora. "Especially on the diary. Chuck wants a woman's input. That's where Shaw's weak— empathy, nurturing, that kind of thing."

I've broken it off with three men in six years, Jess mused. I'm bad with kids. Career first and relationships second. I could be a testosterone exporter. Have to keep my hair long to give a semblance of femininity. "I don't know."

"You can call me in Malibu day or night if you hit problems."

"I've already got one. Hugh. I'm new, I'm from outside the White House, and he doesn't like the plan."

"That's his problem. And you don't have to like him. His wife sure as hell doesn't. We're in the same Stoicism group. Just get the job done." She put her hand on Jess's and quoted Epictetus. "'In peril and yet happy, in exile and yet happy, in disgrace and yet happy...'"

# 6.

The sun was setting. Hoping for a breeze, Cassandra climbed to the White House's top floor, dragged a lounge chair out of the solarium onto the promenade, bummed a cigarette from one of the sharpshooters, and savored it. She was in no danger of being detected: her parents were stuck in the East Room, pretending to listen to an opera singer. She smoked it down to the filter, flicked the butt over the battlements, possibly onto the head of one of the agents skulking in the greenery, opened her laptop, and resumed her blog post.

"And if u ppl have read the iliad u know Cassandra's one of the princesses of troy who always knew what was going to happen but was totally doomed not to be believed by her controlling shit-4-brains father. thank god so much has changed since the bronze age!!! if ur not sure if i'm being ironic, click *here*. u think ur parents r bad, imagine if they happened 2b the leaders of the free world! see july 28 for actual transcript of actual conversation with Most Powerful Man in da Solar System about me taking thong bathing suit on CA trip like it's any of his business. so nice we're still a normal family despite the butlers and nuclear arms. lol."

Detouring further from the rest of the country's normal, she raised a curved finger to her Secret Service agent as if beckoning a waiter, had him get Ernie, the new usher she'd caught watching porn on his cellphone, and inquired with a blackmailer's perfect pitch if there might be any chilled Chardonnay left over from dinner. There was.

"in case u had urself frozen when you died and the heat just thawed you out and you're wondering what's with the weather, ITS TOTALLY SCREWED, just check out the link to the article about trees in virginia spontaneously combusting. i predict penguins swimming up the potomac by next year but my name's Cassandra and NOBODY BELIEVES ME! i also predict that the FREE PARTY will totally kick ass in november especially with all u guys GETTING OUT THE VOTE! would u rather be free or have TOTAL DOMINATION over yr lives thru drug laws, wiretapping, censorship, penalties 4 certain sexual preferences, wasteful foreign wars, INCOME TAX WITHHELD FROM PAYCHECKS, etc. if ur old enough to vote SPREAD DA FRICKIN WORD! if ur not u can still help out big time. click *here* 2 check out the names of the bands supporting us. then 4 a laugh check out whos signed with the Republican label! ROFL!!!!! I mean who the hell—"

*   *   *

"—are the Footlighters?"

Chuck Thorne looked up from his computer. "Patrick!"

It was just past eight in the morning. Thorne's administrative assistant, small and quick as a minnow, had barely entered his West Wing office and started his caffeine therapy. He noted the tenor of his boss's voice, gave a *sotto voce* "Gotta go" to his inamorata in the Bureau of Engraving and Printing, closed his cellphone, and presented himself like a bellhop. Thorne motioned him to close the door.

"Cassandra's got six hundred thousand friends on MySpace, plus the maximum number Facebook allows, plus her own blog, which has so many readers she's got Microsoft advertising on it. Half the money from that she gives to the Free Party. They're taking votes from us, especially at colleges, and we don't have any votes to lose. She's a wind in our face instead of at our backs. Make something happen."

Patrick's angelic features darkened. He was in love, in a mood to embrace humanity, and suddenly felt he'd stepped into *The Godfather*.

"Make something happen?"

"Don't call Gordon Liddy, but you know what I mean. Technical difficulties. Sites overloaded. Something."

Patrick nodded uncertainly.

"We also can't take a chance on her finding out about the president. Two weeks at the Malibu house without bumping into him isn't going to work. Talk to Heather. Try to get one of the grandparents to take her for a week. Maybe a week each. It'll look good with FFI."

Patrick's thin lips registered doubt. Along with its anti-abortion and traditional-marriage elements, the Family First Initiative encouraged families to call prodigal elders home, trimming the government's Medicare bills. The program was supported by government-dispensed information for in-home caregivers. Bathing and taking temperatures was one thing, but kitchen table surgery was proving a problem. All two million copies of the *We Can Handle It!* brochure series had been recalled after the less than satisfactory experience of the Maine couple using *Collapsed Lung? No Problem!* Patrick had overseen the filming of the Shaws taking each other's blood pressure readings. Modeling a close-knit extended family had posed a much bigger challenge for the Shaws, with the president's parents bitterly divorced and Bianca's in and out of the news as they entered and exited rehab clinics. None of the four seemed to care for Cassandra.

"I'm not sure if—"

"Butter 'em up. The president and Bianca are too busy, she's acting out, needs a grandparent's steady hand. Old-fashioned values."

Patrick swallowed. The president's father was currently dating a thirty-six year old former *Playboy* Miss February.

"I'm not so sure the old-fashioned values line will have much effect," he spoke up. "It's not like any of them are still milking their own cows. It might not be something—"

"Figure it out!" barked Thorne. He knew the mad rush to prepare for the trip was getting to him. "Send Cassandra to camp! Send her into space! But she can't be in Malibu the whole time—got it?"

Patrick nodded.

"Next item! Get 'em a dog."

Thorne swiveled in his chair, grabbed a red, white, and blue collar off a shelf, and tossed it to Patrick.

"Do they want—"

"They don't, but I do. A golden retriever. They need an image transfusion."

Patrick pulled out a pen and added this to his list.

"Tell the press it used to be a guide dog for the blind. Owner died, it wandered the streets, the First Lady fell in love with it at the pound."

Patrick cleared his throat. "You don't see a lot of golden retrievers at the pound," he offered gingerly. "You mainly see pit—"

"Which is what makes this story so miraculous, right? Which is why they decided to name it Milagro."

"They did?"

"Spanish for 'miracle.' "

Patrick jotted notes.

"Next thing. The press. The First Lady and the president's double will be on Air Force One, plus doubles for his doc and the football carrier. But no press whatsoever. Talk to Gil, Angie, everybody. It's got to be clear. He wants two weeks of absolute peace and privacy. Time to reflect. A spiritual retreat. No interviews, no photos, nothing—until the last day."

"But you know they're going to want—"

Thorne stood up. "I'm late."

Patrick stared at his pad with its list of forbidding chores, like those assigned to a fairy tale hero. "I'll get on it."

He retreated to his room before Thorne could ask for a hair from the head of a man not of woman born. Thorne passed his doorway a minute later, touched antennae with congressmen, generals, favor-seekers, and deadline-beaters on his way to the door, and hopped into a cab. He got out at one of the Secret Service's buildings, where he was accompanied by an agent on a journey horizontal and then vertical that brought him at last to a garage in the basement. Before him stood the just-arrived president and his entourage of agents, slowly orbiting a well-worn gray minivan. Thorne joined the moving circle.

"It's a Chevy Astro, seven years old, thoroughly refitted," stated Karl Lindblatt, the president's Special Agent in Charge. Big and pale, he opened the side door. The passenger area held a single seat in the center and a bench seat behind. "Reinforced windows. Armored. Tracking equipment. Drop line, full communications capability. Self-healing gas tank, secure air supply, run-flat rims, same as with the Beast." Like a gallery docent, Lindblatt gave the group a minute, then moved around to the driver's door, climbed in, and inserted a key. The engine roared to life. "We put in a turbodiesel V-8," he called over the noise. "Not much on mileage," he addressed the president, "but it'll get you over the Rockies."

Shaw gave no reaction.

Lindblatt turned off the engine and stepped down. "We didn't have to do much to the exterior." He ran a finger over the ratty raccoon tail affixed to the radio antenna. Mutely, he showed off the body's age-appropriate dents, pointed out the borders between imperfectly matched paint, and lingered at the Marine Corps decal and the much abraded image of an alien's head.

"We wanted a vehicle that wouldn't attract attention. No brand new Escalade or Suburban, especially these days when most people are getting by on older cars. Plus we wanted something that would blend in anywhere in the country. No bumper stickers from local radio stations or sports teams." He pointed out the "I ♥ Border Collies" decal they'd added. "We'll carry license plates for all states on the route."

Thorne and the president gazed at the rear license-plate holder. "'Don't Drive Faster Than Your Angel Can Fly'?" recited Shaw.

"Yes, sir. But don't worry. The group's small, but we'll have a full complement of angels watching over you. Three shifts, same detail except for Agent Boyce taking Agent Denny's spot. There'll be an agent sleeping in here, making sure it's secure. I'll remain your SAIC."

Shaw tried to think of Lindblatt as a hovering angel but had trouble imagining the man's massive body leaving the ground. Looking in the passenger window, he found his eye traveling the splits in the upholstery. "It'll be a switch from the usual, that's for sure." He stepped back and cast a wistful glance at the nearby row of black Suburbans.

"Blending in was the priority," stated Lindblatt.

Shaw touched his toe to a rusting wheel well. "Mission accomplished."

"What's the motorcade going to look like?" asked Thorne.

Lindblatt consulted a small notebook. "Lead car, follow-up, tail car, all unmarked, two agents in each. Fenster from WHCA in the follow-up, in charge of communications. Agent De La Cruz here will be driving Chevy One." A thick-necked agent raised his hand. "Aside from him and the president, there'll be me, Doctor Weiss, and Major Rinaldi carrying the football. Farther back, the president's media team, three cars, two passengers in each. More than two in a car attracts attention. Farther back, we'll have a WHCA truck, a CAT team in two vans, and sixteen additional agents." He closed his notebooks. "Barebones, but we think we've got it all covered."

"What about lodging?" asked Thorne.

"Same groupings in hotels."

"We're staying at hotels?" the president asked sarcastically. "Things are looking up."

"Or whatever lodgings are locally available," Lindblatt clarified.

Thorne wondered if a president had ever stayed at a KOA, and from forty years in the past he heard his wife scream when she'd come on the snake in the self-service laundromat's drier. Maybe the trip wasn't such a good idea. Then again, if Shaw managed to kill a snake, it would be huge, worth fifteen points in the polls minimum, the inverse of Carter flailing at the rabbit. Maybe they should plant a snake, already gravely wounded... He made a note to have Patrick look into it.

When there were no more questions, Thorne accompanied the president to his limousine.

"So you heard what he said. New ID for everyone on the trip whose name might be known to the public." Thorne smiled. "And that definitely includes you. Got a new name in mind?"

"Not really."

"Something a little bit close to Scott Shaw would be good. Makes it not so foreign. Easier to remember."

Leaning against the car, the president cogitated, eyes narrowed. Half a minute passed.

"Scutt," he spoke at last. His eyes closed. "How about Scutt... Shrave."

Thorne inhaled slowly, working to keep his feelings out of his face.

"With respect, Mr. President." He paused. "'Scutt' is…is not a name one hears often."

"Fine!" erupted Shaw. "Then you pick it out!"

\* \* \*

Hugh pulled another beer from the cooler. "This is crazy!" It was 1:40 in the morning. He pried off the bottle cap. Coffee put him to sleep, alcohol kept him awake. "'He walked among us'—but not through a single southern state?"

Barry glugged from his third Frappuccino. Jess was working on her second Red Bull. They were in election headquarters on K Street, windows still closed against the steamy air, the air-conditioner chugging heavily. Hugh walked up to the huge United States map like a geography teacher, a mailing tube in his hand instead of a pointer.

"He's gotta go to Florida! He can't win without it. And Virginia's suddenly up for grabs, too." He smacked Richmond with the tube.

"And they give a great tour at Williamsburg," said Jess, "but we're fine in Virginia. And Florida, too. We need to head north. First stop has to be Pennsylvania."

"You can win without Pennsylvania. You can't win without Florida."

"If California goes the other way," Barry said, "we're gonna need 'em both."

"We're in cars, not planes!" Jess gestured toward the map. "We can't hit the whole country in twelve days. And Klaus says Florida's solid."

"Klaus says all kinds of shit!" Hugh hit the floor with his tube. It was Cora who'd sold Thorne on Klaus Krober, over Hugh's objections. He knew that dueling pollsters were as bad as having two divas onstage, but out of catlike curiosity and gut-level distrust he'd called up the RNC and gotten their latest numbers from Mark O'Malley, which showed Florida in question and the border states beginning to buckle.

"The guy speaks in numbers and has a German name, so you see a scientist in a lab coat at Mercedes, handing down truth." Hugh swigged from his beer. "But this isn't engineering—it's politics! Numbers lie here! He's asking a hundred and sixty-one questions for god's sake! It's like taking the LSAT. People will say anything just to be done with it. And my German-built Audi's in the goddamn shop!"

"He's thorough," Jess defended him.

"He's a creepy Bavarian voyeur. Peter Lorre should play him in the movie." Hugh walked the room. "Before your time."

Barry opened Klaus's latest poll and scanned the questions. "'Do you feel anxiety about the possibility of a president whose family originated in southern Italy?' " he read aloud.

"He's a Freudian, not a Republican!"

"'Have you felt a desire to shop for clothes more frequently than normal during the past month?' "

"And what's that about?" asked Hugh.

"It's about consumer confidence, obviously," said Jess.

"Next week I swear he'll be asking about underwear. 'What phrase best describes your feelings about cotton bikini—"

"Forget him!" Jess waved her arms. "Let's talk about Pennsylvania."

"Let's!" agreed Hugh. "A lost cause. Right up there with the Confederacy."

"Seventeen percent unemployment," said Barry. "The unions hate us. The governor hates us."

"The goddamn Quaker Oats man hates us."

"We've still got a chance there, according to Klaus," said Jess. "And since we can't count on California, we have to have it. It'll be a daring raid into the—"

"What are you, Robert E. Lee?"

"He was a pretty good general."

"And he got beat at Gettysburg."

"The parallels are a little rough," said Jess. "First, we took Pennsylvania four years ago."

"Second, he had Traveler and you've got a Miata."

Barry belched. "Then again, we're doing Ohio for sure, so it's on the way. It's a thousand miles down to Miami. Shaw just told the country to conserve on gas."

Hugh smacked a table with his tube. "This isn't a family vacation! And another thing—there's no jobs in Pennsylvania. He'll never get hired."

"I've got an uncle in Erie," said Jess. *"He'll* hire him."

"I take it back. It *is* a family vacation. And *I've* always wanted to see Lancaster County. Can we go?"

Barry stretched. "Unfortunately, it's beautiful downtown Pittsburgh you need to go to. The biggest job retraining center Shaw funded is there. He can see how it's doing, from the inside."

"I'll say. If he loses in November he'll be going there for real."

"Or," said Barry, "you head over to Philly. The Foundation's supporting a homeless shelter there."

Hugh smirked. After the blow-up over the combined $330 in charitable contributions on the presidential couple's tax forms two years before, a foundation was slapped together with their names on it, a place their corporate friends could loudly and piously drop their contributions into the collection basket. Funds had poured in, the bulk flowing out to enterprises coincidentally located in swing states. Instead of earmarks, Fiore was calling them "almsmarks."

"Hold on," Hugh spoke up. "Virginia's got a Foundation project. A breast cancer center in Roanoke. Near Lynchburg, so we could do the Jack Daniels tour, too."

"Wrong Lynchburg," said Jess. "Jack Daniels comes from Lynchburg, Tennessee."

"Gotcha," said Barry.

"Didn't know you were old enough to drink."

"Maybe there's a lot you don't know."

"I know Florida sure as hell needs us," said Hugh. "And that Lynchburg's in the Tennessee Fourth, where we had a retirement and could use a boost on our way *back up* from Florida."

"Plus, with Tennessee you'd get Dollywood," Barry threw out.

"Hershey's Chocolate World," countered Jess.

"Holy Land Experience!" crowed Hugh. "Orlando. Live crucifixion *and* resurrection daily."

\* \* \*

Two mornings later, a scant few hours after a kama sutra session with his girlfriend that opened his third eye but left his other two now at half-mast, Patrick hoisted his gaze from his computer and hooked it on the screen of the TV across his cramped office. *Good Morning America* was showing the Olympic athletes entering the stadium the night before. The sound was off. Patrick lost himself in the ceaseless, mesmerizing scissoring of legs. The chairman of the Seattle Olympic Organizing Committee then came to the podium and flapped his jaw. Faces on jumbotron screens bloomed and faded. Next came the wattle-throated president of the IOC. Then President Shaw took the podium, his blond hair like a flag caught in mid-wave. While he mouthed the words opening the Games, Patrick produced an alternative soundtrack under his breath.

"All is lost. My jockstrap is on backwards. Please pray for me." The crowd around the president applauded.

"Massive fraud and a blizzard on election day will be required for my reelection." The crowd stood and cheered.

"Go UCLA." Fireworks went off.

Patrick lowered his eyes, took another swallow of his triple-shot latte, grabbed an energy-supplying handful of M&Ms, each with the presidential seal, and resumed the labors at hand. Thorne had decided to start the trip in Pittsburgh, then to follow I-70, the route of indecision, through the key toss-up states of Ohio, Missouri, and Colorado, then to pass through New Mexico en route to three days in California. Patrick was tasked with lining up jobs and coordinating with the Secret Service. Temp agencies would have been perfect, since Shaw would only be working a day, but he'd found their labor pools so full that none were taking new applications. If the president weren't hiding his identity, there'd have been no problem, but he was. Patrick opened Craigslist's Pittsburgh page and picked his way among job openings.

"Dynamic self-starter, hardworking, dependable..." Not a good fit, he said to himself.

"Tile setter, experienced..."

"Line cook, minimum two years..."

"...willing to roll up sleeves and turn around well-loved amusement park." In a day?

"Must know Photoshop, Power Point..."

"Clean record, Commercial Class A license..."

"Eighty words per minute..."

"Enjoys working with children..." Patrick paused, then pictured the president's jaw clenching whenever his daughter was mentioned.

On the TV's crawl, he saw that Pretty Boy Nussbaum, the foreclosed-upon bank teller, had struck again, this time a savings a loan in North Platte, Nebraska. Patrick returned to Craigslist and clicked over to Accounting and Finance.

"MBA or CPA required..." Only a bachelor's.

"Establish, maintain, and coordinate the implementation of accounting and accounting control procedures." Sounds too hard.

"Accounts Receivable Specialist, strong resume..." Not likely. Cutting tax in-flows was Shaw's specialty. Patrick glanced dourly at the stack of reports on his desk. Smokers were the only constituency deemed safe to tax—cartons in D.C. were up to $102—but the grim-voiced Heritage study on top of his pile warned that smokers were giving up the habit as well as dying out. They were a limited resource, like fossil fuels, possibly good for only another decade. Patrick sighed. One crisis at a time.

"Dynamic individual with three years LAN/WAN network experience..."

The Olympic flag was brought into the stadium by eight bearers, among them an anti-oil activist representing the environment, and a Nobel-winning, capitalism-bashing writer from France, representing culture. Who'd stacked this deck? Patrick clicked the TV off with his remote and returned to work. He tried the "New Today" listings in the Pittsburgh *Post-Gazette* classifieds.

"G-tube and trach exp required..."

"Broad knowledge of disabilities and rehabilitation regimens..."

"Proficient in Solid Works 3D CAD, MS Word, electronic file management..."

"Outstanding leadership qualities..." He stared at the words, considered while chomping another handful of M&Ms, then moved on.

\* \* \*

Six hours later, a short distance away across Lafayette Park, a black Lincoln Town Car coasted sedately to a stop beneath the columned portico of the Hay-Adams Hotel. One bellman opened the passenger door while another unloaded the trunk's collection of reinforced hard-shell luggage. Their owner, tall and slim, fashionably earringed, with a red goatee and matching loose silk shirt, emerged out of the air-conditioning into the heat, cast an eye on the ragged assembly of the unemployed chanting slogans in front of the Andrew Jackson statue, and entered the frigid lobby with relief. A plump female behind the desk announced, "I can take care of you here." He strode forward, then passed her in favor of the striking Scandinavian-looking clerk farther down, busy typing but with no customer before her.

"Checking in. Victor Bascombe." His voice was grainy with fatigue.

The woman continued typing without lifting her eyes or speaking.

"Silent 'b,' silent 'e,'" he added. "Rather like you."

She gave no acknowledgment, appeared to come to a stopping place, and apparently typed his name into the computer.

"You'll be staying two nights with us?" she asked pleasantly.

"Two nights with you sounds absolutely delightful."

Blond hair barretted to the side, blue eyes calm, she ignored the remark and examined his reservation. "Nonsmoking. Checking out on the fourth."

Her struggle to remain professional excited Victor.

"A room with a view of St. John's, if you've got one," he said.

She made no reply, but her fingers began tapping. "I have a room with one king bed facing St. John's, at four hundred ninety-nine dollars a night, plus tax."

The doors to the street opened, admitting a hotel guest along with a megaphoned voice calling "Ho, ho, hey, hey, eat the rich with Hollandaise." Victor cocked his head toward the park.

"The natives are getting restless," he noted. "I'm just in from Africa, where the natives are much better behaved, actually."

"Shall I put the room in your name?"

"Please." Price was no object; the Reelection Committee was paying. "And if you could have the kitchen send up a plate of crepes suzette and a bottle of Roederer, that would be lovely." The door opened again, letting in the ruckus. He wondered if, in the weeks he'd been gone, "Eat the rich" had become more than a metaphor. He'd avoid crossing through the park.

"Would you like to put incidentals on a credit card?"

His eye descended along her jawline, then circumnavigated her mouth. He leaned closer. "You really have quite a fascinating bone structure."

"Incidentals on a credit card?"

Victor's red eyebrows drew together in conference. "Actually, I've got a different idea."

He waited for her to inquire. She didn't oblige.

"How about you pay the incidentals and I put you in my next film."

She paused, lips pursing slightly. "I'll leave the incidentals, then."

Victor simulated a pained expression. "We've hardly met, and already we've fallen into this cold formality, all business. Do you feel it, too?"

# 7.

At 7 a.m. on August 4th, the presidential minivan left the Washington Monument in its rattling driver's-side rearview mirror. It was Monday. The trip wasn't scheduled to end until two Fridays later. Heading up the G. W. Parkway, the president made out a trio of sculls on the Potomac, the rowers facing astern, unable to see what they were headed toward. He identified.

His seat, centered for safety in case of an accident, was comfortable, but the two roof-anchored seatbelts crossing his chest made him feel strapped into an electric chair. The session the evening before with Lola, in charge of his makeup, had likewise had a whiff of death, then rebirth: his blond hair falling in clumps on his shoulders, the shamanlike mixing of dyeing potions and the complex rite of their application, new clothes laid out for him, then Thorne's revelation of his new name. The glasses he was now looking through put a fuzzy brown frame around his field of vision, a grating annoyance. Likewise losing his week's vacation. He looked down at his carefully scuffed work shoes, rubbed his hands on the knees of his jeans, stared at the "Bassmaster Classic" logo on his t-shirt, and asked himself, Who the hell am I? He didn't feel like Scott Shaw. Then he remembered: I'm Matt Dawes. As advised, he did a set of ten mental repetitions of the name, then ran his hand for the fiftieth time over his brown crew cut and false mustache, glad he couldn't see either. The vehicle holding him likewise bespoke a violent break with the past.  After eleven years spent in spotless limos, he found his gaze stuck on the large stain on the van's blue shag flooring.  The White House was the only pre-owned element in his world, a rare instance in which something used by others carried prestige. He idly opened his armrest's ashtray, saw a pair of butts looking back at him like surprised lovers, and quickly closed it. He wondered what tale lay behind the deep gouges in the roof, though he had no more real desire to know than he wanted to meet the people who'd slept before him in tonight's hotel bed.

Agent Lindblatt, riding shotgun, turned in his seat. "Would you like to hear the radio—" Shaw could tell he was about to say "sir," but finished instead, after an anguished grinding of mental gears, with "Matt." They'd all been instructed to use it, lest an audible "sir" in public cause someone to question Shaw's identity.

"Sure, why not."

"Very good—" Lindblatt let the "sir" die on his tongue. He turned on the radio.  Trumpets blasted from the van's six speakers, causing Major Rinaldi, behind the president, to jump and put a motherly arm around the black bag containing the military's nuclear attack plans.  Rapid-fire Spanish came from the radio.  Shaw had recorded a campaign ad in Spanish but only after hours of retakes and with the text spelled out phonetically in phrase book fashion.  Agent De La Cruz, behind the wheel, had helped him and still recalled seeing "Es-TA-doze You-NEE-doze" on the teleprompter. Lindblatt punched one of the radio's preset buttons. Another Spanish station, a woman singing "*por favor*" over and over.

"What's that mean again?" Lindblatt asked De La Cruz.

The driver rolled his eyes.  "Please."  And people complain about Hispanics living in linguistic ghettos, he thought.  English was the biggest ghetto of them all.

"Thanks."

"*De nada.*"

Lindblatt gave him a puzzled look. He punched another button, landing them on a Spanish Christian station. De La Cruz then grabbed the tuning knob and used his evasive driving training to steer wildly around Spanish, rap, rock, and religion, finally stopping at an announcer delivering sports news.

"Thanks," said the president. The baseball scores, however, stimulated none of his usual reflexes. Even the breathless review of the Redskins' preseason game barely engaged him. He was on Charon's boat and had left his old life behind. It was all unjust, he complained to himself. The Democrats had played by the same fiscal rulebook when they'd been in power, sent their kids to private schools and skied in the Alps, but Dave Dabney, their candidate, wasn't washing dishes and plunging toilets. Shaw fumed, then tried to take his mind off the subject by saying "Hi, I'm Matt" ten times. He reminded himself not to ask for people's vote.

Sports gave way to traffic on the radio, then a feature on the nation's reborn interest in darning.

"Music?" Lindblatt asked him.

"I really don't care."

Lindblatt tuned in a country and western station. De La Cruz released a long-suffering sigh, conspicuously audible, and took advantage of Lindblatt's brief call to headquarters to lower the volume. The scene would never have taken place in the Beast, Shaw reflected. The trip's informal air was already affecting behavior. In place of the usual suit and tie, both agents were in shorts and polo shirts. No one was wearing the usual armored vest, difficult to disguise under hot weather attire and too likely to ignite curiosity. The story would be that the five of them were friends on a fishing trip, a claim supported by the rods sitting on their luggage. When Shaw had entered the van, De La Cruz had hummed "Hail to the Chief" under his breath, hoping the others would join, only to be shushed by Lindblatt. Dropping customary respect was the price of protecting his identity.

Behind the president, Dr. Arnold Weiss, compact and spectacled, never before seen in shorts, flipped idly through a magazine as if seated in another doctor's waiting room. Beside him, Major Rinaldi had traded his Class A uniform and beret for nylon shorts and a black t-shirt. The man suffered from allergies and sniffled once every thirteen seconds by Shaw's watch. Struggling to turn around in his seat, intending to stare Rinaldi into silence, he found the major's eyes closed and headphones over his ears. The president couldn't recall the Army's motto, but felt sure this wouldn't make a good poster. He faced forward again. Rinaldi sniffled. Shaw wondered what hour and day he would crack on.

An endless string of ads led Lindblatt to change stations. He paused at a talk radio program.

"What I'd like know is when the president is gonna take his wooden head out of his wooden—"

Lindblatt gave the dial a desperate turn, delivering them to a station broadcasting in an Asian language.

Shaw cocked his head. Was this really his country? Just then, the dialless phone hidden in the compartment attached to his seat rang. The president opened the top and picked up.

"Yeah?"

"Chuck, Mr. President. Just checking in. How's it going?"

Shaw snorted. "We've only been on the road fifteen minutes."

"Haven't started Car Bingo yet?"

"What's up?"

Lest the president feel isolated and forgotten, Thorne briefed him on the typhoon in the Philippines, heatstroke deaths in Houston, the dollar's fall against the yen, the North Sea oil spill, the Chihuahuan town whose whole police force had been decapitated, and the porn industry's demands for a bailout.

Shaw gazed blankly at the cars coming into Washington. What drew people here? he wondered. The steady diet of disasters certainly held no appeal for him. Traffic was scarce in the other direction. The road not taken. Maybe he was headed the right way after all.

"Plus the Russian famine's getting worse," Thorne added. "We've got all four horsemen of the apocalypse riding this week."

"Bingo," said Shaw.

"And stay away from tomatoes. There's another E. coli outbreak. Mainly west coast."

They'd already driven through a McDonald's on Constitution Avenue, where Lindblatt had picked up two sausage burritos, devouring both. On the console lay the meal's detritus, among which Shaw made out a bright triangle of tomato.

"We're on it," he said.

\* \* \*

Six cars back, Kyle Eckersley, 24, still dealing with acne, zipped along Interstate 270 in a silver Ford Econoline van, with Victor in the passenger seat. As Victor's usual sound man was back in Equatorial Guinea, laid low by sleeping sickness, Cora had lent him the stringy nerd behind the wheel from her pool of production people. Since the photographer's Porsche 911 was in Los Angeles and Kyle's ancient Civic wasn't up to the trip, Cora had rented them the van they were riding in, with space for their equipment and the capability to serve as a conference room. Kyle's eyes were wide with excitement. A D.C. native, he'd never driven cross-country before. Beside him, Victor slouched, a baseball cap over his face, unhappily awake, his body still on West Africa Time. From beneath the cap's bill emerged his red goatee and the words, "So was Boyce really screwing Bianca?"

Kyle had no idea but appreciated being asked. He dredged his mind for gossip. "I think I heard she's got a thing going with her personal trainer."

Victor felt jealousy drip into his veins. When he'd filmed ads during the campaign four years back he'd tried to catch the woman's roving eye, without success. With his own eyes now closed, he imagined undressing her in a changing room, then found his fantasy interrupted by flashbacks from his hotel stay. He'd struck out with the desk clerk at the Hay-Adams, had fared no better with his Haitian maid, the breakfast waitress, or the ravishing concierge, all of whom claimed to be happily married. Had marital peace suddenly broken out? Was he losing his touch? He felt ready to return to Equatorial Guinea, where the president's aides had plied him with women as unthinkingly as with bottled water. He craved escape.

"I need some music," he said.

"Go for it."

A thief had attempted to snatch Victor's iPod on 14th Street the evening before but had only gotten away with his earbuds. He fished the device out of his pants pocket, searched the compartment between the seats, then stared at Kyle. "Where's the damn dock?"

The driver shrugged. Victor repeated his search.

"Maybe it didn't come with one," said Kyle.

"You gotta be kidding."

"It's got a CD player."

"I don't believe this!"

"You bring any CDs?"

Victor gawked at him. "Did I bring any CDs? Did you bring a buggy whip? And the fucking flint tools?" His eyes widened and his pale cheeks turned splotchy.

Kyle felt his palms moisten. He'd never met Victor, but his reputation traipsed up and down the halls of Cora's consulting firm. They were barely into Maryland. Somehow, he thought, they had to hold it together all the way to Malibu.

"There's an exit!" shouted Victor. "Half a mile! Get off and I'll buy some earbuds."

"Are you crazy? I have to follow Greyhound."

"Who the hell's 'Greyhound'?"

"The Secret Service car ahead of us."

"So tell Greyhound we're both getting off."

"But we can't. It's not in the plan."

"What fucking plan?"

"We're not getting off till Bedford, Pennsylvania. Two hours. A bathroom break at Burger King. The Secret Service has it all checked out."

"Are you're kidding me?"

Kyle shook his head. His Boy Scoutish obedience maddened Victor.

"I can't believe this!"

Kyle needlessly adjusted the rearview mirror. After a half mile of silence, he piped up, "At least we've got a radio and CD player."

Victor's head lolled sarcastically. He folded up his long body and leaned back in a modified fetal position, head toward the door. "Have I driven a Ford lately?" he mocked morosely. Fifteen seconds passed, then came the answer. "I'm never driving another Ford again for the rest of my fucking life!"

Kyle drove. Ten miles later Victor, still unable to sleep, turned in his seat and faced Kyle. "Is that Jess seeing anybody?"

Kyle shrugged.

Victor glared at him in frustration. "Did they give her a new name?"

At last, a question he knew the answer to. "They had to."

"Why?"

"Might be recognized. She's been on talk shows a few times. Her name turns up in blogs."

Victor thought. "What about Trevor?"

"Same story."

"And the eye shadow queen?"

"Lola?"

"Yeah."

"Her too."

"Are you bullshitting me?"

"I heard her talking about it."

"She's sure as hell not on *Meet the Press*."

"She was in *Ladies' Home Journal* this year. "And I think maybe in *TV Guide*. And she was married to some Hollywood star. Used to get her name in the papers."

The car in front changed lanes, Kyle following. Victor was silent. Then he sat up straight and burst out, "I was on Esquire's list of 'Ten Young Filmmakers to Watch'!"

Must have been a long time ago, Kyle thought. He kept his eyes locked on the van. "Sorry," he croaked.

*　*　*

"His hair didn't take the dye too good, had to do it twice, poor baby. He looked miserable as a dog getting a bath with the garden hose, so I sang him some hymns to pass the time." Lola crossed from speech to singing. "'The locks of His head are as grapes on the vine, when autumn with plenty is crowned...' It had hair in it and it just came to me. I think it helped." She took a hand off the wheel to lower the mirror and check her own dyed blond bouffant. "His came out a little brittle, like he'd washed it with bar soap—did you ever do that? I used semi-permanent instead of demi-permanent, just in case things went kinda squizzy, so maybe with doing it twice it'll get him to the end of the trip, but you never really know, you know? I still can't get used to him dark."

Jess waited to see if more thoughts were coming. Despite two uses of "squizzy," she was still unable to deduce its precise meaning in Lola's lexicon. "At least he'll get a break from the dumb blond jokes," she said.

By the end of the trip, she knew that she herself would be more than ready for a break from Lola—sixty, sweet-natured, devoted to Shaw, but apt to see the world solely through the lense of beauty care. The one news story she seemed to be following was the war in the Congo, a humanitarian disaster with tens of thousands of deaths and displacements that apparently also threatened to cut off supplies of a key ingredient in mascara. What else, Jess mused, should she expect from a woman who'd told *Ladies' Home Journal* that the right to look one's best was protected by the Constitution? She was a walking sampler of beauty products but no paragon of pulchritude—short, buxom, with a low-slanting brow and a frog's wide mouth, her loose-fleshed throat protruding from a pink ruffle-sleeved blouse. Jess guessed it was her maternal nature, not her looks, that drew Shaw to her, given his harpy of a mother. Lola had been doing his makeup since his days in the California legislature and had moved to Washington at the cost of her third marriage so as to stay with him. Surrogate motherhood clearly could work in both directions. She herself, alas, had a mother and didn't feel the need for another.

Her BlackBerry rang. Agent Kerrigan was calling.

"Poodle, this is Greyhound. What's your position?"

Jess wondered if she should take offense to the code name given to the only car containing women. She peered ahead at an approaching sign.

"We're coming up on Exit Twenty-nine. Sharpsburg." They'd needed to gas up, then had had to return to Lola's apartment for a forgotten travel bag, causing the motorcade to leave without them.

"Are you keeping it at sixty-five?" asked Kerrigan.

Since Jess's Miata didn't have enough luggage space, they'd taken Lola's fourteen-year-old black Buick Regal. The car no longer lived up to its name and its driver was prone to slowing down while talking, speeding up during the silences and passing all the cars who'd recently passed them.

"We're working on it."

"Using cruise control?"

Lola could hear Kerrigan's words. "Tell him I gave up on cruise control twenty years ago when I accidentally turned it on and I shot through a parking lot at forty miles an hour. Sorry but no thank you."

Her voice and Oklahoma accent were both strong. Jess was sure Kerrigan had heard. "We'll keep an eye on the speedometer," she said.

"And how's my special boy doing?" Lola asked loudly.

Shaw's entire staff had worked to expunge that phrase from her vocabulary, given its scent of mental retardation and Lola's penchant for giving interviews.

"Tell Luane he's doing fine." Kerrigan hung up.

"I don't care for 'Luane'," Lola stated flatly.

Jess wasn't particularly thrilled with being Joyce Goffstein, or with their cover story: a mother and niece going to Disneyland for the first time. Their names and situation had both issued from the riotous imagination of the Secret Service. Jess felt stuck in an idiotic sitcom that would last two weeks instead of thirty minutes.

"Maybe we should work on our characters a little," said Lola. "Practice talking to each other like they would, before we stop for lunch. So we'll be ready."

Jess squinted painfully at the thought. "Why don't we just be who we are?"

"Cause we're connected to the president! Can't give anybody any reason to think he might be anywhere nearby."

Jess knew the rationale but had no appetite for play-acting. What she had was 89 emails in her Inbox and a list of thirteen calls to make.

"Let's make it simple," she said. "I'll work in PR in Silver Spring, you have a hair salon in Falls Church. No White House connection. Same private lives."

Lola sighed in disappointment. "I thought I'd get rid of my first and third husbands."

"Go for it."

"And what about our family. You and me. We need to know the details. Are you the daughter of my brother or my sister?"

"Do you have a sister, in real life?"

"I've got three—"

"I'll be the daughter of the oldest, okay? Cut and paste me into that actual family. Family trips, siblings, all the details we'll ever need. That way you won't have to make anything up."

The corners of Lola's lipsticked mouth slowly rose. She took her eyes off the road and gave Jess a mischievous grin.

"You squizzy little vixen, you! Having sex with Reverend Boland all those years, then having the babies in secret..."

\*   \*   \*

"Of course we mention Maryland. So what if it's Democratic? We're trying to show he's president of the whole country. Rich and poor, east and west."

Hugh sat in Trevor's Lexus SUV, a pillow on this thighs and his laptop on the pillow, his fingers poised to continue composing the president's diary of his trip.

"Right you are." Trevor looked through his gold wire-rims at Interstate 70 but as a speechwriter saw at the same time his proposed words set in type. "Though small," he declaimed in his patrician accent, "Maryland has always possessed a big—"

"Hold on, hold on. Small-state syndrome. They're sensitive. Never tell 'em they're small."

Trevor's brow furrowed. "Isn't it obvious?"

"Of course it is. But you gotta pretend it's a secret. Like when Michael Jordan visits the White House, he's not Black. Or tall."

Trevor tried again. "As we crossed the great state of Maryland..."

Hugh typed, then shook his head. "It's a diary, not a convention speech. More personal."

Trevor sipped his cold coffee. He cleared his throat. "Never had I seen Maryland look lovelier than on this August morning..."

Hugh thought of the jungle of graffiti covering Frederick's closed factories and the blocks-long bread line he'd just glimpsed outside Hagerstown.

"Wow. Wonder what he was smoking?"

He took in a cornfield, the plants scrawny and brown, an army of the dead. Neither the drought nor unemployment were as severe in the South. If they'd headed to Florida first they could have shown a rosier...Hugh stopped his thoughts from going down that painful route, then noticed that in place of the news, burbling in the background since they'd left, a voice was singing on the radio. He turned up the volume. Bruce Springsteen was finishing *Brother, Can You Spare a Dime*, followed by commentary, then the crackly Rudy Vallée version from 1932.

"Can you believe this is back on the radio?" he said. "What's next—black and white movies? Zeppelins?"

"Your polio idea would actually have fit right in."

"Hold the thought. Might need it later."

Hugh's eyes were slapped by a long series of "Fiore for President" yard signs that someone had stuck in the grass embankment, then a full-size billboard reading "Time For Change—Time For Fiore," with an army of voters on the march behind the huge head of the sandy-haired candidate, shown in a denim work shirt, no tie, thick lips in a determined pose.

"He looks a little like Mao," said Trevor. "Maybe we should be working on that instead of the Mafia angle."

"Get somebody to publish his damn autobiography as a tiny paperback with a red cover." Hugh considered. "Problem is, you start saying he's Italian and Chinese and a Commie, he's too evil to be real, which makes us look desperate."

"Which we are."

"True." Hugh exhaled. "It's gonna take something huge to turn this one around."

"I'd certainly say we're trying something big." It wasn't every day that he carried a fake driver's license. Instead of Trevor Hirakawa, he was now Rodney Takahashi, a name he felt sure he'd trip over. "No car of mine's ever had a Secret Service code name before."

"And what's with 'Terrier'?" Hugh wondered if Archibald were behind the choice. "We're little yappy nuisances?"

"Or, alternatively, proud flushers of foxes. There's usually a terrier with the hounds on a British fox hunt."

"You don't say."

"The name comes from *terra*, Latin for 'earth.' Chosen because they could squeeze into—"

"Hold it, Trev. Latin isn't gonna help us here. We need to make our prince into a pauper, remember? Let's put Cicero back on the shelf and tune into the common folk. Ever read *Us*? The magazine?"

Trevor shook his head.

"Just like *Foreign Affairs*, except with actresses instead of superpowers. And more pictures. You might like it." Hugh looked down at his laptop's screen. "Now let's get to work. Maryland. More down to earth."

Trevor cogitated for a quarter mile. They passed their first Shaw banner, on the side of a barn, the plastic ripped into ribbons and defaced with spray paint. Trevor's inner Samurai and moon-viewing poet were released together. He cleared his throat. "The van carrying me sliced across Maryland like a filet knife splitting the belly of a cod."

Hugh's eyebrows shot upward. "Wow. Better! Maybe a little too down to earth. But I'm interested. People might actually read this thing." His fingers scurried over the keyboard. "Keep it coming."

# 8.

Victor filmed the "Smile, You're in Pennsylvania" sign through the car's open window, observed by a pair of snickering giants on a road crew and feeling like the rankest of tourists. He likewise documented their highly undramatic passage onto the Pennsylvania Turnpike. The bathroom stop at the Burger King in Bedford, PA, by contrast, was a tense, awkwardly choreographed number that felt drawn from the world of espionage, the travelers passing each other in the hallway without acknowledgment, wondering which feet in the stalls belonged to Secret Service agents, finding meaning in glances, throat-clearings, coughs. The president entered, sandwiched between agents. Checking his false mustache in the mirror—thick, sandy, neatly trimmed—he felt it gave him the manly look of an old-time baseball player but might also conceivably be seen as gay. He suddenly wondered what signal was being sent by the man noisily jingling coins in both pants pockets while discharging his splashing fountain of urine. Shaw left quickly without drying his hands.

Their lunch at the Subway thirty miles outside Pittsburgh was in the same minor key. Hugh felt himself in the cafeteria scene of a prison movie, the team of tunnel diggers and dummy carvers sprinkled about the noisy room, touching eyes. For the president's agents, who were accustomed to him eating only food prepared and served by his stewards for safety's sake, it was a shock to see Shaw bite into his Sweet Onion Chicken Teriyaki sandwich. Lindblatt put the presidential doctor at the same table and personally inspected Shaw's container of onion rings, then tried one himself, analyzing the taste like the savviest of wine snobs, before allowing the president to eat one. It was the first time Shaw had eaten with the mustache in place, conscious when he dabbed it of its lack of sensation, like a prosthetic limb. He feared it might end up in his sandwich and possibly his stomach. Lola, three tables away, locked her gaze on him, nodding minutely to let him know all was well.

Afterward, the same cast checked in at the Hilton Pittsburgh, publicly using their false names for the first time, anxious as novice counterfeiters. They walked off to their several floors with studied nonchalance, then began arriving half an hour later in staggered order at the president's suite. In one of the two bedrooms, the local field agents and advance team conferred with the travelers. In the living room, in an antiqued desk chair, sat the president.

"Phone number?" Jess quizzed him.

"567-3000."

"Area code?"

"412."

"County?"

"Allegany."

"Zip code?"

Shaw thought. "Damn." He glanced at his index card.

"15222." Jess was planted before him, clipboard in hand. Lola stood behind him, scissors clicking, evening the hairs over his ears. Lindblatt and Boyce looked on. The room was luxurious, with the sun bouncing off the Allegheny out the window. Hugh arrived with Trevor, exclaimed over the vista, and was shushed by Lindblatt and asked to step back from the glass. He and the others who might be known to the public hadn't been given disguises, but were encouraged to wear sunglasses and hats and to avoid being seen with the president. Personally, Hugh had felt he'd have attracted less attention inside Subway without his oversized Ray-Bans and his khaki cap with its neck-protecting flap, redolent of the French Foreign Legion.

"Social Security number?" Jess continued.

"646-888-2848."

"Good. Work experience?"

Shaw searched his packed memory. "I was a busboy in high school. After graduation I took food service classes at a vocational school funded by private industry at no taxpayer—"

"Let's cut that," said Hugh. "We're not after the guy's vote."

"Never hurts," Jess replied.

Trevor took a seat. "It's like witnessing. A little obnoxious but studies show that word of mouth—"

"And speaking of that," Hugh interrupted, "everybody in the country knows what he sounds like. We're running ads here right and left, on TV and radio. So tell me—why aren't people going to recognize his voice?"

Jess's lips munched on each other. She sighed. "I don't know."

"You don't know?" Hugh smacked the side of his head. "The whole point is he's incognito and you don't know?" He paced. "What the hell did Peter the Great do?"

Lindblatt held his finger to his lips.

"Maybe he mumbled," whispered Jess. "Or he just didn't talk much." She turned toward the president. "It's a listening tour. You're not here to give speeches."

"So cut the line about vocational school funding," said Trevor.

"Unless it comes up naturally," said Jess.

It occurred to Hugh that if the trip flopped, he'd look like a sage and Jess would be out on her ass. Unfortunately, if Shaw lost the election, Hugh's own reputation and employment prospects would take a major hit. He moved forward, eclipsing Jess, standing head to head with Shaw like a boxer's trainer.

"So keep your voice low. Don't try to be the life of the party. And stay away from your stock lines."

"I really don't think 'Peace through power' is going to come up washing dishes," Jess said. She crowded Hugh. "So don't be mute. Try to get us some good audio in the break room. Joking with the common man. Hearing their concerns."

"But no Washington references," Hugh reminded him. "You're from here."

"I'm from here."

"And remember to call the manager 'sir.'"

"He knows that!" hissed Jess. She reminded Shaw, "No one's going to call you 'sir.' You're going to call them that."

"It's different," said Hugh.

"I get it! I'm not stupid!"

"Don't move, hon." Lola fussed over his false mustache. "This one little corner keeps wanting to come up."

"Terrific," Hugh moaned. "That's all we need!"

"Voices," cautioned Lindblatt.

"And accent on the positive! You're scaring him!" Calmly, Jess addressed the president. "It's a busy restaurant near the Amtrak station. They need someone right away, so you're looking good. And we've already got an agent on the staff."

"Agent Kerrigan, Mr. President," said Lindblatt. He'd changed into jacket and slacks, the outfit he'd wear while walking down the street behind Shaw and entering as a diner. "Can't miss him." Shaw was six-two and well-built, but dwarfed by Kerrigan.

Boyce joined the half-circle around the president, anxious to repair his dented image. "We've got three secret cameras already in place—two in the kitchen and one in the break room. We'll be watching you like a hawk the whole time."

"You've got your locator, right?" Lindblatt asked.

The president exhibited on his palm the small black plastic device that beamed his whereabouts, then returned it to his pocket.

"Your wire's working fine," Lindblatt continued. He patted the mic just under the collar of the president's plaid button-down shirt. "Just remember it's there. And the transmitter."

Shaw reached around to the small of his back, where the matchbox-sized transmitter was taped to his skin.

"You've got Kerrigan," said Boyce. "There's the cameras. There's your mic."

"And if anything were to go wrong," Lindblatt said, "which it won't, we've got six more agents and two vans parked a block away, and fourteen—"

"All right, all right." Jess looked at her watch. "His appointment's at one-thirty. It's show time. Let's go."

\* \* \*

The minivan cruised sedately through downtown, slowed almost to a halt while passing the long red awning of Stan's Place, turned at the next corner, and disgorged the president, then Lindblatt ten seconds later. The sun was hot. It pressed into Shaw's scalp through his sparse head of hair, as foreign as the sight of people on the sidewalk passing him without a glance. His reflection in a shop window was jarringly strange. The neighborhood was similarly unfamiliar. He'd campaigned in Pittsburgh four years before but had been somewhere in the suburbs. Alongside the nervousness about the chore ahead he felt oddly buoyant, with no aides jabbering in his ears, Lindblatt out of his sight to the rear, and no moving parade of agents clotting his route ahead. He bestowed a hearty smile on the unshaven man selling apples on the corner. He had a sudden impulse to stray from the plan and enter the ice cream shop across the street, dispensing heart attacks to his handlers. He hadn't needed to campaign for the nomination, had scarcely been out of Washington in months and then only in the usual arenas and convention halls, rarely stepping off the red carpet. The sun's sizzle on his head, the rumble of trucks, the smelling-salts scent from a door opened on a hair salon all made him feel as if he'd awakened from a coma. A few doors ahead, he sighted a figure sleeping on a length of cardboard. Approaching, he saw it was a woman, wrapped in a filthy sweater, wisps of hair dancing about her sunburned cheek. He stopped, reading with interest her lengthy tale of woe, written in faultless cursive with a Sharpie on a scrap of sheetrock, causing Lindblatt to do some unplanned window-shopping at a wig shop to avoid passing his protectee. Shaw reached in his pocket and lifted out the coins he'd been issued. He picked among them like a foreign tourist and dropped a quarter into the can beside the sign, feeling pleased to be of help. The woman's eyes snapped open.

"That all you can give?"

The president halted. He'd been trained to deal with hecklers but not the ungrateful homeless. He cast about for a reply, his mind as blank as during the 2010 debates when Jim Lehrer had asked him the gotcha question about Lesotho, then he saw Lindblatt striding rapidly forward with a hand on the gun under his jacket. It occurred to Shaw that a hail of bullets ripping through an unarmed unemployed reading teacher and mother of four might not be the best start to Operation Compassion. He reached back into his pocket, gave the woman another nickel, waved off Lindblatt even though they were supposed to seem strangers, and moved on down the sidewalk.

"A nickel?" the woman called after him. "Are you kidding me? Do you know how much a cup of coffee costs?"

Shaw realized he didn't. Into his head came a line from his last weekly address: "We're a proud people, reluctant to take charity." He reminded himself to talk to Hugh about that, marched four doors down, and entered Stan's Place. The restaurant was large, still busy with lunch customers. It gave off a meat and potatoes feel—old linoleum, waitresses to match, no danger of finding "chipotle" on the menu or of leaving hungry. He fended off the hostess's offer of a menu, told her his errand, spotted Agent Kerrigan bussing tables, and was led through the kitchen to an office, given an application, and told to wait. He filled it out, cribbing twice from the index card bearing his biography, then sat, eyes roving. Waiting for others was for him a bizarre inversion of the normal. Then again, there was nothing else he had to do—another anomaly.

The big-boned African-American manager burst into the room, simultaneously drying his hands on a towel, introducing himself simply as Keller, and speed-reading the application.

"A lot of restaurant work."

"Yes, sir. My first job, in high school, was as a busboy, actually. Right here in—"

"I don't got time to hear the fascinating story of your youth. What

I'm trying to find out is why you're still washing dishes after all these years. Are you dumb? Lazy? You steal? Doing drugs?"

The president's head spun. Not even Sam Donaldson had poked so many holes in him at one thrust. Before he could answer, Keller put a thick finger under a phone number on the application, reached toward his desk phone with his other hand, and dialed.

"Yes, a Mr. Matt Dawes is applying for work with me and gave you as a reference. What have you got to say for him?"

A block away, in one of the Secret Service's communications trucks, Jess cleared her throat nervously, studied the three monitors, none of which showed Keller or the president, then spoke into her cellphone.

"Dawes was... incredible. You really want this guy." Her free hand raked her hair. "He's got a vision of... kitchen logistics, you know, that's really outstanding."

Eyes rolling, Hugh mouthed the phrase "kitchen logistics" to Trevor.

"And what's a forty-two-year-old white boy still doing washing dishes?"

Jess floated up from her seat, passed Agent Boyce, and wandered the confined space.

"Hygiene!" she declared. "He's a huge believer in it. Always has been." She realized she'd lapsed into candidate-speak, talking about his record. She could feel the manager wavering and switched tacks. "It's a calling for him. He feels called by God to serve, and to serve Him specifically in the kitchen."

She wiped the sweat off her brow and stopped in front of one of the fans. Hugh mouthed the words "called by God" to Trevor, wincing as if he'd swallowed a mothball.

"Is that a fact?" Keller sighed. "Thanks for your time."

He hung up and studied Shaw. "I had a washer quit two days ago and another this morning. So I need somebody right quick—starting now. What I don't need is no proselytizing preacher in there shoutin' the Lord's word at my cooks! Understand?"

The president hadn't been able to hear Jess and looked baffled. "I'm not really a religious person—"

"You're not?" Keller's brows lowered.

"They pretty much make me go to church."

"They make you? They who?"

Shaw realized his slip. He racked his brains for a way out. "What I meant was—"

Keller stood up. "I don't know what your game is, but I don't have time to find out." He grabbed a freshly laundered apron from a stack and tossed it at the president. "Let's get working."

Listening via Shaw's microphone, Jess pumped her fist and shouted "Yes!" The screens, banks of equipment, and the difficulty of the operation gave the truck the feel of NASA Mission Control. They'd successfully placed a president in employment, but no chorus of cheers accompanied Jess's.

"'They make me go to church'!" Hugh's hands levitated, palms upward, asking the Supreme Being to explain.

"Fortunately," said Trevor, "it wasn't on film."

"But we're recording all the audio! So there's that to worry about!"

Jess approached Agent Pratt, in charge of the equipment. "We're not going to need that audio, okay?"

The man, perspiring in his long-sleeved shirt and tie, had a blocky by-the-book face. He seemed to struggle to process the request.

"It comes under 'superfluous documents,'" said Trevor. "It's not covered by the Presidential Records Act and it's not going into the National Archives. No problem to delete."

The man exchanged looks with Boyce, then gave a reluctant nod. Jess wondered if he were a Fiore supporter.

"But then when we spill the beans in Malibu and everyone who hired him finds out, and the manager remembers..." Hugh's head fizzed with foul possibilities.

"We're fine," said Jess. "Shaw can call him on the phone and tell him it was all playacting."

Hugh cracked his knuckles. "And let's pray that 'called by God to clean' never shows up on the Internet."

"I know, I know. Next time I'll—"

"The guy asks for a reference for a dishwasher and you tell him he's Superman, Martha Stewart, and one of Christ's apostles rolled into one."

"I just wanted him to get the job! Okay?"

"Not okay! Impossible expectations! With a rep like that he'll be lucky to last till three o'clock!" It was embarrassing to disparage the president in front of the men sworn to protect him, but Hugh figured they'd heard worse from Shaw's own wife and daughter. "And come to think of it, how's it gonna look time after time when God's gift to humanity doesn't show up the next day?"

"It's not like they invested years of training." Jess sat back down. "We'll tell them what was happening later and send 'em signed photos. They'll not only understand, they'll be thrilled, trust me. Business will go through the roof."

Trevor nodded. "They'll be building display cases for his time cards and aprons."

"And his toilet brushes," said Hugh.

"There he is," said one of the agents.

All gathered around the middle monitor. The view took in one of the stoves, a sink, counter, and the dishwashing station. A blond male in his twenties, skinny and listless, was explaining the machine's operation to the president. They ran a load of dishes, the racket covering up the conversation.

"Turn the sound up," ordered Jess.

Agent Pratt complied.

"No tips," Shaw's mentor could be heard saying. "No overtime. They take six bucks a day out of your pay for food, even if you don't eat nothing. If Keller finds any silverware in the trash, it's five bucks a piece, so watch it. You punch in over there." He nodded to his left. "Lockers in there. You got a lock?"

The president shook his head. He looked concerned. "You mean people you work with would actually—"

"Man, where you from?"

"Me?" The president froze. His staff did the same. Then Shaw's mouth puckered and relaxed in familiar fashion. "I'm from here."

His co-worker seemed to accept this and wandered away. The dishwasher finished its cycle. The president opened it, disappearing in a cloud of steam. His agents and aides settled in to watch, scooting chairs close.

"World's longest and most boring photo op," said Hugh after an hour.

Trevor returned from the ice cream shop and looked up at the screens. "Rather like watching the ocean. The dishes come in. The dishes go out."

"Which fits, 'cause the audio he's picking up sounds like a Cousteau documentary."

Jess dug into her pistachio almond. "I wish I could enjoy it."

"What's wrong?"

"The garbage disposal for starters. What if a fork goes down there and then flies up in his chest?"

"Not likely."

"Not likely? He already mangled that spoon."

"True." Hugh licked the ice cream off his own spoon. "Then again, a scar or a burn wouldn't hurt. Could help him compete with Fiore's fingertip."

Boyce and Pratt gave Hugh a look.

"Theoretically," he added. He refrained from mentioning Thorne's snakebite idea.

"Let's not go there, okay?" Jess pictured a fork buried in Shaw's forehead. "It shouldn't be about who's got the most stitches. It's not a sympathy contest."

"You're too young to remember *Queen for a Day*."

"But I remember *ER* and I really don't want the president there. And frankly, the kitchen looks dangerous. Like what's going on there?"

She leaned toward the monitor and pointed with her spoon at a junction box high on a wall. A pair of thick wires emerged from above it, tied in a knot. "Can that be right?"

Boyce peered at the screen, conferring a knowing nod on her complaint.

"I'll bet the place hasn't been inspected in years," she went on.

"Talk to Trevor about it," said Hugh. "He wrote our position on regulatory agencies run amok."

Trevor nodded, taking credit.

"And if Shaw gets electrocuted," said Jess, "or the dishwasher explodes and his face comes out looking like a fricking wonton—"

"Then we'd have the sympathy contest sewn up." Hugh ignored Boyce's glare. "Fiore would have to lose two limbs, minimum, and even then—"

"Actually," said Trevor, "we should use the safety angle. In his diary." He opened his laptop, looked up for inspiration, then began typing. "'I noticed no work-caused scars or missing digits on the jovial staff, who impressed me with their competence.'"

"Competence," said Hugh. "Perfect! That'll take care of Fiore and his finger. The guy wasn't a martyr to worker safety—he was incompetent. A klutz."

Trevor typed on. "'I'll never forget Mario, whose pride in his crew's safety record fueled a fierce distaste for unneeded inspectors, unions, and—'"

"Whoa, Trev. We're for unions, remember. For two weeks, anyway."

Jess turned her eyes on the rightmost monitor. "And check out that fan on the ledge. I swear it's about to fall into the tub of water."

Boyce leaned close to the screen. He nodded to Pratt, then texted Kerrigan.

"Point taken," said Hugh.

The back of a bearlike cook came into view. He set something in the meat slicer, prepared to cut slices, then turned around and spoke to someone. Jess shrieked and pointed. The man wore a black eye patch.

"Okay, okay." Hugh stared at the man. "Maybe we'll skip worker safety."

He sent a glance at Trevor, who reluctantly lowered a finger onto the backspace button.

The afternoon passed slowly, broken only by the drama of Keller digging through the trash can into which the president cleared tubs and coming out with two spoons and a fork. After the lunch rush, Shaw tackled the metal mountain of pots waiting in a sink.

Hugh yawned. "It's like Andy Warhol's *Sleep*, only with water."

"And you can't fast-forward," said Jess.

Trevor watched the Olympic high hurdles on his iPhone. Pratt brought in pizza. All dug in, the conversation drifting away from the president. Then Boyce pointed at a monitor.

"Check this out." He turned up the audio.

The president was in the employees' room with Kerrigan and a grand-motherly African-American woman who'd been doing food preparation.

"...two fifteen minute breaks plus your meal?" she was saying. "Who told you that?"

"It's right there." Shaw pointed to a poster on the wall.

"They don't give you no breaks here."

"But it's the law, right?" Shaw turned to Kerrigan, who shrugged. "I just thought we could relax a little—"

There was a bang off-screen. Kerrigan reached instinctively for his shoulder holster, then dropped his hand.

"Relax?" asked the woman.

"Maybe talk about any concerns you might have about the direction the country's—"

"You gonna get my ass fired. That's *my* concern!" The woman left.

"Oh, well," said Hugh.

Kerrigan sat down heavily on a chair. His apron was too small for his giant's frame. Bussing tables and mopping floors weren't in his job description and he had the weary look of a man who's unexpectedly had to tend to his toddlers for a day.

"How 'bout you?" the president said to him. "Anything you'd like to share?"

"Not him!" Hugh shouted.

"Me?" asked Kerrigan.

"Why not?" said Shaw.

"Did they work something out beforehand?" Jess asked.

No one had an answer. Kerrigan seemed taken off-guard.

"Well, let's see."    A pause.    "Being from Pittsburgh...like yourself..."    Another pause.    "I'm concerned, you know...with steel tariffs, naturally..."

Hugh wailed in disbelief.

Jess turned toward Pratt. "We're not gonna need this, okay?"

*  *  *

Kerrigan's shift ended at eight. The restaurant closed at ten. Fifteen minutes before, the last of the seven different agents posing as diners entered, hanging on while the president cleaned up in the back, uncomfortable at breaking the Service's policy of having an agent close by him at all times. Keller shooed the agent out at 10:40. At 10:55, after finishing the evening's dishes and scouring another stacked sinkful of pots, the president punched out, staggered through the back door, and was ushered into the waiting minivan. Ten minutes later he shuffled into his room at the Hilton to find Victor and Kyle there, with lights, camera, umbrella, and a chair in one corner. Lola rushed forward.

"How's my sweet boy?"

Shaw collapsed onto the bed. "Ready for sleep."

Lola began unlacing his shoes. "You poor dear. Tell me all about it." She sniffed. "You smell like..."

"Chicken-a-la-King," said Kerrigan.

The president reached groggily toward his mustache.

"Don't do that, hon! We've got filming to do."

"Tomorrow," murmured Shaw. "All I want's a shower and bed."

"I know, darlin'. But you can't take a shower till we're done."

Victor stepped forward. "We're looking for that sweaty look, Mr. President."

"We're going to film the diaries right after work," said Trevor. "While everything's still fresh in your head. Just you, talking straight to the camera."

"Jess's idea," said Hugh.

"And it's a good one," she defended herself. "Like on reality TV. It'll look private and intimate. You'll build trust with the country. Then we'll splice in footage from your jobs and the trip."

"I'm really pretty beat." Shaw's voice was slurred with fatigue.

"No worries. Nothing long."

"And nothing fancy," added Victor. "We're looking for that homemade feel. The leader as an anonymous man of the people. Your story's their story. Like Pancho Villa or Castro."

"God, I hope no one's recording this," said Hugh. Kyle, who'd been checking his equipment, conspicuously unplugged his mic.

The president threw an arm over his eyes to block the light.

"What am I supposed to say? That I got docked fifteen bucks for the goddamn silverware?"

"It's all written," said Jess. "We did it while you worked. All you have to do is memorize it and say it to the camera."

"Memorize?" the president mumbled weakly. "No teleprompter?"

"If people saw your eyes moving left to right, then they'd know it was written."

"And some of them," said Hugh, "might wonder out loud whether the words were really coming from your innermost heart."

Jess opened her bag and pulled out the draft. "It's short. You'll see. We'll take it a sentence at a time. Here goes. "It's after midnight, but I don't think I can sleep, my head's so full of impressions and insights from my first day on the job." She looked at the president. "Now you try it."

Shaw's lips moved silently.

Hugh turned her way. "I told you—shorter sentences."

"It's really just one long paragraph," she said to Shaw. "Two minutes, tops."

"We could even cut a little," said Trevor. He looked over Jess's shoulder. "'My first day on the job was one I'll remember the rest of my life.'"

Hugh edged between them. "'My first day was unforgettable.'"

"'I love my job,'" Trevor topped him.

"Too sugary," said Hugh. "People won't relate. They hate their jobs."

"Speaking of which, let's get this damn thing recorded," said Victor.

"Right." Jess looked at her sheet. "We're not gonna start rewriting. We're going with this." She cleared her throat and spoke with the exaggerated clarity of an elocution teacher. 'It's after midnight, but I don't think I can sleep, my head's so full of impressions and insights from my first day on the job.'" She waited for her student's response.

Lola leaned toward him. "Look at that," she whispered. "The poor baby's sleeping. All worn out."

All gazed at the president, his mouth gaping slightly, his plaid shirt stained under the arms, left thigh wet from a spill. The scene resembled a deathbed gathering, until Victor released a disgusted sigh, snapped off his lights, yanked the cord from the socket, and noisily started breaking down the set.

"And that's a wrap," he said. "Nice work, everybody. See you at the fucking Academy Awards."

## 9

The next morning, the president presented himself at the Ronald Reagan Job Retraining Center, just across the 9th Street Bridge. He was handed an application and clipboard, wondered what awaited behind "Waste Disposal," "Mine Safety," and other available fields, turned it in, took a number, and sat beside Lindblatt on a battered metal folding chair in the former bottling plant with several hundred other hopeless looking hopefuls. It took him only three minutes to read the Pittsburgh *Tribune-Review*, shrunk to comic-book size and only six pages long. After that, he read the Center's brochure featuring his own smiling face and upbeat quotes from satisfied customers, then switched to fanning himself with it, and after three hours waiting for his interview and aptitude test, left.

"Compassionate Conservatism needs to put a little speed on," Shaw told his advisors. They'd put the time to use by interviewing retraining instructors.

"So what did you find out?" asked the president.

"That there's a reason India does our customer service," said Jess. "It's harder with Americans."

"Not in our national character," said Hugh. "Complaining's more our thing."

"Uplifting," said Shaw.

They got better footage following the Ohio River to the north: small towns, brick courthouses, hay fields, broad-shouldered barns. North of Edgeworth, Victor filmed the president fishing, a Steelers cap on his head and a contented look on his face despite having nothing but a sinker on his line. They moved on, then spotted a river cleanup crew, halted, managed to insert Shaw and Lindblatt into the group of at-risk youth, and documented in detail the president pulling sodden mattresses, fishing line, undergarments, and rusted appliances out of the river.

"I'm not sure we're really gonna want to show this to the country," said Hugh. They watched as Shaw wrestled with a mossy toilet.

"Not exactly 'Morning in America' material," Trevor said.

"The point is he's working to improve things," said Jess.

"Maybe a Bonus Feature on the DVD," said Hugh.

Shaw worked for two hours, returning to his van disgusted by the hundreds of pounds of junk he'd pulled out but invigorated by the labor of doing so. People never see a president really moving his muscles, he realized. He'd show the country he could do more than sign bills and tap a golf ball into a hole.

They crossed into Ohio, changed license plates, ate dinner in a fish house in Youngstown, then checked into the Radisson. Shaw was yawning. Lola sat him down, put adhesive remover on his mustache, and pulled it back a centimeter at a time. He felt released. He showered. When he emerged from the bathroom in pajamas, he found his aides gathered near one of the queen beds.

"He walks up," said Hugh, "opens the drawer, finds the Gideon Bible, smiles, opens it—"

"Wait. That means he didn't bring a Bible on the trip." Jess shook her head. "No way. I say he shows the camera the Gideon Bible, he smiles, he puts it back, then he picks up his own Bible—"

"Which he's bookmarked in the New Testament," added Trevor.

"Way in the back. Makes it look like he's read everything before that."

"Better idea!" said Hugh. "He opens the drawer. We zoom in. No Bible. He frowns. He takes his own Bible from his bag and reads from that. Then, in the morning, he leaves *his* Bible in the drawer! *Then* he smiles."

Jess thought. "So what does he read the next night?"

"The Gideon Bible."

"Meaning he doesn't have his own for the rest of the trip?"

Shaw, sitting on the room's other bed, pulled back the covers, slipped between the sheets, called goodnight to Lindblatt, grabbed his eyemask from the bed table, put it on, and blindly turned off the lamp.

*   *   *

"Then we blew the morning in Youngstown," Jess said into her phone. "We had a volunteer gig lined up at the Boy's Club, but there was a TV crew doing a story, so we left. Couldn't chance it. So we drove to Akron."

"And?" asked Cora.

Anxious to stretch her legs, Jess had walked down the rutted farm road in her shorts and sandals, dirt infiltrating her toes and a deer fly circling her head. She waved if off for the twentieth time, then used her hand as a visor against the sun.

"Nothing. No work."

"Lockheed Martin wouldn't hire him? They've got a division there and we're sure as hell hiring them. Cluster bombs, Deepwater, the Ares rocket..."

"I wrote him a new resume but frankly I just didn't feel comfortable giving him an advanced weapons engineering degree."

A rough-edged sigh traveled west from Washington.

"The same way," Jess went on, "we don't really want him designing a bridge that might, you know, fall down in the future. I'm trying to stay away from situations that might lead to lawsuits or funerals."

"What about Goodyear? They're in Akron. We let 'em write the goddamn bill on tire disposal."

"About to lay off another fifteen hundred people. Only job they had posted was Employee Termination Supervisor. The last one was strangled, so there were safety concerns." Jess jigged like a sailor, trying to get a pebble out of her sandal. "How's Malibu?"

"Cold. I'm wearing a sweatshirt and fleece pants."

"You're kidding me."

"I wish. The weather's seriously screwy. They're having snow flurries in the Sierras already. The beach is a couple of miles away and I hear it's like Wales in the winter. But otherwise things are okay. The golden retriever's a hit. Young and rambunctious. Helps distract the press from the president. That and the First Lady in a bathing suit during a break in the clouds."

"No thong, I hope."

"Not a thong, but not exactly bloomers, either. You should have heard the cameras clicking."

"Chuck's not gonna be happy. Any volunteering gigs? Maybe get her on the local news, cleaning oil-soaked birds or something?"

"Never an oil spill when you need one."

"I'd never noticed that."

"But I've got something else in mind. Bianca in the kitchen."

"Yeah?"

"Counter-intuitive, I know. But it's where we need to go. Motherly. Domestic. Part of the film for the convention. More later. Where are you?"

Heat waves shimmied above the tomato fields surrounding Jess. In the distance she made out a moving multicolored row of pickers.

"Ohio. Somewhere very far from a Starbucks." She'd spent her entire life in D.C. and New York and found the flat landscape flowing away in all directions faintly disquieting.

"How is it?"

"Ohio?" Jess's voice was parched and croaky. "It's a hundred and fifty fricking degrees. Everything on the menu's fried except the coffee. And there's no work." She slapped a mosquito, smearing blood on her calf. "So we're out in the boondocks trying to get him hired as a farmworker. Not easy."

"That's not entry level enough?"

"For machines, maybe. They don't use humans to pick corn and soybeans. And with the other crops, it's turning out to be tough."

There came the creak of Cora's desk chair reclining. "Jesus."

Jess turned around and saw the president, flanked by De La Cruz and Lindblatt, walking toward the cars. Hugh preceded them. "Talk to you tonight."

She walked back at high speed and confronted Hugh. "So?"

"Not hiring."

"Not even with De La Cruz's Spanish?"

"Same as the other places. Thought we were La Migra, I'm positive."

Who could blame them, thought Jess. Three guys, all with necks like tree trunks, two of them as white as Wonder Bread, one in Bermuda shorts, wanting to pick tomatoes? She wiped the sweat off her forehead. "How many more places are we going to try?"

"How about none."

It was 3:15. They got back in the cars, backed out of the grid of farm roads they'd entered, and pulled into a roadside restaurant named Lulu's. They entered in three groups, Jess and Victor with the president and Lindblatt, the latter two peeling off toward the bathroom.

"I've been following your work," Victor addressed her.

"Yeah?"

They sat at a booth, where an age-spotted waitress dealt them menus. Victor studied Jess's slim nose and comely mouth. French-looking, he thought. Rich brown hair dancing on her chest. She seemed a perky Girl Scout leader, refreshingly wholesome after Equatorial Guinea's sullen prostitutes. How to get into her tent?

"Cora's obviously impressed. And I can see why." He picked up a menu and said casually, "You seeing anybody?"

Jess had known the conversation was leading here. "You asking me or my cover, Joyce Goffstein?"

Victor smiled. "Either one." He wondered if that sounded too desperate.

"Well, Joyce is married. Five kids. Husband's a cop, on the jealous side. And she's not really a fan of earrings on men." Jess picked up a menu. "And I'm giving celibacy a try and liking it."

Me, too, thought Victor. Minus the "liking it" part. Maybe she'd get to the same stage.

"If you're ever in the mood to fall off the wagon, let me know."

Nothing, Jess knew, would keep her truer to her vow. "I'll do that."

They studied the food offerings in silence, like a married couple. The president and Lindblatt joined them. Victor decided to show Jess some of his own work in action and caught the others' eyes.

"See this?" He touched the black pen in his shirt pocket, speaking softly enough that the two mountainous local men at a table across the room couldn't hear. "It's a camera. We'll get a life-on-the-road scene without attracting any stares."

"So what do you want me to do?" asked Shaw.

"Just act normal," said Victor. "Look at the menu. Order. Look out the window."

"Tyson made a big donation last week," whispered Jess, "so you might want to think about ordering the fried chicken."

"I thought we were just getting drinks. If we're eating, I want a burger."

"Eating's better," said Victor. "More sensual. Visceral. Shows you've got the same urges as everybody else. You're a man. You're a mammal."

"Talk about connecting with our base," said Jess.

Victor looked into the president's eyes. "Chewing. Swallowing. Sucking food from between your teeth. It's all good." He removed the pen and cleaned the lense on the sleeve of his t-shirt. "Camping out one night wouldn't be a bad idea. Cooking something fatty over a fire. Peeing on a tree trunk at dawn, the steam rising off it with the sunlight behind—"

"Whoa. You're not in Africa anymore." Jess narrowed her eyes at Victor's long face, intense and bony as one of El Greco's. "We're not gonna show him eating his enemies' flesh. And no defecating in front of the Grand Tetons."

"I'm just saying—"

"And I'm just saying it's for the Republican convention. Which is traditionally rated G."

His head swiveling as at a tennis match, the president helplessly watched his aides squabble. Jess faced him. "Like I said, Tyson would really love to see you eating chicken on national TV."

"And like I said, I'd really rather have a burger."

"No bone in a burger," said Victor. "No resonance. Not as primal."

The waitress approached, read their expressions, correctly surmised, "You need a little more time?" and u-turned.

Invisibly from behind Jess's menu, like the voice of conscience, came the words, "You've already got the beef states locked up."

"But I really don't feel like having chicken."

Victor rolled his eyes, then checked that the pen's camera was trained on Shaw. "Rolling."

"Wait a second," hissed Jess. To the president she said, "There was a big new study on red meat last month in *The Lancet.* Even the Surgeon General's changing his tune. Beef's the new tobacco."

"Nice slogan," said Shaw. "You ought to sell it to the Beef Council."

"And they might be dumb enough to buy it." She'd consulted for them the previous summer, at odds with their own ad visionary and his masterpiece, "Better Red and Dead." She was a vegetarian and had given away the sampling of bovine body parts they'd wooed her with.

"With fried chicken," Victor said, "you get to pull off the skin, then eat the flesh, then gnaw on the bones. Then you can then crack 'em and get the marrow."

"What are you?" asked Jess. "A dog?"

"Hey," the president whispered. He looked at his three tablemates in turn. "Read my lips." Then above his menu he slowly mouthed the words, "I want a burger." He repeated the performance for emphasis, watched in bafflement from across the room by the waitress and the pair of local men.

"Hallelujah," she muttered to her companions. She wrote "hb" on her pad. "He's finally decided."

"Damn strange way of showing it," said one of the men.

"What do you expect," said the other. "He's gay."

"Yeah?"

"Pretty obvious. Look at that mustache."

\*   \*   \*

The president left most of his fried chicken on his plate. An hour later and twelve miles to the west, he was bent over between rows of strawberries, picking them into a plastic flat sitting on a low rolling cart. As instructed, he began singing "This Land Is Your Land."

"Cut," said Victor. He was six feet away, camera on his shoulder. "Not so loud. You're not giving a recital, just keeping yourself company." To Kyle, holding the mic boom, he said, "Take off the dead cat. Let's try to pick up some rasp from the breeze." Kyle removed the furry mic cover. "The sound of the real outdoors. Live from Ohio."

The president restarted. "This land is your land..." The words came out in a wavering, off-key mumble, the concentration required to find the right pitches causing his hands to slow, then halt.

"Cut." Victor's head popped up above the camera. "The idea is that you're working and singing at the same time." He tried to rein in his frustration. "How about just humming it?"

"Fine."

Shaw mopped his brow with the red bandana his aides had bought him at a rural store where they'd stopped for a photo op. He returned to picking, accompanying himself with a kazoolike buzz when a mother and waist-high daughter in pigtails suddenly entered Victor's view behind the president, the girl pulling a cart bearing the words they'd covered with duct tape on Shaw's own, "Logan's Pik-It-Yore-Sef." The girl stopped before getting too close to the group of men. She whispered something to her mother behind her cupped hand.

"Because they probably think it's fun to pick strawberries, too," came the reply.

Victor closed his eyes. Kyle drew in the boom, resting his arms. Agent Boyce stepped forward protectively toward the president. The mother bent again to receive another question.

"Maybe the man just bought the camera," she answered.

Victor gave the woman a withering stare.

"Maybe he's just learning to use it, all the different buttons and things. Maybe he wants to practice on something simple."

Victor stepped to the side, wordlessly inviting them to pass, checking out the woman's wares as she did so.

"Maybe the lady's ankles are so fat that she couldn't find a man to marry her," he said within her hearing. "And that's why she has to pick her own goddamn berries."

Hugh whispered, "And maybe some smart, smart viewers are gonna figure out that we're at a pick-your-own and laugh at the president on TV really loud."

"Maybe so. Especially after he reads the dick-brained farmworker diary you're gonna write for him tonight. With the *Grapes of Wrath* quote and the Cesar Chavez cameo."

"I'll get right on it."

"Good." To the president, he said, "Let's forget the song. We won't record sound. So I'll be talking to you, okay? Just pick, then stop, wipe your brow, eat a berry, and we're outta here." Freed, Kyle headed toward the car, anxious to get back to *World of Warcraft* on his laptop. Victor assessed the light, deciding that the late afternoon shadows looked good and implied that Shaw had worked a full day. He ordered Boyce and De La Cruz to pick in the middle distance, showing that the president was working among people of color.

"Sorry," said Boyce, making no sign of moving. "Agents don't carry suitcases or run errands." The First Lady's detail from which he'd come had been criticized for doing so in the past, leaving him anxious to prove that he had the right mindset for guarding the president. "And we don't work as extras, except when the president's safety's at stake. Which it isn't in this case."

"Whatever." Victor sighed. "But you can forget the cast party." He put his eye to his viewfinder. "Rolling. Action."

The president dropped back into his crouch, picked, forgot to wipe his brow, twice pushed his hated glasses back up his sweat-slippery nose, then ate a berry.

"You didn't check for bird droppings or rodent contact," Doctor Weiss spoke up. "Do you want me to go over the disease possibilities again?"

"We don't have an extra twenty minutes," snapped Victor. He was sick of having Weiss on the set, with his Ike-style bald head and apocalyptic lectures. He had him check out the stretch of berries in front of the president, waiting impatiently, then filmed the scene again.

"Cut! C'mon, people! The fucking price tag's still on his bandana!"

He looked at Boyce and De La Cruz, who refused to budge. Kyle was gone. Hugh had drifted off. Rinaldi and the football were in the van. Weiss was searching for animal scat.

The president fumed. "I'm not helpless, you know!" He tore off the gummed tag and threw it on the ground. "Now let's go!"

"Put more berries in your mouth this time," said Victor.

"Why?"

"I want to see some juice."

Shaw felt trapped in one of his wife's fashion shoots from the past, conducted by shutter-clicking tyrants calling out states of mind as if ordering at a noisy deli. He resumed picking, reached for his bandana, wiped his dry brow, then put two berries in his mouth.

"Where's the juice?" asked Victor.

"Not ripe enough," said Weiss.

"There's gotta be some kind of liquid in there."

The president desperately added saliva, trying to produce a strawberry slurry.

"Now let some run out and wipe it off with your sleeve."

Shaw obeyed.

"That looked more like spitting. Or some weird kind of drooling. Start over."

Shaw frowned, stretched, then returned to his squat and began picking. To the rear, Hugh was talking to his wife on Trevor's satellite phone.

"I told you," he said. "It's secret. All I can say is I'm in a major metropolitan area."

The president glanced Hugh's way.

"Forget him!" yelled Victor. "Keep to the script!"

"That?" said Hugh. "Some nut on the street. You know cities." He looked out over the ocean of green. "People preaching on street corners. Talking to themselves. Here's my cab. Gotta go."

Bending at the knees, back straight, in accordance with the dozens of brochures on back pain Weiss had handed him over the years, Shaw scooted his body awkwardly down the row.

"With all respect, Mr. President," said Victor, "you look like a duck. You never see farmworkers working like that."

Reluctantly, the president straightened. He looked for juicy berries that didn't have to be tugged off the vine, judging and rejecting one candidate after another.

"And they move a lot faster," said Victor. "They're working, not shopping."

Shaw bit his tongue. After a minute's searching, he had a handful of strawberries that weren't as hard as crabapples. Sick of them but determined to finish the shoot, he put them in his mouth with as much mammalian gusto as he could muster.

"Good!" called out Victor.

Someone shouted something else. Shaw crushed the berries, worked to usher a rivulet of juice out of the corner of his mouth with his tongue, then turned and saw that everyone was peering off to the side. He straightened up. Victor's camera was tracking a brown stain low in the sky to the north. It folded in on itself, stretched out, bunched up, then divided in two, producing a faint mechanical clatter. All watched raptly as the long cloud passed out of sight.

"Wow," breathed Victor.

"What was it?" asked the president.

"Locusts. Got some great footage."

Hugh popped a soda. "Too bad we can't use it."

"How come?"

"Guess you've been in Africa too long." Hugh sipped and savored. "Our official position is that locust swarms may not actually exist. Could be mass synchronized delusions by wheat farmers who want us to cover their losses."

"Whoa. I thought the camera never lied."

"Special effects? Photoshop? Are you kidding?" Hugh sipped again. "We're recommending further study."

Victor rolled his eyes. "Oh, well."

He pulled a water bottle from his back pocket, drank, poured the rest over his head, then faced the president.

"Take twenty-seven. Berries with mouse turds."

Dr. Weiss failed to smile.

"I can't believe this," said the president.

"We're getting closer." Victor shouldered his camera and put his eye to the viewfinder. "One more time. Juice, sweat, and tears."

# 10.

The motel in Willard, Ohio where the main motorcade stayed was a one-star affair with sagging blinds, a broken ice machine, and a thriving algae population in the outdoor pool that bumped Dr. Weiss's internal threat level to red. He lifted the paper covers off of the glasses in Shaw's room and slowly looked in as if expecting to find spitting cobras. He replaced the pillow with one brought from Washington and dumped the bathroom's complimentary products in the wastebasket. Along with a supply of the president's blood, he traveled with guaranteed-safe containers of the president's shampoo, conditioner, and other potions. Boyce tested the TV, phone, lamps, air-conditioner, and hair dryer. Lindblatt stripped the president's bed to the mattress, inspected all coverings with rabbinical care, pocketed as a tip the quarter he found, and remade the bed. They ate at the steak house next door, Weiss surreptitiously inserting a meat thermometer into Shaw's portion. The president fell asleep an hour later while watching the Olympic platform diving competition.

Operation Compassion left in shifts in the morning, later than scheduled due to a female tourist's noticing the "I ♥ Border Collies" bumper sticker on Chevy One, which led her to quiz Shaw in Helen Thomas fashion about his hastily concocted history with working dogs, followed by a docent-led tour of her wallet photos of her own canines.

Clouds and cooler air moved in overnight. The group's luck changed with the weather. In Columbus, the president was hired at the first stop they made, a busy hand carwash on East Broad Street that Patrick had researched. In his red company t-shirt and Ohio State Buckeyes cap, Shaw worked elbow to elbow with a crew that got a near-perfect score in diversity: Hispanic, Hmong, African-American, and even a Pacific Islander.

"Get as close as you can," Jess instructed Victor, filming with his telephoto through the window of their rental van across the street. "We really need to see those faces."

"Faces? I'm already zooming up into the guys' pores."

"Too bad there's not a Native American," said Trevor.

"The melting pot's always half empty for you." Hugh bit into his apricot Danish. "He'll pick up some Indians out west. Same for Bushmen, Lapps, Neanderthals. . ."

No agents had been hired, so Lindblatt drove one of the motorcade's cars in and asked for the full detailing package, giving him an excuse for standing near the crew or watching from the waiting room for a full three hours. A succession of other agents took advantage of the situation to wash their vehicles and check out the premises. With Shaw's arms in constant motion drying cars, his mic picked up only noise until his lunch break. The advance team had planted a camera in the cramped employee room, where there were only two chairs and no table; workers turned out to eat in shifts out back, sitting on crates in the shade. Lindblatt stood, yawned, and, as if stretching his legs, wandered that way in the president's wake. Jess and the others had moved into the communications truck, ears cocked to the president's audio feed.

"Shaw? I dunno. I guess he's doin' a pretty good job, you know."

The voice was African-American. There came the sound of the president drinking, followed by a soft belch.

"Sure, you hear people rag on him, time to time. 'He don't know shit. He don't care nothin'. He just screwin' his woman while the world burn down. He hate black folks. Let the cities go to hell. If he bring his car in here, we gonna dry it with sandpaper. Then slash his tires. Then cut off his balls. Make him drink wax-stripper, then drop a match down his throat.' Stuff like that. You know. And maybe they're right. Probably are."

The sound of rapid chewing came through the speaker.

"Why you ask? You votin' for him?"

"Me?" The president sucked something up a straw. "I...you know...I haven't made up mind. Not completely."

Shaw got off at three and climbed into the van. Wanting to milk Ohio for as many locations as possible, the entourage drove two hours to Cincinnati. There the president applied at a Jack in the Box for an open morning shift, but had trouble producing urine for the drug test while being watched by the assistant manager. The man offered Shaw a guaranteed clean sample for twenty dollars and fifteen percent of his first two paychecks.

"Thanks but no thanks," his aides heard Shaw say.

" 'We're a nation of entrepreneurs,' " Trevor quoted from the speech he'd written for Shaw's appearance at Wharton. " 'Ready with supply wherever there's demand.' "

Inside the building, the president virtuously zipped up his pants. The assistant manager lowered his offer to ten percent.

"I don't really think I'd be happy here," Shaw said. He glared at the skinny twenty-something, had half a mind to throw him against the wall and make a citizen's arrest, but knew he couldn't get involved with the police. He walked out, furious at the unpunished manager and himself, feeling like Clark Kent helplessly watching a purse-snatching. It was dinner time. The backup plan was to offer his services at a soup kitchen downtown. The offer was accepted, he and Kerrigan mashing potatoes and assembling giant bowls of salad in the kitchen, staying out of the spirited discussion between two other helpers on whether the sun orbited the earth.

"These are our people," said Hugh, eating a sub in the truck. " 'A fine people,' " he added, quoting from another presidential speech.

Jess shook her head. "I know we need the church vote, but didn't Copernicus settle this like five hundred years ago?"

"News travels slow in the heartland. Still on dial-up."

"And with Fiore being a Catholic," said Trevor, "he can brag he's got the edge here. His church arrested Galileo. That's hard to trump."

"Maybe we should try." Hugh considered. "What if we showed Shaw, I don't know…Something even more prescientific. Praying to the sun. Maybe talking to a river."

Jess wrinkled her face. "I'm not seeing a lot of temples to the sun around. What I am seeing is a lot of little white Protestant—"

"Carving something. An image of an animal."

"It's the evangelicals we need, Hugh, not the Druids."

"Sacrificing an animal."

"Are you crazy? We just gave them a dog!"

"Ohio's still in play, okay? I'm finding us any votes I can!"

That night, Hugh called the latest of the president's press secretaries, Gil Olivares, in Washington. He'd come on board four months before, his cinnamon skin and rolled r's meant to answer the charge that the administration was more country club than cross-section; that he'd been a member of a country club in his native San Antonio had been his first hot potato.

"Day labor tomorrow," said Hugh. "Latino land. So it's potentially huge. If we get some good footage, it could swing Colorado and New Mexico and even California. So be my Berlitz. What's he gonna need?"

"Spanish tutor to the president. Never knew this was in my job description."

"And I never knew I'd be posing as a traveling bank examiner."

Gil took a deep breath. "Okay. Greetings. *Hola* or *buenos días*. Either one…"

Hugh began writing, one eye on the hotel room's TV, where Mahmoud Fazel, the blind Muslim weightlifter from Pakistan was readying himself. He'd lost his sight in the accidental drone attack on Peshawar, his nephew leading him by the hand toward his bar with its massive weights, their slow-moving entrances reviled by the right as political pity-mongering.

"How would he say 'I'm from here'?"

"*Soy de aquí.*"

"And Weiss wants him to learn 'Does it have tomatoes in it?' The E. coli thing."

Fazel put his hands on the bar, then ran them to the weights and back to find their correct position. Between his dark glasses and thick black beard, his facial scars were conspicuous.

"You watching the Olympics?"

"Yeah," Gil replied. "PR disaster. I'm gonna need a shield at tomorrow's briefing."

"Maybe you should sign on with Al Jazeera. All the bad news on your plate turns to gold."

Grasping the bar, his body low, head down as though prostrated in prayer, the weightlifter mumbled inaudibly.

"We really need this guy to get caught with steroids," said Gil. His previous work had been in sports broadcasting.

"Or bratwurst and beer. Write him up for a fatwa."

The weightlifter's body jerked into motion, hefting the bar to his waist, then his shoulders, elbows quivering. He gathered himself, muttering again, then propelled the weights upward with a shout, bringing his legs together for a tense, tipsy moment as he held five hundred sixty pounds triumphantly above his head. Then he roared and let the barbell crash to the ground.

"I knew football was sublimated warfare, but weightlifting?"

Gil sighed. "Now for the goddamn Pakistanian anthem."

"If they can find the music. And a belly dance orchestra."

"I just turned it on. Was that for the gold?"

"Yeah," said Hugh.

"Fabulous."

"It'll pass. Same in politics. The country's got the attention span of a gnat. Swimming's up next. Relax."

They returned to beginning conversational Spanish. Hugh passed the lesson to the president the next morning over breakfast. They then drove to a Home Depot west of downtown, where Shaw and Agent De La Cruz emerged from the van and joined the end of the line of Hispanic men hoping to get hired as day laborers. They tried to blend in, leaning against a low wall, heads down except when a big pickup passed, Shaw's face protected from the already fierce sun by a Reds baseball cap. Listening in the communications truck across the street, Hugh looked up at the video on one of the monitors.

"I don't believe it. There's other white people in line."

Jess stood and peered at the screen. "My god." She looked shaken. "That's definitely not going in the film. Way too depressing."

"We have nothing to fear but fear itself, and taking jobs that illegal aliens used to do."

Bleary-eyed after a night of Lola's sleeptalking, Jess returned to reading the news on her BlackBerry: Vasectomies were up, indicating deepening loss of faith in the country's future. Vice President Coburn, campaigning at a Virginia food bank, had demanded that the Ukraine sell us wheat. A Pensacola woman who'd moved her aged father home from a VA hospital, in line with Shaw's Family First Initiative, had been found guilty of dismembering him, selling his organs on eBay, and continuing to collect his Marine Corps pension. The half million members of Friends of Cassandra had pledged to carry her posts and podcasts in the wake of cyber attacks against her sites. Pretty Boy Nussbaum had robbed another bank. The CEO of a bailout-reaping investment firm had been thrown out of his eightieth-floor window by an angry mob. Jess looked up. Hadn't they jumped out windows on their own during the Great Depression?

Through the speaker came the sound of Shaw clearing his throat. She glanced at the monitor and saw the president facing the straw-hatted man beside him. "Show time," she said.

"*El temperatura...*No. *La temperatura...Es...*No. *Está?*"

"Jesus." Hugh winced. "We went over this at breakfast!"

"We've been telling the country he speaks Spanish for years," said Trevor. "If this ever gets out—"

"It won't," Jess vowed.

"*...está extremelamente...*No. *Está muy...muy...*" He paused. "*Hoy, la temperatura está muy...alto. Alto? Elevantando? No...*"

De La Cruz stepped forward, unable to bear any more. "*El dice que hace mucho calor hoy.*"

The man before them grunted matter-of-factly.

"Try something else," Jess prompted. "Something we can use."

As though he'd heard her, the president cleared his throat again, thought for a moment, then confidently unfurled the statement, "*Soy de aquí.*"

His interlocutor's eyebrows lifted. "*De que parte?*"

Shaw's eyes expanded. He glanced at De La Cruz, then back at the man. "*Otra vez?*"

"*De que parte de la ciudad eres?*"

The president inhaled. "Say again?"

"Where do you live in Cincinnati?" De La Cruz translated for him.

Shaw racked his brains. He'd campaigned often in Columbus and Cleveland but didn't know Cincinnati as well.

"East side?" asked the straw-hatted man in serviceable English. "West side?"

The president's frustration with the conversation boiled over. "Then what the hell were we doing talking in Spanish?"

"Cut!" shouted Hugh.

All three men were hired an hour later. With his aides and agents in discreet pursuit, they rode in a truck bed with five other men, De La Cruz keeping a protective arm in front of the president in lieu of a seatbelt. The truck wound its way through the western suburbs, passing developments ravaged by foreclosure and finally stopping before an Italianate mansion, where the crew spent the next five hours installing a sprinkler system.

"He looks happy working," said Jess. "Moving his body."

The van was parked two doors away. Hugh observed. "Maybe this is the vacation he didn't know he needed."

Jess aimed an ear toward the speaker. "The sound of shoveling's good, too."

"A hell of a lot better than his Spanish."

Posing as a curious neighbor, Victor ambled nonchalantly up the sidewalk and stopped to observe, recording the scene with his pen-camera. He pretended not to recognize Lindblatt, walking one of the bomb-sniffing dogs, lingering in similar fashion. Avoiding Spanish, the president dug trenches and sweated in silence, wondering what his wife was doing at that hour and whether it had been wise to leave her with his double for two weeks. In the truck, Hugh trolled blogs. Escaping the heat and tedium,

Trevor had driven to a pricey German restaurant for lunch, cleaning his gold wire-rims' lenses with ice water, opening his laptop and checking the posts on the Asian-Americans for Shaw website, stopping by the three Margaret Thatcher fan sites he frequented, then composing that night's diary between sips of chilled Gewurztraminer.

"It was then," he wrote, "I knew for certain that I wouldn't trade this moment, eating a simple bean burrito, for the fanciest state dinner. Relaxing in the shade—"

A Hispanic water steward refilled his glass, the man's nameplate reading "Ignacio."

"—with my new friend, Ignacio, who seemed surprised at my command of the Spanish language."

His venison arrived. He saved his work, then took out the copy of *Us* that Hugh had bought him to put him better in touch with the common man. He scanned the headlines: "Brianna Snubs Kylie." He wondered idly who they were, along with Shawn, Terry, Jen, Tim, Cory, Kris, Heidi, Adam...He intended only to skim the articles, but found the texts so shrunken that skimming was a full reading. After finishing it and his meal, he reopened the president's diary and resumed writing, feeling the magazine's influence.

"We found we had much in common, and that both of us were closely following not only the presidential campaign, but the Latin Grammy Awards, whose winners will be announced the very week after the election. What an exciting time for our nation! We spoke enthusiastically of Juanes, Kany, Julieta, Fito, Gloria..."

\*   \*   \*

Victor was waiting in the president's hotel room when he entered. Dispensing with sound so he could talk to his subject, he tracked Shaw across the room, squeezed into the bathroom behind him, and filmed him washing his hands at the sink.

"Good! Keep it going! Now back to the soap."

"But they're clean," Shaw protested.

"Don't move your mouth! More scrubbing! It'll show how dirty you got."

The president sighed. Through clenched teeth he muttered, "I know how to wash my own hands."

"Maybe we should call the book *He Washed Among Us*," said Hugh.

Victor ignored him. "Now let me zoom in on the nicks on your right hand. Too bad you didn't break a nail."

"A real shame," said Shaw out of the camera's sight. He dried his hands, than dutifully sat under the lights for his diary taping, staring at the teleprompter he'd insisted his staff use. Jeans and t-shirt conspicuously sullied with dirt and grass stains, he did a run-through of the text.

"Ignacio complimented me on my use of the sumjuctive verb endings, which so many—"

"*Sub*junctive," Trevor corrected him.

"Sumjuctive."

"Sub-JUNC-tive," said Hugh. "Like 'junk.' Shouldn't be too hard to remember. Just think of this film we're making."

"Thanks for the morale boost," said Jess. "Appreciated."

"Take him off the credits," tossed out Victor.

"Please, I insist," Hugh said.

The president squinted into the lights. "Would all of you shut up?" He sighed. "I've got a killer headache, and I swear I'm gonna have skin cancer from the lights by the time this trip's done."

He began again from the top. Victor conferred with Lola, who licked her finger, dragged it over the dried mud on the president's left knee, and transferred the smudge to his brow.

"Brown badge of courage," said Victor.

Shaw pressed on. "Working beside my new friend, Ignacio—"

"Whoa," Jess halted him. "I don't know about 'my new friend, Ignacio.' Haven't we already had 'my new friend, Mario' and 'my new friend, Latanya'? It's sounding too much like Sesame Street."

"Or like one of those serial killers," said Lola. "You know, the way they go state to state, making friends."

"Point taken," said Trevor. "'My work mate, Ignacio.'"

"Work *mate*?" Jess shook her head. "I don't think so."

"Partner?"

"Are you crazy? We're not after the gay vote."

"Not us," said Hugh. "We're going after the Spanish teachers."

"Can you say 'work mate' without snickering?" Jess asked the president.

"Colleague?" said Trevor.

"Too white-collar."

"Buddy?"

"Too friendly. They were only together a few hours."

"Chum? Teammate? Associate?"

"They were crawling around in the dirt, not a boardroom."

"The point is that they were working together."

"'My new ditch-digging associate'? C'mon."

"Doesn't sound natural."

"Not this again!" said Shaw.

Victor gave a loud whistle.

"Hey!" he shouted. "You know what? If you guys want it natural, then tear up the fucking script! Try letting him say what he's really feeling!" He started his camera and put it on the president. "Give it to me raw! Straight from the heart!"

Shaw seemed at a loss, as when he'd been asked his Cincinnati neighborhood. Then his false mustache twitched.

"Straight from the heart?" His breathing sped up, his ears reddening. His glasses slid down his nose. He grabbed them and threw them across the room.

"Well, here it is. I'm sick of the whole goddamn thing!"

The group froze. The words ricocheted around the room. Lindblatt, arms raised to warn them about volume, said nothing. There came a collective exhaling.

"I didn't say it'd be usable," said Victor.

\*　\*　\*

Jess scratched the taping. No sooner had she given everyone the evening off then Chuck Thorne called and put them all back in motion. The president's slot the next day in Indianapolis had fallen through. They'd skip Indiana and no-chance Illinois and head straight for perennially close

Missouri. Thorne had lined up an 8 a.m. job at a clothing factory in St. Louis—a plum for showing Shaw as a friend to immigrants and unions and peeling off some of Fiore's votes.

They checked out and piled into the cars, Shaw finding himself envying the commoners he'd worked with that day: no advisors or fake name or frantic schedule or daily diary...In the seat behind him, Major Rinaldi slept. His constant sniffling had led Shaw to practically order Dr. Weiss to give the man something for his allergies. Weiss's concoction had worked but had knocked out Rinaldi, in charge of the equipment that could launch the next war. Shaw prayed it wouldn't be needed that night. He inserted his earphones, began Lesson One of the *Spanish for Gringos* audio Jess had handed him, and promptly joined Rinaldi in sleep.

They crossed the Mississippi at 10:25. Six cars to the rear, Hugh said through a yawn, "It's Friday, this must be Missouri." The Arch gleamed in the moonlight to his right. Then below it his eye took in the vast, mismatched collection of tents and tarps stretching endlessly along the river.

"Wow. I heard they swept the homeless out of Seattle for the Olympics. Maybe this is where they sent 'em." The scene partook of both a Middle Eastern market and a Civil War encampment. Hugh glimpsed a homemade Fiore sign taped to a streetlight, then the official version a block later on a giant 14' by 48' billboard.

"What's the latest from Klaus on Missouri?" he asked Trevor.

"We're down nine points."

"And we're calling that 'undecided' on our website?"

"It's only August," Trevor said. "Plenty of time. A touchdown and a field goal and it's ours."

"Wonder what Shaw's come-from-behind record was?" Hugh headed for sportsstatsjunkie.com on his phone, juked his way through its the maze of information, and stared at the numbers he'd come looking for. "Oh, well."

The president's group spent the night at the Union Station Marriott, which should have been bustling on a Friday night, but wasn't. People didn't have the money to travel, Shaw realized. The eerily empty halls and the thunderstorms that rolled through past midnight gave him the sense he was sleeping in a haunted house. He received his security briefing the next morning via secure phone, reviewed the present tense of Spanish -er verbs while showering, traveled ten blocks, and at 7:55 walked into the ancient brick building that housed Millennium Manufacturing.

"Wonder what millennium we're talking about?" Hugh asked Trevor.

"Does look a little Victorian," said Jess.

"Or medieval," said Trevor. They moved into the communications truck. The workers entering the building's rusty metal door were nearly all Hispanic and Asian. Falling in behind them, the president and Agent De La Cruz were hired at once. Thorne had served in the Marines with the factory's owner, and without mentioning the true identities of the applicants, had asked if there might be short-term work for them. The owner was pleased to comply, as people usually were when receiving a call from the chief of staff of the President of the United States.

Hugh picked through the open box of doughnuts and sat on his usual folding chair. Through the speaker flowed Shaw's footfalls and the piercing squeak of his dolly as he unloaded boxes of buttons and zippers from a truck.

"No video?"

"Lindblatt is posing as an EPA inspector," said Jess. "He'll put some cameras in place."

Hugh winced at the dolly's squeal. "That's good, cause the audio isn't thrilling me."

Inside, De La Cruz had been put to work, against his wishes, two floors above the president, sealing stacks of blouses in plastic. Below, the president trundled back and forth to the delivery truck at the loading dock. Neither could know that the secretary who'd shown Lindblatt into her boss's office had caught a glimpse of his shoulder holster, had returned to her desk, snatched up her phone, and whispered to the Peruvian supervisor on the ground floor that an immigration raid was about to take place. A diminutive Paul Revere, the supervisor strode rapidly down the aisles, sending the feared words *La Migra* left and right. The illegals in the room fled toward the loading dock, where the Guadalajaran driver, talking on his cellphone while his truck was unloaded, comprehended the situation, hung up, remembered being caught sprinting up the block during a raid in

Houston, and windmilled his arm like a traffic cop, directing escapees into his nearly empty truck. Inside, just turning with his dolly stacked high, the president was bowled over by the human flash flood.

"What was that?" asked Trevor.

"Sounded like Shaw dropped his dolly," Jess replied.

Hugh bit into his crumb doughnut. "Be just our luck if he gets fired before we get any video."

Fifteen seconds later, the driver had yanked down the cargo door. He scrambled into the cab, put the truck in gear, and gunned it down the alley.

"And now our audio's breaking up," said Jess.

"Again?" said Trevor.

Agent Pratt, on a stool, communing with his coffee thermos, still groggy from his storm-interrupted sleep, let the remarks wash over him. He was sick of Shaw's aides and their constant squabbling, and tired as well of the audio problem, a frequent issue when the president's upper body was in motion, as it was that day unloading boxes. He gave it a minute to see if it fixed itself.

"Audio's gone entirely," said Jess.

Behind her, Hugh was grateful for the vacation from the dolly's squeaking. He took another bite of doughnut. "No loss there."

# 11.

The truck turned and the human cargo within was thrown like a wave against the driver's-side wall. It was black inside. The truck was midsize. Shaw had no idea how many people were inside it. All he knew was that some number of them were splayed on top of the dolly that was crushing him. He had a flashback of being on the bottom of a dogpile in football. This, by contrast, was co-ed, without pads, and played on a splintery plank floor. The air was filled with exclamations in Spanish. Shaw picked out *La Migra* several times and suddenly deduced what had happened. He pressed the dolly's metal slats upward as if trying to force open an iron maiden, while the group, as in a game of anatomical pickup sticks, gradually disentangled itself. At last he was able to turn onto his side, felt one of the zipper boxes being shoved into his ribs by his neighbor, then was swept toward the passenger side with all the others when the truck turned again. The sole of a shoe was digging into his jaw. He started to yell, then wondered if he'd be taken for an immigration agent. He grabbed the ankle, unsure of the owner's gender, and forced it downward, eliciting a female's "*Suéltame!*" Beneath him, the transmission gargled. He could feel the truck accelerating, but didn't sense they were going at freeway speed. He'd been often in St. Louis, but only in visits measured in hours and couldn't begin to guess his present route.  Speculation in Spanish flickered about him as the passengers again separated themselves, bobbing like shipwreck victims as the truck took a series of potholes.  Staying low, a few of them blindly finding the waist-high U-hooks and hanging on, they bounced along for another five minutes.  The truck turned, braked, and halted, the engine still running.  A traffic light, Shaw thought.  Then the cargo door's clasp rotated crisply and the door shot up.

"*Bájense!*" shouted the driver.

The crowd of twenty scurried to the opening.  The president, on hands and knees, was last.

"Could you tell me where—"

The driver gaped at him, astonished, but seemed to have no time to understand and pulled him out by the arm.  "*Rápido!*"

Shaw squinted against the light and climbed down into a narrow alley.  The driver yanked down the cargo door, hoisted himself into his cab, threw a "*Suerte!*" over his shoulder, and drove on.

You're welcome, Shaw thought.

The air smelled powerfully of well-aged garbage.  He looked about him.  Most of the group had exited the alley in the direction the truck had taken.  He headed that way.  Dilapidated brick buildings, commercial on one side, backed up to the puddle-pocked alley as to a latrine.  Black plastic garbage bags lay in deep drifts on both sides.  The president heard snoring and saw just ahead a man and woman next to a grocery cart packed with belongings, the pair sprawled atop an expanse of black plastic as if on a vast king bed.  Vaguely, he recalled mention of a garbage strike in the Midwest.  St. Louis?  Or was this business as usual here?

He rubbed the knee that the dolly had ground against and set off, hobbling.  Dueling Spanish radio stations twined in the air above him.  Over a door to his right a hand-painted sign proclaimed "*Carniceria El Cerdito.*"  This was followed by "*No Estacionarse,*" then "*Peluquería Marisol.*"  Beyond Lesson One of *Spanish for Gringos*, he told himself.  He had trouble making out the letters in a sign farther on, then stopped.  His hands jerked up to his face.  His glasses were gone.  He glanced behind him on the ground.  They weren't there.  Must be in the truck, he realized.  He was sick of wearing them and hoped his handlers would let him return to contacts. For the moment, without either, his distance vision was limited. Then his hand shot into the right front pocket of his jeans. His locator was gone. Must have slid out in the truck, too. He unfastened the top button of his khaki work shirt, unclipped the mic, and peered at it. Its tiny head had been crushed and hung weakly from its wire. He tapped it with his finger, then blew on it, said "Mayday" several times, then "Can you hear me?" He broke off when a Latino man with a tattooed neck emerged from a door, gave him a long look, and tossed a garbage bag onto the pillowy mountain growing out of his dumpster.

Shaw moved ahead purposefully, as if on his home turf, trying not to limp and appear vulnerable. He switched from speech to thought. You're fine. You're bigger and stronger than these people. Nobody's going to mess with you. Plus you're their president! Then he began wondering if he could prove it. Without the blue contacts he'd worn for decades, his eyes were brown. Lola had just checked his scalp that morning for signs of blond roots and found none. Ripping off the false mustache would help, but without adhesive remover it might take his lip with it. Every card in his wallet had "Matt Dawes" on it. He pictured himself surrounded by gangmembers, desperately feeding them White House trivia—the movie theater in the East Wing, Situation Room gizmos, POTUS and FLOTUS, things the movies got wrong—while their skeptical leader held a gun to his head and guffawed.

All you need is a phone, he told himself. He hadn't been allowed to carry a cellphone out of fear that the line wasn't secure and that the device could tell others his whereabouts. That, as it happened, was exactly what he needed to do. He came to the end of the block, veered right, then hit a commercial street and turned onto it. Civilization, though not the one he knew. The line spoken suavely by the tuxedoed male on the tequila billboard across the street was in Spanish and lost to him. To his left, the free newspaper stacked in a wooden holder was *La Voz del Interior*. The store before him was titled *Estética Unisex de Gabriela*, evidently a beauty salon. Wasn't St. Louis at the center of the country? It seemed from where he stood more like a hinterland, a just-acquired colony only partially absorbed into the empire. A mother with her brood trailing her like ducklings passed him, the woman with the Virgen of

Guadalupe on her t-shirt, her son's sporting *Viva Las Chivas*. The president walked past a scissor-gated used furniture store, a bar with *Cerrado* in the high window, two empty buildings sporting *Se Vende* signs, and came to *Comedor Familiar de Carmen*. The smell of food was an international language. It was open. Surely phone lines had reached this far. He went in.

A TV high on the wall blared in Spanish. The cloth-covered card tables with folding chairs held a single male diner bent over his breakfast, a fork in one hand and a scoop of corn tortilla in the other. He looked up at Shaw and chewed on the sight. A female toddler in diaper and stained t-shirt waddled out of the kitchen and did the same. Shaw was president of their country but felt more like an intruder. He looked for a phone, didn't see one, approached the kitchen entrance, and tried in vain to attract the attention of the woman within, bent over a sink with her back to him. The whole incognito thing was working too well, he thought. Where was the rich baritone voice announcing his entrance, then the four ruffles and flourishes on bugles and drums? "Hail to the Chief" had come to feel like an overplayed song on the radio, something he dreaded hearing—except at that moment. The president cleared his throat for the fourth time. The woman didn't hear this over the clatter of her work but turned toward the stove in the course of her duties and suddenly noticed his presence.

"*Sí?*" Her face was dark as a strop.

With exaggerated clarity, Shaw stated the sentence he'd had much time to mentally assemble. "*Necesito uno teléfono.*"

The woman fixed him with a suspicious gaze. She pointed toward the street. "*Cuatro cuadras.*"

The president looked blank.

"Four blocks," she translated.

Shaw rolled his eyes and felt his internal pressure building. "*Es muy importante!*"

She considered, then walked past him, barely up to his shoulder, a bellrope of black hair behind, and drew a cordless receiver from below the small counter. Being twice her size and white apparently came with advantages. Shaw was pleased to accept them.

"*Una llamada local?*"

Shaw realized her meaning. *"Sí!"* he assured her.

The woman handed him the phone and puttered nearby, making certain, he felt sure, that the number he dialed had no more than seven digits. He smirked and wished he could tell her that he commanded a three trillion dollar budget and could cover any long-distance charges. He looked down at the keypad. Then it dawned on him: he had no idea what number to punch. Aides and secretaries always placed his calls, personal calls included. He had no idea of his wife's or daughter's numbers, much less Chuck Thorne's or Hugh's. And good luck trying to get through to the Secret Service, much less the White House.

Thinking, he looked up, and found his eye snagged by a pinstripe-suited car dealer on TV, his voice fast as an auctioneer's and enhanced with echo effects. Everything about the man inspired distrust, and yet seemed strangely familiar to Shaw. He couldn't follow the salesman's Spanish, syllables clacking like castanets, but he also couldn't tear his eyes off his dyed pompadour and whitened teeth. The sight of him engaged a gear in Shaw's brain and set it slowly rotating. The ad ended. Slowly, the president put down the phone.

*"No teléfono,"* said the president.

"No?"

Shaw felt dazed. He floated over to an empty table and sat. The woman looked concerned. She picked up her daughter and approached.

"Food?" she asked.

The president considered. He knew what he wanted. It was only nine o'clock, but being incognito came with advantages as well. "Could I get a beer?"

* * *

When the president's audio signal hadn't come back on, Agent Pratt in the communications truck had texted the news to Lindblatt, who was pretending to be an EPA inspector and couldn't be seen wearing an earpiece. As Lindblatt was trying at that moment to talk his way past the manager and onto the floor to put cameras in place, a job the advance team hadn't had time to accomplish given the sudden itinerary change, he'd ignored the buzzing in his pocket while arguing for a long-overdue inspection. It was more than a minute later when he'd pulled out his phone and read "No POTUS audio." He'd returned to the toad-faced man before him, whose maddeningly slow delivery and elusive phrases, he'd come to realize, veiled the offer of a bribe in exchange for skipping the inspection. Lindblatt had curtly declined. This had been seen as a sign that the offer of $500 and anything he liked in XL had been insultingly low. The manager had raised his offer to $1000 and a complimentary frolic at one of the city's finest houses of prostitution. Lindblatt had excused himself from this negotiation to call Pratt, telling him to send Agent Boyce in to fix or replace the president's mic. Each linkage in the chain of communications had consumed time, and by the time Boyce entered the front door, Shaw had departed. The sight of Boyce—another well-built stranger—confirmed for the doubters among the employees that there was indeed a raid in progress and set off a secondary scramble toward the building's various doors. In the midst of this chaos, Boyce searched for the president, sweat pressing out his palms, and reported his failure to find him to Lindblatt, who called in backup. Vans and SUVs disgorged agents front and rear. The street and alley were blocked off, the building was sealed and searched from rooftop to basement incinerator. Lindblatt passed the grim news to his superiors, picturing himself forced to stand in a pillory on H Street to be spat on by agents entering Secret Service headquarters. Jess saw herself as the butt of a *Saturday Night Live* skit.

The president's locator had stopped transmitting at the same time his mic had. The Secret Service caught up with the truck Shaw had been unloading at another garment factory, across the river in East St. Louis. The driver, continuing his route as if nothing were amiss, admitted to having transported the fleeing workers but claimed not to have noticed the president, swearing he'd dropped the illegals at the Greyhound station and that he'd taken them under duress, with a gun held on him. A search of the cargo area turned up the president's glasses and the crushed locator but no other trace of him. The scores of policemen and agents combing the blocks around the bus station had so far done no better.

"Why the hell doesn't he call?" Jess demanded. She and Hugh and Trevor were pacing outside Millennium Manufacturing, praying Shaw would pop out of a trash can or turn a corner. "Or take a cab back here. Or go to a police station. Anywhere!"

Hugh might have enjoyed seeing her suffer if he weren't more frightened than he'd ever been.

"The whole goddamn idea was always crazy!" he screamed at her.

"It was a good enough idea that both our bosses liked it!"

"Peter the Great. Jesus Christ! Ivan the Terrible roasted people alive. Does that mean we oughta do it, too?" He'd called Thorne, who'd already heard, at high volume, from Archibald. "Do you have any idea how many heads are going to roll because of this?"

"And mine's gonna be first, so get off my case!"

"And what the hell's Victor doing?"

With his camera on his shoulder and Kyle beside him, boom mic held high, they were recording the ongoing search.

"He said it's in case Shaw turns up," Trevor reported. "And we all laugh about it later."

This outcome seemed suddenly even more remote to the three of them.

"The blooper reel," said Hugh. "Crucial to national security. What a team."

Jess's phone rang.

"What happened?" shouted Cora from the line's other end.

Hugh watched Jess's eyes well up.

"I don't know what happened! Nobody does!"

"Well, somebody blew it! It doesn't really matter who, cause if Shaw doesn't come out of this alive, you and I are going to have our names carved in stone next to John Wilkes Booth and Lee Harvey Oswald!"

Jess broke down crying, Hugh and Trevor turning chastely away.

"Carved in stone," said Hugh. "Like Mt. Rushmore, only different. Wonder where they'd put it?"

"St. Louis would be logical," said Trevor.

"No fucking mountains."

"Unless it's more of a theme park."

"Assassin Land."

"Who'd want to kill or kidnap somebody unloading boxes of zippers?"

"True," said Hugh. "But then where is he?"

Trevor, like everyone else, had no answer.

\* \* \*

Two Tecates and a basket of pan dulce later, the president went into the restaurant's bathroom, peeled his transmitter off his lower back, wrapped it and his mic in paper towels, and deposited them deep in the metal trash can. He opened his wallet and found he had $34 in cash. He paid his bill with this, and his taxi ride to a mall two miles away. He grabbed a cart on his way into Target and proceeded to put into it a towel and washcloth, soap, toothbrush, toothpaste, sunscreen, a digital camera, a pocket-sized voice recorder, a notebook and pen, a six-pack of water and three bags of chocolate chip cookies. He paid using the credit card he'd been issued with Matt Dawes's name and likeness, then used the card at an ATM next door to take out $200. At the Verizon store further on he bought a prepaid phone and $20 worth of minutes. He found a bench in the shade. He remembered the number for the Malibu house but couldn't risk it; Cassandra had worn out her welcome with all four grandparents in four days, been dumped in Malibu, and might pick up one of the extensions, as she'd been caught doing, gathering fuel for her blog. Instead, the president called his mother, who had Bianca's cell number in her address book, Shaw masking this errand under detailed inquiries about her health. He next called Bianca, got her voice mail, and instructed her to tell Thorne and Archibald that he was perfectly safe and would see everyone in Malibu in a week as planned.

The First Lady had been up late the night before, laying siege to the handsome stand-in for her husband who'd flown west on Air Force One. His willingness to take part in that deception didn't carry over into adultery; his imperviousness to her come-ons suggested to her mind either advanced training in brainwashing resistance or the direr possibility that her charms were fading. She'd drowned that thought with a bottle of Pinot Grigio, never hearing the Final Jeopardy jingle she'd downloaded as her ringtone for unknown callers. By the time she'd awakened and listened to the message, head still fuzzy, and passed the curious news to Thorne, it was past noon in Washington and the president's chief of staff had been hanging from tenterhooks for hours, twice dipping into his wife's comprehensive collection of anti-anxiety drugs. He relayed the report to Archibald.

"He doesn't want protection?" the Secret Service director boomed. "He doesn't have a choice!"

"He told Bianca he doesn't want anyone with him. He said the trip was a mess, he was sick of being told what to do, but then there'd been a mishap and now he had a better plan."

"What the hell kind of better plan?"

At the moment those words were careening down the line, the president was shooting along Route 50, heading westward, a bag of cookies and a United States map both open on the passenger seat of a silver Dodge Grand Caravan. He'd felt like Rip van Winkle in the rental agency, having to ask the gum-snapping clerk to explain XM radio to him—stations with names instead of frequencies, whole stations for devotees of Martha Stewart, Jimmy Buffett, Catholicism, *Playboy*. Most amazing of all was the pleasant female voice of the GPS that had guided him faultlessly to the on-ramp for I-44, informing him of upcoming turns, then dinging at the moment he needed to begin turning the wheel. Having scarcely driven since becoming governor, and with his blurry distance vision, he was grateful for all the help he could get. He was now in rolling country west of the town of Union, glad to be off the interstates and on his own, tuned fittingly to Channel 16, The Highway, singing along with George Strait on the chorus of "It Just Comes Natural." The minivan was big enough to sleep in if need be. He'd picked up a sleeping bag, pillow, lantern, and more food on the outskirts of St. Louis and felt a glow of self-sufficiency. The song ended. Shaw hopped among the news stations and stopped when he heard the words "In this morning's weekly radio address, President Shaw called on Americans to help each other during these difficult times." Clearly, his disappearance hadn't been leaked, and never would be. A five-second clip of his speech followed. Shaw burst into laughter. What dupes, he thought. The newscaster, the listeners, the whole country. The address was stale, not fresh-baked that morning, recorded weeks before in preparation for his trip. It epitomized the layers of fakery smothering everything he did. He snapped off the radio, grabbed his recorder from his shirt pocket, and continued where he'd left off.

"And the strange thing is that it took a car ad on TV to show me the truth. But the truth comes through many…you know…places. Whatever. And watching that car dealer give his memorized spiel, with his voice coming out with that weird echo sound, I'm telling you, I saw myself. And it hit me. Everyday Americans, the ones I'm here to meet, are sick of slick, and doctored, and phony. I believe you want more from your politicians, and especially from your president." He thought back to Victor's instruction the day before. "I believe you're hungry for someone who'll give it to you raw and real for a change. Which is why I'm going to finish this trip the way I should have started it—alone. No speechwriters and aides writing my lines. No makeup. No pros doing sound and lighting." He clicked off the recorder, picked up his camera, took his own picture at arm's length, as he'd often seen his daughter do, then resumed recording. "That picture's probably not even in focus. But you get the point. You elected me, not a bunch of Washington consultants. And if you like my style, out of focus but honest, I'm hoping you'll give me your vote."

He turned off the recorder and grinned. Let Thorne and the others put that in their pipes and smoke it, as his father liked to say. And that included Archibald and all the rest of the coddlers. Shaw knew that the president had the power to order Secret Service protection for anyone; surely that gave him the power to lift it as well. Teddy Roosevelt had ditched his detail and tramped the Sierras for days with John Muir, not only none the worse for it but inspired to protect the country's grandeur for all time. Who knew what legacy his own trip might produce?

He ate another cookie and turned on his recorder before he'd entirely finished swallowing. "Man that tastes good. No script here. Just these audio postcards from a journey through the real America. Not the trip that my staff used polls and focus groups to lay out. And not the America my opponents are always visiting, the one that's full of complainers and cynics." His radio address returned to his mind. "But the good-hearted and generous country that's still here, under our feet and in our hearts." He raised his eyes, impressed at his own powers of invention. "A country that's—"

Ahead on the shoulder, he sighted a woman walking listlessly with her back to traffic, a pack on her back and her thumb extended.

"The kind of place that when our fellow citizens are in need, we lend a hand, no questions asked. And I think this fact-finding trip of mine will bear me out. Starting right now."

Shaw braked, eliciting a honk of protest behind him, and pulled over. In shorts, skinny as a weed, the hitchhiker accelerated into a trot. The president lowered the passenger window.

"Hey, there." He gave her the hearty smile of a rescuing knight and saw she was only a teenager, maybe sixteen, her face sallow and freckled. She looked to be outweighed by her backpack. "How about a ride, young lady."

"Thank you, sir!" She beamed at him, her incisors leaning like loose fence pickets. "You are so kind! Nobody around here picks up hitchhikers."

The president fumbled and found the switch that unlocked the doors. "Is that right?" He watched as the girl pulled the side door open and dumped her backpack inside. "I've always believed we all have a responsibility to help out others in need."

The hitchhiker opened the passenger door. "You sound like a good person. But you sure do look tired."

"I do?"

"I bet you've been driving a long time. I've got my license. Want me to drive?"

"Now that's kind of you," the president replied. "I'm fine, really. I'm just—"

He stopped. The girl was holding an automatic pistol on him. Her narrow face wore a twinkly smile.

"Oh," said the president.

# 12.

"And another thing!" the president yelled into his voice recorder. He waited while an eighteen-wheeler rolled past, sandblasting him. "Easy access to firearms! That's gotta stop! I don't give a damn what the NRA says!" He paused, wondered if such heresy was wise, but was too angry to care. "And what about values? I mean, the van and my wallet I can understand. But the cookies? All of 'em? Even after I asked?"

He'd been standing, thumb out, for an hour. A blond in a red convertible descended the slight hill ahead and passed him with such immaculate obliviousness that he wondered if he'd ceased to fully exist. At the very least there'd been a flagrant destiny mix-up, leaving him hitchhiking like his petite carjacker, standing at the spot she'd walked to from God knew where, unwillingly taking her up life. His cellphone had been left behind on the passenger seat under his map. He'd luckily had his recorder in one of his work-shirt pockets and his camera in the other. On his wrist was the cheap Timex bought for the trip. He'd thought to grab his water on his way out the door, but otherwise had nothing but the clothes he stood in: shoes, jeans, and his long-sleeved khaki shirt. She, meanwhile, along with food, drink, air-conditioning, and 247 satellite radio stations, had his cash, his Visa and ATM cards, and the cheat sheet he'd kept folded in his wallet with Matt Dawes's biography and his ATM's PIN number. He thought back to the motto on Chevy One's license plate holder, "Don't Drive Faster Than Your Angel Can Fly." He seemed to have done exactly that.

Three hours later, he'd have traded a kidney to be driving at any speed whatsoever. He'd moved ahead to a "No Littering" sign, its pole festooned with wind-borne trash. He'd leaned against it for a while, then eventually sank into a sitting position, his energy sapped by the sun and the thousands of cars ignoring his need. His water was long gone. He was considering gnawing a nearby chunk of wood into a crutch to hold up his right arm and its extended thumb, when a homely Dodge, decades old, swung into view, driven by a single male. The car was redolent of an earlier era of trust and concern for the less fortunate. The approaching driver's round face reminded him of a kindly history teacher he'd had. His own features brightened. He sat straighter, held his arm higher, attempted to look more worthy of trust. The car blew by him. On its rear bumper was the sticker "Strength, Self-Reliance, Shaw."

The president gazed hopelessly before him. Across the road stood a hayfield studded with drying bales. Behind him stretched pasture. He could make out no sign of a town he might walk to. Burning, headachy, mouth parched, wishing he'd grabbed his hat from the van, he was passed by a beer truck and driven nearly mad by the scene on its side of amber bottles reclining with feminine languor in ice, condensation coursing down their curves. He fantasized one of his White House stewards stepping forth from the asphalt's heat waves with an icy lemonade on a tray. Hardly able to summon enough saliva to swallow, he couldn't bear his thirst any longer, searched for a pebble, cleaned it off in his palm with a spatter of spit, then popped it in his mouth. He'd heard of this from his childhood Boy Scout leader. He envisioned Dr. Weiss gesticulating wildly, while Victor, always trying to draw out Shaw's inner cave-dweller, gave him two thumbs up. The stone tasted of dirt and made a clatter against his teeth, but seemed to get his mouth's juices flowing. His stomach growled and he noted an impulse to snatch at the dragonfly that hovered curiously before him. *Too primal*, he thought. *Closer to the Donner Party cookbook than The Boy Scout Handbook.* He wasn't there yet.

By 5 p.m. he was considerably closer, and found himself recalling with interest the summit in Cancun and the Mexican president's song of praise to roasted grasshoppers. He needed food. He walked down the road, crested a hill, and thought he glimpsed a cornfield ahead. He prayed it wasn't a mirage or a product of his poor vision. It wasn't. The field was unfenced and set back from the road, the plants tightly spaced, a jungle without perceptible rows. The drought had laid only a light hand here. Shaw's eager eyes picked out upturned ears and sent the news to his salivary glands. He waited until a string of cars passed, reluctant for his rural shoplifting to be witnessed, then inserted himself among the leaves, moved forward a few feet, and snapped off an ear. Desperately, he husked it, sank his teeth into the kernels, chewed—then spit out what he'd taken in. The corn was dry and strangely bitter, like no corn he'd ever tasted. Had he wandered into Monsanto's test fields? He tried another ear and found it even worse. He popped his pebble back in his mouth and sent it circling to rinse out the taste, then took advantage of his privacy and emptied his bladder. He tried for a nonchalant look as he exited the field, ambling back to the road like a man absently walking the corridor to his office. He continued down the highway. A quarter-mile on, he passed a sign in front of the field that read, "Promoting America's Energy Independence Through Corn." Goddamn ethanol! Made from some inedible strain. He'd spoken in favor of it all over the Midwest, especially in Missouri. It had seemed like a good idea at the time.

He stuck out his thumb and walked, facing the traffic, then backed into a pothole, launching himself into an extravagant stumble and fall, to the hilarity of the children cooling their heads out the open windows of a passing church bus. The confetti of their laughter fell upon Shaw, who bounced up and briskly dusted himself off, feeling like a circus clown. He was literal-minded by nature, lacked the required enzyme for producing humor, and was unaccustomed to being laughed at except at the points in his speeches where his corps of jesters had inserted laugh lines. This wasn't the White House Correspondents Dinner. He glared at the pothole, pulled out his voice recorder, tested it, then yelled into the minute microphone slits, "And infrastructure problems in this country are real!"

He continued down the road, thumb out, his back to traffic this time, watching rocks and holes, realizing he'd taken up the carjacker's modus exactly. He disliked this, but needed to find his way to a town in case he wasn't picked up. He hoped that the sight of him walking would be a point in his favor with drivers, demonstrating a self-reliant spirit. Half an hour later it occurred to him that drivers' takeaway might be that he'd stink of sweat and could likely walk to wherever he was going. The sun bore down on his head. The skin under his false mustache was tormenting him as well. Lola had always removed and reapplied the mustache after half a day. He was dying to do the same, then suddenly realized: he had nothing to reattach it with. Lola's tube of spirit gum, with its strange scent of liniment and pencil eraser, lay somewhere behind him. He didn't know how long he could stand his upper lip's itching, wiped the sweat off his face with his forearm, then reached quickly toward his nose. He'd rubbed the mustache off. He found it on his sleeve, loosened by time and his sweating skin. He turned away from the road, scraped the remains of adhesive from his lip, and stuffed the mustache in a pocket. He wondered if he looked dangerously like himself without it and his glasses. He walked on, then noticed a broken pair of sunglasses in the weeds. He snatched up the single arm and its attached lense, and was intently studying his curved image in it when a horn sounded. A rattletrap pickup had pulled onto the shoulder behind him. A thick-chested man with an unchecked gray beard was at the wheel, with a German shepherd patrolling the bed. Shaw dropped the lense and ran toward the lowered passenger window.

"You busy doin' your makeup or you want a ride?"

"A ride!" The president saw that the passenger seat and the floor in front of it were buried beneath a welter of tools and fast food packaging. The driver hiked a thumb toward the rear.

"Don't mind Samson. He don't bite. Except for homosexuals. Don't know how he knows but he does, so you might want to think real hard about it before getting in."

Shaw had nothing to declare on that count and walked confidently back to the truck's gate, followed by the dog. He was wary about invading its space. He held out the back of his hand for inspection and wordlessly informed the animal that he'd signed the California Defense of Marriage Act. He stepped onto the bumper and gingerly climbed over the side, the dog's gigantic head moving over him, apparently assessing his claim. The truck lurched into motion, Shaw savoring the sensation of air moving over his head. Buoyant with gratitude, followed by the dog, he moved forward to the center window connecting the cab to the bed and slid it open.

"Thank you!" he shouted over the wind and engine noise. "You're a true American!" He reached into his pocket. The driver's head turned his way and was lit by the flash of Shaw's camera.

"What the flamin' hell?"

An oncoming car honked. The driver blinked off the flash and regained his lane.

"God bless you! You'll be remembered! You might even be famous!" He pictured the man's densely whiskered face filling the jumbotron screen at the convention, a down-home St. Nick blessing the proceedings. Then he checked the photo and saw the gnarled anger in the man's startled features. No amount of digital plastic surgery would make it usable. Shaw had nearly promised him a cover on *Time* and was now glad he hadn't. "Anything's possible," he added vaguely as a verbal consolation prize.

"That's for damn sure."

The president squatted behind the window. He cycled through settings, disabled the flash, then took another picture of the scene, getting the road ahead, the man's plump hands on the steering wheel, and the back of his bald head, a safer subject than its front.

"I'm going to California, by the way," he announced. The driver grunted. "Malibu, actually." The president smiled and removed his head from the window, as if having instructed a cabbie.

"And I'm goin' about three miles down the road."

Shaw's face fell. "You're kidding. Only three miles?"

The driver snorted. "Think I'm your goddamned chauffeur?"

Shaw felt tempted to inform him that he was indeed accustomed to and deserving of a chauffeur. He gazed out at the pasture passing on his left. He tried to pump uncomplaining gratitude into his heart and voice.

"Well, I'll take it. As long as there's a town."

"There ain't."

"No?"

"Not where I'm turnin' off. But you can walk to Medina. Easy."

"Yeah?"

"Four and a half miles."

Shaw retracted his head and wondered if he had the strength. Looking down into the cab as if it were a display case, he scoured the offerings and picked out among the passenger seat's clutter a half-eaten bag of potato chips. He stuck his head back through the window.

"I want to thank you again for picking me up. You're a saint in my book. I know you couldn't know it, but I haven't eaten anything, not a meal anyway, since morning. So I just wanted to say, you know, if you had any food you could spare, anything at all—"

The driver released a noisy sigh, glanced right, picked up the chips, regarded them and the price of sainthood bitterly, and tossed the bag back at the window, hitting the president in the forehead. The bag bounced back onto the bench seat, spilling half its load. Shaw's arm shot through the window and snared them like a frog's tongue. Reaching back blindly, the driver slid the window shut and latched it. Through the glass, the president made out the muffled words "Pushy bastard."

Five minutes later, the truck was heading northward up a farm road, raising a squall line of dust, and Shaw was again walking down Route 50. By the time he approached Medina the sun was setting and so was the president's ability to walk. The town was announced by a water tower featuring the snarling head of a giant-canined tiger, evidently the high school mascot, below which growled the black-lettered warning, "You're in Sabercat Country!" This was followed by a weather-beaten sign bearing a sword and fez, a lion's profile, and other service groups' totemic symbols. Hazy memories of Anthropology 101 drifted through Shaw's sunstruck brain. His nation might be hurtling through a new millennium, but clearly had a hairy foot planted in the Stone Age. Maybe Victor had been onto something after all. Or maybe he'd walked all the way to New Guinea.

The smell of grease returned him to America. A McDonald's stood before him. He had no money other than a nickel and two pennies but was frantic to pass through the arches to the promised land of fats and carbohydrates. He entered, closed his eyes a moment to enjoy the frigid air, and at once attracted the suspicious stare of the big white-mustached man wearing a badge reading "Manager." Shaw had heard that the elderly had been thrown back into the job market with the crash of their retirement accounts but hadn't seen the phenomenon in person before. The man looked less than pleased with his lot. Hoping to disengage his eyes, the president studied the overhead menu, mentally gobbling the images of meals, glossy as pin-ups, while racking his brains for a plan. There was no Help Wanted sign in the window. He felt sure that the hard-visaged manager wouldn't agree to a quick food-for-labor exchange. He wondered if he should ask him outright for a handout, then heard in his mind's ear the heavily spiced phrases he'd attached to welfare users in the past: "free lunch fanciers," "rats in the granary," "panhandling paragons of parasitism." The aromas blowing over him from the kitchen were driving him wild. He turned abruptly and headed for the bathroom, where he drank from the faucet, washed his face, squeezed wet towels over his head and down his back, then had an idea. He exited the store and went up to the payphone outside the door, dialed the operator and succeeded in getting her to connect him with a free 800 number for Citibank's Visa cards. Moments later he was explaining that his card had been stolen, he'd been without food for nine hours and had walked who knew how far, that a replacement card had to be delivered to him immediately and that he needed the woman to instruct the cashier at the McDonald's to accept his order and take payment by phone—at which point he suddenly realized that he'd been addressing a recorded female voice.

"Son of a bitch!" he burst out. The woman's speech, complete with the sound of a keyboard in use when she looked something up, was infinitely more lifelike than he recalled from the era back when he placed his own calls. He felt as if he'd asked a store mannequin for directions. "I don't have time for this!"

"I'm afraid I didn't get that," spoke the voice. "If you don't hear the option you need—"

"Listen! I was carjacked and robbed!"

There was a pause. "I think I heard you say you'd like information on our cash back and rewards program. Am I right?"

"No, you piece-of-shit robot!" Shaw felt both strange and liberated to be yelling at a machine. The approaching female customer gave him a wide berth and entered the store through the Out door.

"Sorry, my mistake," cooed the machine, generously admitting responsibility as well as passing over his outburst. If only his wife behaved as well, thought the president. "Let's try again." Her silky voice gave him the distinct impression of a woman who was shapely and single. "What can I help you with?"

Shaw struggled to control himself, caromed through the labyrinth of options, worked his way to a human at last, and poured his story into another female ear, this one with earwax.

"For purposes of verification, could I please have your mother's maiden name," she spat out at high speed.

"Griggson." The robots sound like people and the people sound like robots, Shaw reflected. He felt like president of Alice's wonderland.

"I'm afraid that doesn't match our records," said the woman.

"What?"

"That's not what we have on file, sir."

The woman had a pungent Boston accent and a runny nose. Shaw half-missed her disembodied predecessor.

"Well, your goddamn files—" And then he remembered. The account was for Matt Dawes. The Secret Service had given him a fictional mother with a fictional maiden name, both on the cheat sheet in his missing wallet but nowhere in his memory.

"Ask me another question! Maybe I'll know the answer!"

"Maybe you will," said the woman, her voice barbed with mockery. "But unless you can give me your mother's maiden name, I can't send you a replacement card. As I'm sure you can understand."

"You're kidding me!"

The woman exhaled powerfully. "I'm afraid, sir, that you may be kidding me and trying to gain unauthorized access to this account. In an effort to protect Mr. Dawes—"

"He doesn't exist! And neither does his mother!"

The elderly couple who exited just then gave the president matching mystified looks.

"I beg your pardon?" asked the voice at the other end.

Shaw ended the call. He went back inside, mosied around, considered pocketing a handful of ketchup packages, but saw the manager's eyes bolted on him. Not worth the chance of his mug shot on the cover of People. He turned and headed again for the door, noticing with keen interest an abandoned tray with its logjam of uneaten fries. The sight spurred him to circle around toward the back of the restaurant. He had no other choice. He'd eat leftovers. It wouldn't be so bad, he told himself. He'd have swallowed those fries in a heartbeat. When you couldn't see the people who'd started the meal it was easier to finish it.

He spotted the dumpster between the slats of a fenced enclosure. It would smell bad there and he might be interrupted. He'd grab a garbage bag—brand new, germ-free plastic, he reminded himself—and head away from the road, toward the trees in the distance along what seemed a creek, where he could feast in private on his kill. He scouted the area, sauntered coolly toward the fence, looked behind him—and saw the manager, watching him from the back steps, a cordless phone in one hand. The president barely broke stride, passing the enclosure as if he hadn't noticed it was there, taking with him only the scent of garbage.

"I'm dying of hunger in my own goddamn country," he said aloud. It was 8:20 by his watch. Shaky as a fever sufferer, he shuffled down a tree-lined street into town, his progress tracked by a series of porch-sitting sentinels. Shaw was used to being watched, but not by people who weren't smiling, weren't waving, and weren't taking photos. A mother clapping to her toddler's dance through the sprinklers came down off her steps and led the child toward the house before Shaw's approach. His walk was becoming a zombie's stagger, his eyes as hollow as his stomach. He was sweat-stained and dirty and could feel himself being judged. He thought of the Christmas Eve death by taser of a homeless wanderer by three St. Louis cops. Any minute, he felt sure, a police car would pull alongside him. If Jesus ever came back to earth, he thought, he damn well better come in a motorcade.

A grandmotherly dachshund-walker probed him discreetly when she passed. From an open front door came the scent of chicken, raising the president's determination to a pitch he'd never experienced in sports. There was food in this town and he was going to eat it. Maybe the locals were right to fear him. He was one against the world and felt far more dangerous than when tough-talking North Korea. He was ready to kill with his own hands to survive.

He moved on, the town small but heavily populated with churches. The main street he walked down was a cafeteria of Christianity with choices for every taste, from raw, dirt-on-the-roots worship to overcooked Unitarianism. Shaw reached the single commercial block and found choices in food were much more limited: a breakfast-and-lunch café and a small grocery, both buttoned up. He stood before the latter, burning holes into its jolly "Come Back Again!" sign, cursing small towns' early hours. Then he saw this for the advantage it was. Business owners had gone home for the night. He continued to the corner, backtracked up the alley, and found the back of the grocery. He heard no activity behind the stucco wall encircling the house and yard across the way, opened one of the dumpster's heavy, creaking lids, and folded himself over the side, hoisting out boxes and plastic bags. He felt like a bear in Yosemite breaking into a car trunk but was beyond caring, as he was beyond minding that he dined that night on a loaf of wheat bread from which he first tore off mold, a similarly afflicted package of sliced Swiss cheese, two labelless cans of sardines for his fish course, and a cornucopia of culls from the produce department. His beverage was a heavily dented 32-ounce can of tomato juice which he succeeded finally in puncturing against the dumpster's sharp corner, holding the can over his head and aiming the spurt into his mouth like wine from a bota bag. He'd tell Dr. Weiss about it, someday.

Not bad, really, he summed up when he was through, and belched in acclamation. The peaches had been ripe instead of rock-hard and the sardines had been a serendipitous treat. Bianca hated the scent of fish and he'd been forced throughout their marriage to take his occasional tin of smoked herring outside as if he were puffing a cigar. Being on his own had its points. He tucked the unfinished tomato juice can behind a shrub, left the alley, and strolled through the town's small grassy park in the dusk, the air cooler, a trio of skateboarding boys cavorting on the sidewalk under a streetlight like the swallows above. Never had he felt food's revivifying force so strongly. He'd fully regained his gusto for the trip, then, like a gambler, lost it just as quickly when he needed a bathroom. The park had no facilities. The nearest church doors were locked. No other businesses were open. The gas station back on the highway was too distant. He returned to the privacy of the alley and squatted over a pizza box behind the grocery. He used a hotrod magazine for toilet paper, threw the mess into the dumpster, washed his hands in tomato juice, and drank what was left in the can. Red in tooth and claw, he thought, and wiped his mouth. So be it. He was in Sabercat country.

* * *

He slept under the bushes bordering the back of the elementary school's main building, out of view of dog-walkers and porch-sitters but not unnoticed by the local mosquitoes or out of earshot of the nearby freight trains, which were active as hamsters during the night. He woke up for the seventeenth and final time groggy and bitten. Head on his forearm, he watched the sun rise. It was the first time in three and a half years, it occurred to him, that he wouldn't begin the day with a briefing. Instead of a whirlwind tour of the world, his eyes took in a spider, delicate and daffodil yellow, busy with its web just above him. He wondered if it was making repairs due to his intrusion and felt a strange solicitation for its welfare. The creature was one of his constituents, unlooked upon until now, an attic trinket he'd unknowingly inherited. He sent it the thought, I'm your president. The message caused no pause in its work. Mind blank, he observed it. There was nothing else he needed to be doing. The realization descended upon him like grace. Had Teddy Roosevelt felt the same in the Sierras? Time was passing, but not in the increments his aides kept such exquisite track off. He picked his camera off the leaves where he'd laid it and snapped a picture of the sunrise. Then he took one of himself and viewed it, using the camera as a mirror. After getting used to the false mustache and glasses, the sight of himself without them was jarring. His hair was still short and brown, but the rest of his face was too recognizably his. He needed to reattach the mustache. Dried tomato juice streaked his chin. Meditation gave way to listmaking. He needed a shower, hot coffee, a hat, cash, a cellphone, a clean shirt... None of these would be waiting in the grocery's dumpster. It was time to look elsewhere.

He got up and washed his face at the school's water fountain. In the sandbox he spotted a half-submerged cap. It was small, orange, and showed

Spiderman on the front. He couldn't afford to be choosy. He ripped the headband squeezing into it, then walked the three blocks to the center of town where he found what appeared to be Medina's only bank—not simply closed on a Sunday, but shuttered by the FDIC. He'd planned to call Bianca and have her wire him money here. Were the locals using pelts for currency? He crossed the park toward the library, a sturdy dowager of pale brick, and stopped before the sign listing its hours:

| | |
|---|---|
| Mondays | 11-1 |
| Thursdays | 3:30-4:30 |
| Saturdays | 12-3 |

Something had to be done about library funding, he vowed. No wonder people thought the sun orbited the earth. A pay phone stood beside the library's walkway. He'd have Bianca send the money to Kansas City. It would probably take him a day to get there, at which point the banks would be open. He'd continue the trip, meeting people and places without his entourage's interference, but enjoying a slightly higher standard of living.

He picked up the receiver and was pleasantly surprised to hear a dial tone, dialed o, then was caught off guard when a male operator greeted him. When had men become operators?

"I need to make a collect call."

"Number?" The voice was deep. Shaw felt as if he were waltzing with a member of the wrong sex.

"It's my wife's cellphone," he said, then it hit him that the only place he had the number was in his own cellphone, which he didn't have because it had been left in the van, which he also didn't have…He wanted to spill his story, but doubted he'd get any maternal sympathy from the hairy-chested operator. The man confirmed Shaw's guess when he impatiently stated, "We can't make collect calls to cellphones." Thanks for your concern, the president thought. He didn't want to call the Malibu house number, then he remembered the time zones. Cassandra would be sleeping. The WHCA operator answered, accepted the charges, then passed the call to the First Lady's deputy chief of staff, who reported that Bianca was still sleeping. Shaw gave her his request for $500 to be sent to Western Union Kansas City and repeated that he was absolutely fine. He hung up.

He felt better, but less than fine, and set off down a deeply shaded street of two-story clapboard homes, much lived-in and generously porched, an architectural class photo from the 1920s. He knew that each one of them held nearly everything on his scavenger-hunt list, and that none of those items would ever be missed. A cup of coffee? Five minutes of hot water? Foggily, from the prep work before his Russian trip, Marx's slogan rose into memory: From each according to his ability, to each according to his needs. Through a screen door he smelled bacon frying. He sighed, stomach growling. Too bad I'm in Missouri and not Moscow, he thought.

Two houses ahead, a white-haired woman in a robe teetered down her front steps, one hand gripping the iron railing, presumably heading for the newspaper on her walk. The president sprang forward, seeming to race her for the paper, deftly snatched it off the ground and presented it to her with a courtier's smile.

"There you go, ma'am. And can I take this chance to ask if you might have any work I could do for you, in exchange for something to eat?"

The woman regarded him, wide-eyed as an owl, clutched her powder-blue robe at the throat, and mutely shook her head.

"Or maybe not food. Maybe just a cup of coffee and a spare shirt, if you've got one." He assumed she had a husband or son. Did she think he meant one of her shirts? A disturbing idea, but there was no time to rephrase; she was backing away, the rolled newspaper held like a truncheon. "Or just a quick shower." A mistake, Shaw instantly realized, to have her imagine a naked male in her bathroom. And the image of Spiderman on his hat, scaling a skyscraper, one hand inside an open window, couldn't be helping. The woman was hoisting herself hurriedly up the steps. "I can mow lawns, wash windows, clean gutters." He'd leave payment out of it for the moment. "Anything you need."

The back of the woman's robe disappeared through the wooden door. The president heard the click of a lock, then a second click. The next one he heard might be from a gun. He moved on, stuffed his hat in his back pocket, but had no more luck with the twenty-something bathing her Malamute or the man high on a ladder scraping paint from his clapboards. Shaw was disappointed in his citizenry and thought back to his teachers reading him fairy tales in which kindness to travelers and strangers was always rewarded. Hadn't these people heard the same stories? Then he remembered the unpronounceable-acronymed RPFSLS, Remove Pagan Filth from School Library Shelves, a national group whose leadership had visited him during his first term as governor. He recalled that he'd given them ten minutes in his office, that he'd made a faintly off-color joke cribbed from *Who Says Conservatives Don't Have a Sense of Humor?*, and that the room had gotten very quiet. His aides had urged him to endorse their program. He guessed it had been a success.

He trudged up a block sporting three For Sale signs and wondered how many houses around him were in foreclosure. Then he rounded a corner and came upon a couple and their two young daughters, clearly dressed for church, heading out their front door. He gave his pitch, made no mention of showering, and offered to have their lawn mowed and leaves raked by the time they returned from worship. From habit, he nearly extended his hand to the children to shake, but pulled back in time. The wife deferred communication with strangers to her husband, a square-shouldered, prosperous-looking redhead in a seersucker suit. The man bestowed a nod and smile upon Shaw and wordlessly guided his flock around him.

"I just need a little work," the president pleaded. "I'm not asking for a handout." As if begging were a disgrace to Christians, despite the New Testament's praise of poverty. "I'm from here," he said, then adjusted the claim. "From around here."

They walked on. The younger girl, blond and beribboned, her hand in her mother's, turned and looked back until receiving a meaningful tug. Shaw stared at their backs, disgusted.

"And didn't Jesus say to love your neighbor?" He raised his voice to cover the widening distance. "He sure as hell did!"

The accusation hung in the cool air. The parents increased their speed and executed a sharp turn at the corner. The president shouted, "Or maybe that was Buddha!"

He meandered on. He needed coffee, felt sure he smelled it around him, heard it perking, then wondered if he were hallucinating. He gave a rambling appeal to a teenaged boy washing a truck, who called his father, who said, "Not today."

"He walked among us," Shaw murmured, "and starved to death."

He altered his pitch with the gray-haired gardener he found kneeling on a foam pad. Food and clothes and hot water, he'd realized, were too intimate as tender. He asked for money instead.

"I've got a dream job waiting in California," he informed the woman. "All I need to do is get there." He decided to expand his services as well. "And I can do more than just heavy work. I've got experience with finance. Budgets." He halted before he blew his cover, but wished he could. Like God proving his powers through miracles, he was tempted to borrow her phone and order an Air Force flyover. "Legal stuff. That kind of thing."

The woman's heart-shaped face took Shaw in. She was thin, without makeup, in shorts and a battered straw hat. She gave no sign of fear.

"A little free advice. Never go into politics."

The president labored to seem uninterested in the comment. "And why's that?"

"You're a terrible liar."

Shaw's lips wrestled with each other. Maybe he needed his speechwriters after all.

"Were you to have a job waiting in California, and were you needing to get there quick, and cheap, and were you to actually be from this area, as you said, you'd know exactly where to go."

The president's eyes lit. "Where?" He knew he was admitting guilt to the lying charge but didn't care.

The woman's gloved hand pointed left. "Down by the river, west of town. Where the hobo jungle is." She returned to work. "Probably get a meal, too. Pretty decent quality, from what I hear. Right organized down there. You give it a try."

"Thank you! I will!" Shaw felt like giving her a kiss, possibly even an ambassadorship. "I'll pay you back some day," he promised.

She wagged her finger at him. "A terrible liar."

# 13.

Dewey Archibald—eyes grainy, lower lids hanging like hammocks—had been awake for thirty-one hours, all of them spent inside Secret Service headquarters. The building's placid exterior gave no hint to the world of the panicked anthill within. Exiting the elevator and reentering his office, he glanced down on H Street and was astounded by the Sunday pedestrians' restful pace. The scene breathed the repose of an Impressionist painting of strollers along the Seine. Somehow he needed to keep that calm intact. He felt like a party host who alone knows that the guest of honor has just slit her wrists upstairs.

It was noon but there was no time to eat. He found his hound's-tooth tie crumpled on a chair and reknotted it around his neck in the pursuit of normalcy. The Service prided itself on composure built on the rock of preparation. Agents trained for assassins who might use rifles or poison gas, RPGs or knives, who might strike while the protectee was in a car, giving a speech, skiing, on the water. They practiced scenarios on a city-street set worthy of Hollywood and had their own model of the front of Air Force One so as to train for runway attacks. But no one had prepared for the situation currently before them: neither an assassination nor a kidnapping, but a presidential disappearance in which the protectee himself was apparently an accomplice. His brain dull and bald head sweaty despite the air-conditioning, Archibald found moments of comfort in the theory that the scene around him was too unreal to be real.

His cellphone jingled gaily. It was his wife, again. He'd boomed to all and sundry that there could be absolutely no STDs—spousally transmitted disclosures—in this case. His wife had sounded suspicious when he'd called her the evening before and told her he'd need to stay over to catch up on work. The line sounded like an adulterer's and he'd stepped into the part with a stammering delivery, feeling as if he'd been acting in a bad soap opera. Archibald jammed the phone in his pocket. He couldn't stop to talk now. He'd make it up to her when he had time—after the hearings, the thousand-page report, the weighing-in by *60 Minutes*, Lewis Black, and Weird Al Yankovic, then the news conference announcing his resignation, at which point he'd have all the time in the world.

The St. Louis field director phoned in, then Lexington's, followed by a fourth conference call with the FBI, followed by the vice president's call, during which the Deputy National Security Advisor showed up in person. Archibald felt he was in a waking nightmare set at a mad railroad station, with unannounced trains arriving left and right. When the phone lines fell quiet for fifteen seconds, he placed his own call, to Chuck Thorne. In place of "hello" he opened with, "You sweet-talking soft-soaping son of a bitch."

"Nice to hear from you again," said Thorne.

"You promised me this goddamned trip would be a gift."

"I know I—"

"And you were right—like the Trojan horse was a gift."

"Dewey, listen."

"You also compared it to balm of Gilead." His secretary brought him a fax, which he scanned while talking. "But I'm telling you, it's feeling a whole lot more like napalm."

"Look, I'm as—"

"Like hell you are. But you're going to be when I testify at the hearings, and write my memoir, and blog and flog your sorry ass—"

Thorne let him run, like a marlin. Two minutes later he began reeling in. "So what's the latest?"

"Still at large."

"Nothing new?"

"Nothing that makes any sense." Archibald stood where his head would catch the air-conditioning and stared across the room at the United States map on the wall. "Went to Target, got cash, bought a phone, rented a van, bought a sleeping bag, all in St. Louis. The next thing we know he's at a Denny's in Mt. Vernon, Illinois. Then Louisville. Then Morehead, Kentucky." His voice rose with each geographical point on the line. "He told the First Lady he'd show up on time in Malibu. But he's heading *east*."

Thorne could be heard drumming his fingers. "It's been a long time since he's driven."

Silently, both men considered whether Shaw might have his map upside down. In the current climate, anything seemed possible, and in a flash of prophecy Archibald beheld the future: the scandal causing the breakup of the Service, counterfeiting going to the Treasury Department, fraud to the hated FBI, while protection, like an orphan in a melodrama, became a ward of the distantly related and unsavory Department of Defense.

"Where'd he spend the night?"

"No motel charges," said Archibald. "He must have paid cash. Or maybe slept in the van." He sat at his desk.

"Can't you find his location through the cellphone?"

"If he'd turn it on, we could. But it's off. Maybe it died."

"No calls?"

"Just the one to the First Lady. So far."

Thorne exhaled noisily. "Well, we're keeping a lid on it here. Believe me."

"I already tried believing you." Archibald's secretary returned with more papers. He glanced at the top one. "Looks like he did some catalog shopping last night with his Visa."

"Yeah?"

"An Xbox. Twenty-two video games. *Batman. Brutal Legend. Vampire Queen: Brooklyn Edition. Grand Theft Auto.*"

"No kidding."

"A fifty-inch plasma TV."

"Must be for Malibu."

"A bunch of movies. *Public Enemies. The Little Mermaid*." Archibald skimmed, then asked himself aloud, "*The Boys of Playgirl?*"

Both men pondered this in silence.

"For Bianca," Thorne spoke up. "She's a big movie buff."

It didn't sound like movie buff material to Archibald. He turned a page. "He also went to a site called BikersRUs."

"Wow. Who knew?"

"You're his damn chief of staff. You're supposed to know every-thing." Archibald read further. "Bought a pair of low-rise leather pants."

"What?"

"Plus a zip-front leather halter."

"Bianca's got a birthday coming up. Maybe it's a gift."

"And a full-length leather skirt."

Thorne considered. "What size?"

Archibald squinted at the sheet. "Small." He looked up. "Couldn't fit Bianca. Too tall. Or Cassandra. Somebody's got his card."

"And probably the van. Why else would he be driving east?"

"Gotta go." Archibald hung up, suddenly energized. Then he realized that if Shaw no longer had his ATM or Visa card or phone, it would be infinitely harder to find him. His eye swept the vast expanse of the United States on the map. He'd need twenty-thousand agents beating the bushes. And as Thorne had underscored when he'd made his pitch for the trip, the Service was stretched thin with other commitments.

Why the hell, he thought on his way out the door, couldn't Shaw be president of Luxembourg?

\*   \*   \*

Sitting at the deserted bar in the Marriott in St. Louis in an afternoon-long holding pattern, Hugh worked on his third Painkiller and felt it was finally beginning to live up to its name. He stared dumbly into the dark rum, the potion glittering with shaved ice like an Arctic sea, and wished he could throw himself into it. As the glass was too small, he was reversing the procedure and pouring the contents into his body. Trevor was beside him, plastic straw in hand, still with enough muscle control to successfully stab at the lime wedge lying like a galleon at the bottom of his gin and tonic.

"Tonight I'm dusting off my resume," he said to Hugh.

"Don't think I'd put this trip on it."

"It won't matter. Everybody's going to know."

"Cora should pay for witness protection for us. Plastic surgery. New past. New name."

"Sounds a lot like Shaw."

Hugh lifted off the pineapple slice that had been impaled on his glass and sucked on it. "I could be a pineapple farmer in Maui. Total new life." He wouldn't mind trading in his doughy build while he was at it. "Maybe come out of it with an Olympic body," he said. His eyes floated up to the TV, where a barrel-bodied Russian in a leotard was getting ready for the shot put. Trevor's eyes followed.

"Would Donna really go for that look?"

"I was thinking more of a swimmer's body. And Brad Pitt's face."

"Plastic surgery's painful."

Hugh sipped his drink. "Not after enough of these."

They went mute when the bartender got close enough to hear and both peered fixedly at the TV, ravenous for escape from their predicament, undermined by news coverage of an activist group's parody of the Olympics complete with archery targets adorned with the faces of CEOs, javelins flung at a straw effigy labeled "Mortgage Banker"...

"Maybe Maui's not really far enough," mused Hugh. The much-tattooed female javelin hurler with the pierced lip looked to him like she'd swim the Pacific to kill someone in the thirty-five percent bracket.

"You think we're headed for a class war?"

"Could be," said Hugh. "And rich Japanese-Americans who write for *National Review* could possibly have a problem." He reached for the bowl of peanuts. "I'd get rid of your gold wire-rims. Go with aluminum. Maybe wood."

The screen showed a guillotine smartly parting the soccer-ball head from a body marked "Do-Nothing Politician." A group of apparently homeless spectators cheered.

"Guess guillotining's a demonstration sport this year," said Hugh. "Forget dusting off your resume. Time to dust off *Tale of Two Cities*."

Trevor watched the activists joyfully kicking the long-mustached soccer ball about, to the hoots of the homeless. "Maybe we were a little late with Operation Compassion."

"Remember your idea to ship the poor to the moon? Let 'em grow their own food? Maybe we should have moved with that."

"The plan wasn't entirely serious."

"Meaning 'still in its rudimentary stages.' "

"Lunar travel would have to come way down in price."

"Unless we packed 'em in like on the slave ships. Which is the model the airlines are already using."

Trevor observed the ragged crowd. "Probably wouldn't work. As the Bible says, the poor are always with us."

"Written before the Apollo landing. It's a new ball game."

Lola joined them, fresh from church, where she'd been praying for the president. Fresh from a brothel, by contrast, Victor and his tagalong sound man, Kyle, entered and ordered, the group eventually moving to a table. In the absence of new developments, they rehashed Old Business.

"You're the one who got Shaw going," Hugh said, pointing his pineapple slice at Victor. "'Throw away the script! Give it to me raw!'"

"Hey, c'mon. The scripts were driving him crazy. Too much fakery. That's why he left. Just like he told Bianca."

"He wasn't faking washing dishes. Or drying cars with the underclass."

"Getting sick after lunch at that taco truck sure as hell wasn't fake."

"Looked pretty real."

"Smelled pretty real."

It was a bad moment for the two plates of gluey nachos to be delivered. Conversation and consumption paused for a moment.

"If he doesn't show up on Friday, how's the radio address gonna happen on Saturday? He's supposed to use it to tell the country about his trip."

"Use a rerun. Nobody listens to those things."

"Or have a guest host."

"Countries don't have guest hosts."

"Sure they do. They're called vice presidents."

"Or splice together sentences from ones he already recorded."

"He'd sound like a robot."

"Which is exactly what he is."

"So stop programming him!" Victor downed his Scotch. "We're the problem. Just like he said. No wonder he ditched us."

Hugh ruminated. "This is Truman country. Maybe it rubbed off. He wants to be his own man, like Harry. Plain speaking. Shooting from the hip."

"Firing MacArthur's ass."

"Right out of *Celebrity Apprentice*."

"Truman did his own whistle-stop tour," Trevor said. "Talking to people from the back of the train. Off the cuff. Not reading speeches. Some people say that's what pulled out the win."

"So let's get out of his way!" summed up Hugh. "He knows more than we do. We can all go home!"

Raised glasses clicked and chimed above the table as Jess strode into the room. Head swiveling, she found the group and scurried over. Her voice was urgent but quiet.

"They found the van. In West Virginia. Fifteen-year-old girl."

"Was Shaw with her?" Hugh tried to calculate which answer would be worse.

"No. Left him on Route 50, heading toward Jefferson City. He called Bianca again. Wants money wired to Kansas City. He's clearly heading west. Which is where Chuck wants us. So get ready to go."

"Are you kidding?" said Victor. "We just got through deciding—"

"Chuck does the deciding. And he wants us back on the road, all the way to Malibu."

"Why?"

"Cause it's clear that's where Shaw's planning to go. If they find him and he rejoins us, great. If not, we take a lot of footage of landscapes and towns, grab some slice-of-life interviews, we're in Malibu for his big arrival scene, we add some diary sessions later, and we're ready for the convention."

"And what if he doesn't show up?"

"Then we keep on driving into the Pacific. Either way, we're going, so get over it. Be in the lobby in twenty minutes." She left.

"Ours is not to question why."

"Apparently not."

"Blacks and women got the vote. But political mercenaries?"

"Still waiting. In the rain."

"Ours is just to spin and die."

The group reluctantly rose.

"I just hope that poor baby finds a way to shave," said Lola. "Cause those whiskers of his are gonna come in blond."

"Our president's whiskers call," muttered Victor, last on his feet. "And we must go."

\*   \*   \*

Marching along the trail through the woods in the afternoon heat, pockets stuffed with plastic bags, the president followed the gangly form of Danforth, who carried a six-foot wooden curtain rod like a Masai's spear. Shaw felt he might be in Africa and found it hard to believe the man before him had spent thirty years in advertising, climbing his way to a crag in the upper elevations of Ogilvy & Mather. Seven figures, eight cylinders, six bathrooms, three ulcers, two personal shoppers…He was bald, with a long professorial face, reading glasses bouncing on his chest beneath a neatly trimmed salt-and-pepper beard. Shaw envied his hat—tattered but wide-brimmed, chin-strapped, vented at the crown—and the water-bottle holder around his waist, a double, fashioned from leather by Danforth himself, tooled with floral designs. His belt-cinched cargo shorts looked two sizes too big and his tennis shoes, perhaps a high-schooler's cast-offs, sported "Ortiz" in black penmanship on the sides. Flecks of his former life still adhered: his Zodiac dive watch, a cellphone holder on his belt, now housing toilet paper wrapped around a popsicle stick…

"There they are."

The president followed Danforth's pointing hand. Woven in among the woods were rows of bent-backed apple trees, half-hidden in the landscape, a ghost orchard from an earlier era. Small red fruit dotted the branches. The men approached and sampled.

"An early apple," said Danforth. "Excellent juicer." He took another bite, his beard bobbing. "Aromatic. Complex flavor. Perky, but not aggressive."

Hard to leave advertising behind, thought Shaw. He finished his apple, then the two started reaching their arms through the barrier of unpruned branches, dropping the harvest into Danforth's collection of two-handled plastic bags. Freight trains clanked and clattered nearby. When the bags were full, the men threaded the curtain rod through the handle openings, hoisted it up to their shoulders, and headed back toward the hoboes' encampment.

"Never used to get this much exercise in a week," Danforth volunteered. He spoke with the loud-voiced vigor of the reformed. Shaw, still athletic, found it hard to match his gait.

"No?"

"Sitting on the train back and forth to Scarsdale. Gardener handled the yard. Pool man. Housecleaner. Dog walker." He patted his lean belly. "Now I'm a staff of one. Don't know how much weight I've dropped exactly, but plenty. Got meat out of my diet. Ulcers quiet. Never felt better."

"So basically, this little downturn's been a good thing." Behind Danforth's back, the president grinned. I knew it, he said to himself.

"In all kinds of ways."

"Tell me about it." Shaw pulled out his recorder, hit Record, and held it in front of him.

"I'm out in the fresh air. Working with my hands. Time for nature. Artistic pursuits. Spiritual pursuits. It's fabulous."

"Glad to hear it."

"Year before last I was in a tent city in Denver. Cherry Hills Country Club, after it went belly-up. Pretty nice spot on the fourteenth fairway."

The president's eyes widened. He'd played Cherry Hills.

"Thousands of people. A lot of 'em well-educated. I never had time to read before. All of a sudden I'm in three different book clubs."

"Is that right?"

"Travel writing, how-to, and Latin American fiction."

Shaw smiled at the red recording light and mentally urged the man on.

"We had classes in leather work. Hammock weaving. People sharing skills just for the love of it. Mushroom identification. Talk about a lifesaver! More useful than any class I ever took at Dartmouth. I really owe a lot to Shaw."

The president's face glowed. He held the recorder farther forward.

"And to his Treasury Secretary. Heckleford."

Shaw smiled. "Jim's a great—"

"And all the other idiots running the economy."

The president drew in the recorder, almost pressed Stop, but feared missing more material he could use.

"You don't know what you've got till it's gone," said Danforth. "And without those jokers I'd never have known how worthless it all was."

Shaw waited for the soliloquy to change direction.

"There've been challenges. Believe me. And it hasn't been great for everybody. Some people don't do well with change. Like my wife."

Shaw's thumb hovered over the Stop button. Apprehensively, he asked, "How's she getting along?"

"Not that great." Danforth moved the rod to his other shoulder. "Poisoned the dogs. Then herself."

The president's thumb went down. He tucked the recorder in his pocket.

"Couldn't imagine dropping out of her wine clubs. Or planting corn in the front yard, like the neighbors. Or the dogs living on some cheap brand of kibble." They walked in silence a while. "She was sensitive. Like animals that need a certain temperature range."

Over two million a year, guessed Shaw. A silent epidemic.

"For me, it was a relief to stop caring what the neighbors thought. Gave up the toupee the first day I hit the road."

The president's free hand went to his bristly upper lip. He needed to somehow reattach his false mustache. And find another pair of glasses. Until then, he'd let his beard grow and hoped it disguised him sufficiently. For all he knew, he'd run into someone he'd invited to stay in the Lincoln Bedroom during better times.

They approached the camp, set among willows and cottonwoods along a creek. Though no Denver, it boasted a solar shower, message board, outhouse, and a selection of books and periodicals left behind by its roving population, curated by a former librarian with a Fiore button pinned to her hat. The president had already found a scratched but serviceable pair of sunglasses in the camp's free box, washed his shirt with a squirt of borrowed Dr. Bronner's, and accepted an offer of biscuits, beans, and scrambled turkey eggs with Danforth. He'd felt uncomfortable repeatedly being on the receiving end of "To each according to his needs," glad he was among strangers, his weekend fling with socialism a secret. Sweating as they tramped up a rise, feeling the pole digging into his collar bone, Shaw told himself he was working off his debt.

He and Danforth were hailed like hunters carrying a deer. Instead of dispensing handshakes, the president gave out apples from the nearest plastic bag to men in shorts emerging from tarp shelters, a smaller number of women, and the occasional family, sometimes complete with grandparents. It struck Shaw that no one he saw was overweight. Certain residents were underkempt, and some could have kept a dentist booked for a week, but as a whole they were tanned, agile, with good posture, exuding the health that the apple orchard's planters had probably enjoyed, a rarity in the XXXL world outside the camp. The hunting-and-gathering life had its rewards.

They hauled their harvest to a wood and metal contraption Danforth had found among the rubble of the orchardists' home site. He judged the apples through his reading glasses, sliced off questionable portions with a pocketknife, and tossed the apples into a metal hopper that fed them into the many-toothed blades that the president turned via a heavy crank. Minced apple flesh fell into a wooden drum. Shaw then exerted himself against another crank, lowering a metal plate onto the apples and sending an amber, sweet-smelling flood spurting out a chute and into a plastic pail. On the way, it was intercepted by tin cups, canteens, coffee thermoses, Fiji bottles, ziplock bags, and children's mouths. Sweaty and still footsore, his blood sugar low, the president pressed the apples dry, then drank his own labor straight from the pail like a character out of Bruegel. He'd never tasted anything better poured by his steward at a state dinner. He nearly said so, but expressed himself with a long, satisfied sigh instead.

"First time?" Danforth asked, as if they were doing drugs.

The president nodded.

"Eat fresh, eat local, like they say. Cider has a way of making converts."

Shaw felt like one. He'd signed the farm bill in March, everyone knowing but nobody saying that we were poisoning the country and ourselves. What was he doing leading that army of fools? Maybe he'd do what had never been done: dare to defy the lobbyists and party leaders and throw Con-Agra and General Mills and the rest of the moneychangers out of the temple. The thought passed through him like lightning, illuminating the same brain centers lit by his decision to leave his handlers behind.

He sat with Danforth in the shade of a pecan tree and took another long swig. "I sure could have used a drink of this yesterday." He wiped his mouth. "Beat as a dog and dying of thirst, and everyone ignored me. And the town full of churches." He passed the pail to Danforth.

"Christianity's great. Too bad it's never been tried." He took a gulp. "Shaw said that."

The president faced him with peaked brows and terrified eyes.

"George Bernard Shaw."

"Right," said the president.

They pressed another batch, saved the juice in gallon milk jugs, had a late lunch of apples, sweet corn, and plums, and rested. Then they returned to the orchard for more fruit, Danforth filling Shaw in on the E. coli scare, Israel's elections, Pretty Boy Nussbaum, the missing Russian sub, and other news gleaned from his transistor radio and the latest leavings in the periodical collection. Drowsy from the heat and the drone of cicadas and his full stomach, the president let the news wash over him. Rome had survived with madmen on the throne; the United States would get along fine without him for a few days. Major Rinaldi and the football were somewhere safe. The vice president had his own football if required. He'd needed a vacation from the news, he realized, and found the hobo life increasingly alluring.

"So where are the old-time hoboes?" asked the president. They reached the orchard and started picking.

"They're around," said Danforth. "Don't mix too much with the newcomers."

"Like Shreveport Sam at the camp?"

"Perfect example. Geography-based nickname. Very old school."

Shaw detected a whiff of condescension.

"Probably not even named Sam. Private. Not a word about his past. Most of us use our real names. Hell, we've got resumes out there, still hoping for a call. Plus you've got conflict over values. Some unhealthy lifestyle choices in the old-timers. Alcohol. Smoking. Snuff." Danforth crawled through a tree's ground-touching branches, gaining access to the apple-spangled room inside. "You run into a lot of after-hours talking and late sleeping. Then we wake them up with group stretching in the morning."

Shaw reached high for an apple, pressing against a screen of branches, one of which sprang back, whipping his cheek and drawing blood. He gave a yelp. Danforth passed him his always handy bandana. The president had felt a boyish envy of his pocketknife earlier and now wished he had a bandana of his own.

"And their reading material isn't always exactly uplifting," the man continued. "Biology, mainly. The human female, specifically. Without a lot of text."

"But they're still riding trains?"

"Oh, sure. Around and around they go. They just don't usually have a destination."

"Well, I do. Kansas City. My wife's—" Shaw halted, sheepish about being able to pick up any sum he desired. "My wife's maybe going to meet me there. If she's saved enough money from her waitress job."

Danforth climbed out of his cage of branches. "Talk to Cavanaugh. Knows the schedules backwards and forwards. Former travel agent. You can pay his commission in cider."

They returned to camp, cut the apples into slices, placed them on a six-story apparatus Danforth had built from oven racks, and dried them over a low fire.

"You ought to do something about that cut," he told Shaw. He disappeared into his tent and returned with a tiny bottle of hydrogen peroxide, into which he dipped the tip of his bandana. "Used to oversee the Johnson and Johnson account," he mumbled while pressing the bandana to Shaw's cheek. It was dusk. The close contact worried the president more for his identity than out of fear of a *Brokeback Mountain* moment. Still, he was anxious for it to end. He thanked Danforth, got up, and left.

He wandered through the camp, and found Cavanaugh, short and spectacled, in a bathing suit and a traveler's many-pocketed vest. He was ensconced in a sagging beach chair, a cane hanging on one of the aluminum arms, and was reading volume 37 of the Harvard Classics—Locke, Berkeley, Hume—by kerosene lamp. In front of him, barnboard planks lay across two fruit crates and served as a table. In front of this sat a stump, presumably for customers. Shaw sat on it and placed on the table a quart container of cider.

"I need a train to Kansas City," he said.

"Excellent choice." The man's voice carried a soft southern accent. He closed his book, was suddenly open for business, glanced appreciatively at the cider, plucked a railway map from an accordion file at his right, and asked, "What class of service were you interested in?"

# 14.

At 1:15 a.m. by the fluorescent specks on his watch, the president finished the trek to the tracks, following Cavanaugh's map. He had no flashlight, but the one-time owner of Asheville Adventure Travel had cheerily mentioned, as if it were part of his service included at no charge, that there'd be a waning moon up at that hour. There was. Before he left the camp, Shaw stopped by a pine tree he'd noticed and attached his false mustache with sap from one of the tree's sticky flows. He carried with him a Piggly Wiggly bag that held cider, apples fresh and dried, sunglasses, a chunk of car mirror for checking his appearance, and a rusted butter knife he'd found near the orchard that might help deter the yard bulls he'd heard about. He'd arrived with nothing, but now felt he was moving up in the world. Having little didn't free you from the tyranny of attachment, he realized, but just transferred it to the basics: a water bottle of heavier-than-usual plastic, a better class of hat. He'd feared the trip might strip him of his capitalist faith, but now, much relieved, he saw that the worship of possessions was basic to the species. When he came down off the mountain, he'd bring the glad tidings to *Forbes* and Georgetown's anthropology department, dismantling the ridiculous idea of a goddess-ruled golden age of consensus and cooperation. The Powerball had its roots in the prehistoric.

Shaw looked down the tracks, then up at the crowd of constellations above. His mind blazed as well. He turned on his recorder.

"I'm telling you, industry could save millions by outsourcing to hoboes. They're well-trained, they're good workers, and they're right here instead of halfway around the world. And frankly, you probably wouldn't have to pay 'em any more than Asians. They might even take pay in tarps, or beans." He thought. "Maybe do the same with upper management. Instead of million-dollar bonuses, hoboes would probably be happy with a nice Swiss Army knife. Somebody really ought to look into it." He stopped. *Newsweek* had praised him as a delegator, but he now wondered if that had been code for "do-nothing." He pressed Record and recast himself as an outraged reformer. "How come nobody's looked into this?"

He leaned against a train signal, facing east. Cavanaugh had told him that a Kansas City-bound freight would stop at 1:30 at this siding for three minutes to let another train pass, which would keep Shaw from having to race alongside, in the dark no less, and leap onto a moving car. The man had called this "Business Class."

"And something else," the president continued into his recorder. "These people are in shape. From walking for miles I guess and chasing after trains and living in fresh air." He thought of his pet project, reviving JFK's Council on Youth Fitness, and his attempt to whip up enthusiasm through Saturday morning exercise sessions on the South Lawn, regularly skipped by the Surgeon General, the portly leaders of both parties, the Joint Chiefs of Staff, and hundreds of other invitees. The program was quietly euthanized. "We're meant to walk a lot, and grow our own food, and harvest it, and move our muscles." He saw the top brass of Stouffer's and Birdseye and Hot Pockets shifting uncomfortably in their seats as the recording was played at the convention. "We'd not only eat better. We'd cut down on obesity. We'd save millions on health care. Make that billions! We'd be busy. Canning, making jam, sorting seeds, reading up on stuff. We wouldn't have all night to sit and eat crap in front of the TV. We wouldn't have to truck so much food around the country, meaning less dependence on oil. And we could stop dumping all those oil-based poisons on our land." He saw Chevron and Dow and Monsanto leaving in protest, but felt Teddy Roosevelt rising up within him and John Muir looking down. Shaw had grown up duck-hunting with his father in the Central Valley, gazing up at predawn skies star-packed like this one. They'd skied and hunted deer and backpacked in the Sierras, feasting on blackberries and fishing for their dinners. His farm-raised grandmother had been a jam-maker and preserver, steaming her windows on summer nights and building a fortress of jars against hunger in her Fresno pantry. The picture was coming into focus, so sharp-edged it almost hurt. "This is what we all know needs doing, right? The things everybody says but nobody does?" He was as sick of lip service as he was of the scripts Jess fed him. In a jolt, he had a vision of his second term's legacy. He'd be a doer, not a delegator or a blatherer. A knight fighting for the land and the health of his people. "It's so obvious it's—"

A whistle sounded. He pressed Stop and peered into the blackness. As if he were having an eye exam, a light looked back at him. Quickly, he backed up and crouched among brush. The light gradually brightened and the train began braking, producing a tuning orchestra's cacophony, finally coming to a hissing halt. From his low vantage, Shaw was amazed at the height of the cars. He emerged, wishing he had his contact lenses, able only to make out tankcars and flatbeds stacked two-high with containers. From the west came an approaching whistle. Shaw scurried beside the train, passed the tankcars, then hopper cars—a last seating resort, according to Cavanaugh—then finally reached a boxcar, but found it closed tight. He struggled in the dimness to figure out how the door opened, felt the rumble of the eastbound train, then sighted a pinprick of orange several cars beyond, moving up and down. He ran ahead and found it came from the lit cigarette of a hobo standing in a boxcar's open door. The president cast aside Danforth's disdain for smoking and gratefully accepted a hoist from the man just as the other train passed, obliterating his "Thanks." He'd glimpsed a mouth missing several front teeth and retained the rough-grained feel of the man's palm. Here was the type of grip-and-grin he was meant for, not the fundraising shakedowns and photo ops cluttering his calendar. And the same for state visits, with their curlicued protocol and rehearsals and seating charts. He took a step and stumbled over a body. The car featured no seats much less seating charts, and no light, with its north door closed to the moon. The president squatted and let his eyes adjust. The floor was bare metal, not the wood amply furnished with straw he'd seen in movies. The rider he'd tripped over, he slowly perceived, was asleep, an empty whiskey bottle cradled to his chest like a stuffed animal. From one end of the car came the soft sound of a harmonica. Maybe he was on a movie boxcar after all, he thought, then he realized the music was by Bach, the same piece played during the German Chancellor's recent visit. White-collar types were clearly being hit hard, he thought. From the car's other end came male voices. Interested, Shaw approached on hands and knees as the train began to move, and leaned up against a wall within earshot.

"The ignorance in this country. It's disgraceful." The voice was of an old man, East Coast, smart and pugnacious. "And you a congressman!"

"Former congressman."

Shaw's heart accelerated. He wondered who it was. He thought of the ex-NFL players who turned up in the papers years later, down on their luck, wanted for mail fraud or kiting checks.

"You took an oath to the Constitution, but you don't even know where it came from!"

"It's been awhile, okay?"

Shaw feared discovery, but was too curious to move elsewhere. He'd taken an oath to the Constitution himself. He turned on his recorder and scooted closer.

"So then tell me. What's scutage?"

"*Scutage?*" There was a pause.

"Forgot to pack your Cliff Notes?" The old man gave a snort. "*A payment in lieu of military service.* So why's it important?"

The train began gaining speed. The congressman gave no answer.

"Cause King John lost Normandy! A big part of his income. And he's got mercenaries to pay. And what's happening with the economy in the thirteenth century? Inflation! So the mercenaries are costing more than they used to. So what does he do?"

The congressman was stumped.

"He raises the scutage rates! And the nobles throw a fit. Taxes are already through the roof and now this. They're mad as hell. Howard

Jarvis in chain mail. They're not gonna take it anymore. And that leads to—"

Shaw racked his own brain.

"Tax cuts?" guessed the congressman.

"Magna Carta! Limits on the king's power! The ancestor of everything, from habeus corpus to the Bill of Rights." The man gave a moan. "What's happened to education in this country? I'm telling you, the government's gotta do something!"

"I already took my turn."

Suddenly, Shaw recognized the nasal voice. Mel Abernathy! The "Venn Diagram of Vice." The only member of both the Bangkok Seven—caught investigating the international sex trade in too personal a manner—and the Makeover Four, who'd accepted lobbyist-paid teeth-whitening, stomach-stapling, and hair implants. Even so, the Speaker had had to pry him out of the House with a crowbar. Things clearly hadn't gotten better since. He was a Californian. Forty-first district, San Bernardino County. Shaw remembered golfing with him during his first term as governor. Both their families had gone on that trip to Bora Bora back then, looking into some issue or other. They'd chatted in the Oval Office after the inauguration and more recently on the putting green. The man might easily recognize Shaw's voice. Carefully, the president drew in his arm, turned off the recorder, and worked his way crabwise slowly toward the door. Half an hour later, when the train stopped again, he poked his head out and thought he saw a figure exit farther back. He climbed down himself, ran along the train, and climbed into new lodgings a dozen cars to the rear. He found an unclaimed piece of cardboard, lay down on it, and used his bag as a pillow, with the dried apples on top. He cast an envious look at the man snoozing against the wall, leaning back on a couch cushion and with a neck pillow made of bubble wrap.

He slept in snatches. The train traveled in the same manner, stopping frequently, adding or shedding cars, stepping deferentially aside for oncoming trains. Riders came and went, passing through Shaw's consciousness like ghosts. Then he awoke with a start and saw light leaking around the closed door. It was morning. The train was at high speed, clacking like a machine gun. He raised himself on an elbow. The man with the couch cushion was gone, along with the rest of the riders save a beefy woman leaning against a duffel bag.

"You know how far to Kansas City?" the president called out.

She gave no reply. One finger was tapping her jeans. Then he made out the iPod wires leading to her ears. Not your father's hoboes, Shaw thought. It was 6:10 by his watch. Cavanaugh had said he'd be there by five. He approached the woman more closely.

"Hey!"

She started and slowly cranked her head his way, puffy-faced and black-haired.

"Do you know how long to Kansas City?"

She focused her half-lidded eyes on Shaw. "Kansas City?"

He nodded.

"Wrong train, bud." Her head fell back onto the duffel bag.

"Are you kidding me?"

The woman turned again. "KC cars peeled off in Jeff City. We're going north. Des Moines."

Shaw moved to the right-hand door and pulled it open a foot. The sun was just rising, dead perpendicular to the train. They were indeed headed north.

"I don't believe this!" he told the world at large. The dream of the clerk counting out fifties melted in his mind, dripping onto the faint memory of Cavanaugh suggesting a car toward the front. The president had avoided Abernathy but had moved so far to the rear that he'd missed his destination.

He opened the door farther and sat back on the other side, looking out, then opened his quart of cider and took two long swigs. Cornfields without end rolled past his eyes. Son of a bitch, he thought. Then something occurred to him while he fished an apple from his bag. He took a bite. By the time he was done and had tossed it out the door, his earlier plan had been tossed out with it. He'd done the right thing without knowing it. The Secret Service would have asked Bianca about his call. They'd have staked out Western Union and the train yard and every block in between. He'd have been snatched up like a runaway child, lectured, flown to Malibu, and put to bed without his supper. He'd never have seen this sunrise or this stretch of America, would never had the chance to chat with the woman in his boxcar. He'd always traveled by plane, only touched down briefly, only knew his country from 30,000 feet. But that was in the past. Let the Secret Service wait in Kansas City! He'd do an end-around through Iowa.

He stood, saw the woman still had her back to him, unzipped his jeans, and peed out the open door. He ate another apple. All his physical needs had been attended to. He felt better, confident about going it alone, and took two photos out the open door.

An hour later, the woman yawned and sat up, square-jawed and stretching the seams of her jeans and a snap-buttoned plaid shirt. Her dyed black hair looked several decades younger than her skin and stuck upward like iron filings. She extracted her ear buds, rolled a cigarette, and lit it. "So what's with the fake mustache?"

The president's hand shot to his upper lip. The mustache was there.

"Looks like the pictures on my walls after goddamn Hurricane Holly."

Shaw's face stiffened. Without lying about inspecting Hurricane Holly he'd have never found himself in this boxcar. He pulled out his chunk of mirror. The mustache was seriously tilted. Not having anything to reattach it with, he tugged it off, wincing, ripping the backing in the process, and nonchalantly tossed it in his bag, all the while ransacking his wits for a reason why he'd been wearing it. He hoped the subject would evaporate on its own.

"Rob a bank?" the woman asked, and gave a raucous, phlegmy laugh that morphed into a quarter-mile-long coughing attack.

"Not really." Shaw wished he could tell her he'd been bailing out banks instead of robbing them, to the tune of three trillion and counting.

"Costume party?" she said and hacked some more.

Shaw was so ready to put the topic behind him that he answered, "That's right," and gave the woman the firm look he'd been coached on before the summit with the Chinese, intended to put an end to the discussion.

"You're pullin' my leg."

So much for his firm look. What was it with this woman? He reminded himself that he was privileged to be visiting with her. "A birthday party, actually. Different theme every year. But anyway—"

"You must have some real interesting friends."

Shaw thought of the Secretary of Defense, a cross-dresser whose highly guarded secret was rated Level 3, "Capable of causing grave damage to national security." The president extinguished the image of the man's jowly face in his mind lest the woman should somehow see it.

"Not really," he said, jamming her brain waves. He scraped at the patches of sap on his lip, aware he must look like he was picking his nose, then noticed that the woman's cigarette smelled odd. "What's that you're smoking?"

"My own little blend. Corn silk, parsley, and northern wood lily." She took a long, savoring draw. "Why? This the nonsmoking car?"

"Not at all. I'd just never smelled anything—"

"What are you—rich?"

The president shook his head strenuously.

"Then why the hell would this smell strange? Half the country's rolling their own. And using whatever the hell they can find." She took another puff. "I think you're lying. About being rich and your damn mustache."

Shaw shook his head again. "Rich?" He prepared to fight the accusation, but had already implicated himself with his fictional costume-partying friends.

"You're one of them smoke snobs, aren't you? Just cause you and your rich-ass buddies can get up off your gold toilet seats and can walk into a store and buy perfect little machine-rolled anal-resplendent cigarettes made from real tobacco with the goddamn Surgeon General's stamp of approval on every pack—"

Approval? Wasn't it a warning? Shaw recalled a Big Tobacco tantrum about something a year before and his administration giving in. There were simply too many details involved in running a country. No wonder he was always delegating. "I don't even smoke!"

"Well I do, and I ain't ashamed. But all the damn excise taxes—" She trailed off into coughing. "Carton was seven-fifty when I started. Now it's over a hundred bucks! And then Washington started taxing rolling tobacco. I can't even remember the taste of the real stuff. Why the hell you think I'm on this damn train?"

Shaw shrugged.

"Headin' up to Minnesota to harvest northern wood lily!" The woman contemplated the twist of paper in her fingers. "Bring home the roots, dry 'em, and grind 'em. What's that song? 'It Ain't Love but It Ain't Bad'?"

The president had no idea.

"Well, it ain't nicotine, but it'll do. Get me enough to make it through the year if I'm lucky. If the drought and the locusts left me any. And the frickin' goons from Philip Morris."

American resourcefulness and perseverance were alive and well, Shaw concluded. He took the woman's picture.

They passed through Osceola, Iowa, where the mucus had frozen in his nose at the rally four years before. All of a sudden it dawned on him that getting off in Des Moines was a bad idea. He'd laid siege to Iowa for months before the 2010 caucuses. Coffee klatches in living rooms, Rotary meetings, doughnut after burger after fish fry after sundae, shaking hands with workers leaving John Deere and Principal and UPS, his hands ungloved despite the -20° wind chill to show he was one of them—though they were all sensibly gloved or mittened. He'd had his headquarters in Des Moines, on Locust. He and the other candidates had haunted the downtown streets; like homeless characters, they were recognized by the locals and known to be prone to striking up conversations with strangers. He felt he'd handed his tri-fold brochure to every last Iowan except the ones on Death Row. The chance of being recognized was simply too great. His right hand examined his jaw and upper lip. His beard was coming in, but wouldn't do much duty as disguise for several days. He'd wear his sunglasses and pull his Spiderman hat low in the meantime—and sidestep Des Moines for safety's sake.

The train lost speed and entered the city, saluted by lowering crossing gates and clanging bells. Without warning, pounding footfalls and shrieks of laughter came from the roof, as if they were passing through a spook house.

"Tweakers, probably," said the woman.

The president cocked his uncomprehending head.

"Meth heads. They get off on crazy shit like that." She began rolling herself another cigarette. "It's Monday. Must be a three-day tweakend."

Tweakends? Trains as amusement park rides? Wood lilies dug up for smoking? Shaw marveled to find his citizens using the country in their own ways, for purposes never intended. He felt like a teacher returning from a minute's absence who hears too much hilarity coming from his room.

The train clanked to a stop in a rail yard. The president climbed down, checked for yard bulls, dashed across four sets of tracks as the woman had advised, and found a Union Pacific car that pulled out twenty minutes later, heading west. Not a bad connection, he thought; he'd had far worse service on airlines. The car was his alone. He opened his bag and dug into his store of dried apples. They were tasty but tough, a stairmaster for the jaws. He gave up after three, washed them down with some cider, then ate two of his fresh apples. He felt healthy, full enough, but unsatisfied. Programming on The Apple Channel was limited. When a pair of shaggy male wanderers entered his car at a stop an hour later, he held out his bag of dried apples, hoping to receive an offering from one of the other food groups in return. The men chewed, setting their beards in motion and causing an audible popping from one of their skulls. Both were burly with congested collages of tattoos on their forearms. One spit out the apple. There was no return offer of food, though both carried bulging knapsacks. So much for "From each according to his ability…" Either they'd never read Marx or Marx had never met their type.

The train lurched into motion. The day was scorching. Shaw sat in a corner and sipped from his cider. One of the men came over, asked for a swig, drank, must have been expecting whiskey, and yelled, "What are you, Johnny fucking Appleseed?" Still, when he returned to his friend he kept the container, holding the president's only drink. Shaw realized the two might be more of a danger than the sadistic yard bulls and wondered if he'd need his butter knife to keep rape off his list of new experiences. Two hours later, when the train approached Council Bluffs, he was dying to get out of the oven of a car and wild with thirst. He'd eaten his last fresh apple. A Burger King sign came into view through the open door. Shaw was ready for a meal made from a cow but felt he'd spent too much time campaigning in Council Bluffs. Then he remembered that just across the Missouri was Omaha, in rock-solid Republican Nebraska, where he'd scarcely needed to set foot. His foundation even had a soup kitchen there. At the thought, his mind's nose smelled meat. He saw mountain ranges of mashed potatoes stair-stepped with glacial lakes of gravy. Omaha it was.

They crossed the river on a railroad bridge. The train had slowed but showed no signs of stopping. Had he boarded an express? He might have asked his companions if they weren't both sleeping. He couldn't chance not seeing another town for hours, and readied himself. He wrapped his bag of dried apples around his camera and recorder and stuffed them in his Piggly Wiggly bag. He crouched low in the open doorway, amazed at how quickly the dirt below was zipping by from close up. Beyond the dirt were weeds, then fencing, then the backs of warehouses. There were no metal rungs, much less a porter with a step. His mind called up the parachuting scenes from World War II movies. He counted to ten, closed his eyes, and jumped.

As if he'd landed on a high-speed conveyor belt, his legs shot immediately out from under him. He fell on his shoulder, then whirled like a spindle over the drought-packed, glass-flecked ground. He'd let go of his plastic bag at once, sparing its contents being smashed, but hadn't been as lucky with his body. His right shoulder was screaming. Then he knew: he'd separated it. He'd done the same in his second season at UCLA. There, he'd been a queen bee, the focus of coaches and trainers and doctors, whisked to a hospital as if the nation's fate hung in the balance. Now that that might actually be so, he was alone, dehydrated, and broke. He climbed painfully to his knees, then his feet. He noticed a sour, nose-wrinkling smell on the breeze, then realized it was coming from stockyards. He'd wanted to get beyond the Beltway, and he'd succeeded. He gathered himself, found his bag, and hobbled toward a downed section of fence.

One hour, eight interrogated pedestrians, and twenty-six blocks later, he dragged himself around a corner and nearly fainted at the sight of the county health clinic. He'd been told the waiting area would be as thronged as steerage on an immigrant ship, the service slow, the probability high of catching something worse than what he'd arrived with, but at least he could get free treatment. He pulled on the brass door handle, then felt it pull back. He looked up. The building was closed. A sign in the neighboring door's window announced the modified, miniaturized schedule resulting from state cuts. At once, the president thought of Bill Getty, Nebraska's governor, an anti-tax firebrand and blood-spattered budget slasher. Shaw doubted he and his jet-setting wife had ever seen the inside of a county clinic, much less actually used one. Then again, Shaw realized, neither had he. The two men had shared the stage in Lincoln in 2010, Getty fond of boasting to audiences of his vigor in guarding "your money," despite the quintuple bypass he'd had while in office, his health insurance paid by the state.

Shaky with fatigue, Shaw pulled his hat brim down to his sunglasses to ward off the sun. He was somewhere on the fringe of downtown. He drained the used plastic Evian bottle he'd found among weeds and rinsed three times to exorcise the horror-stricken face of Dr. Weiss before he'd filled it at a gas station water fountain. He'd begged ice without success from a series of hard-eyed clerks at convenience stores until a female savior had filled a Coke cup with cubes. He'd slipped the cup under his shirt and held it to his shoulder while walking. He took it out now, drank the melted ice, and popped a dried apple into his mouth but lacked the energy required to chew it. He needed aspirin and was ravenous for food, but had no way to buy either. From across the street came the maddening aroma of smoked pork issuing from Bubba-Que. He rested, sucking on the apple slice, then got up in stages and set off. He stopped at the corner in front of a Runza restaurant, the second he'd come across, and stared at the strange doughy object on the sign. What the hell was a Runza? There was a smell of cooked cabbage in the air. Had he jumped off the train somewhere in the Ukraine? He labored up the sloping street. He'd forgotten how hilly Omaha was. Four more queries and thirteen more blocks took him to the county hospital, where the brisk ER clerk heard only the first moments of his tale of why he had no identification, apparently wrote down a code for cases like his, and sent him to a seat. A succession of more gravely injured dark-skinned victims of shootings and stabbings and overdoses leapfrogged him until he felt like a casualty of affirmative action. At last he was seen by a fast-talking female doctor and found out he had a Type I separation, the least serious kind, requiring no surgery. He was given an ice pack, Advil, a sling, and dismissed.

It was after five. He'd asked the ER clerk for directions and now shambled in a daze toward the Scott and Bianca Shaw Family Foundation Feeding Center. He fantasized whispering his name, like Conrad Hilton popping into one of his hotels, the supervisor's jaw dropping, the private table, unlimited servings, private waiter, wine bucket... There was nothing presidential about the reflection he dragged across shop windows. He was filthy, cut up, his shirt ripped at the shoulder, sunglasses cracked. His sling bore Berkshire Hathaway's logo; apparently the health department had been reduced to selling advertising. The bandage the doctor had slapped on the biggest of his forehead scrapes featured Kool Aid's frosty talking pitcher. It seemed another life when he'd campaigned here for a few hours in 2010, breezing about in his Lincoln Town Car, feeling put-upon at having to sample kielbasa and sauerkraut at a Polish restaurant, then dumplings and Pilsner Urquell at a Czech place, then gyros and baklava in a Greek eatery. The memory compounded his hunger. He entered an African-American district: ailing Victorians sloughing paint, the businesses all wearing bars on their windows and doors. The soup kitchen was no exception, a low brown stuccoed building that looked like it might have been a union hall in the past. His name wasn't chiseled in stately serifed letters in marble, but painted by hand in an inflated, heavily leaning italic more suitable for a car lot. He joined the tail of the half-block-long line seeping out of the building's doors, shuffling forward with the rest of the livestock and finally receiving his salad of half-frozen iceberg lettuce, spaghetti lightly daubed with sauce and topped by a single meatball, garlic bread, canned peas, and pumpkin pie. In his fantasy, the maitre d' had been a svelte female, but the real-life stubble-faced supervisor pacing the floor looked more like a bouncer and was intent on keeping the line moving briskly, lending the room the ambiance of a slaughterhouse. Shaw squeezed into an opening at a wooden picnic table that had been retired from long service in a schoolyard. His silverware seemed likewise to be hand-me-downs from one of the earlier ages of man. A male teenaged volunteer, clearly headed for a career other than waiting tables, poured ice tea into his big plastic cup and then over his hand. Despite all of the above, the president held his head over his plate, inhaled, braiding the rising scents into one strand, and said a silent and sincere grace.

He was a righty. Eating left-handed was as novel an experience as gratitude for food. He felt clumsy and conspicuous, his left hand's incompetence keeping him from wolfing the meal too quickly, important since there were no seconds allowed. He ate the meatball straight off, like the cherry off a sundae, noticed an odd taste, and found himself wondering where the food had come from. The bread felt kiln-dried, not just toasted but old. Waiting to be served, he'd looked into the kitchen and seen a row of cans of peas, all heavily dented. He thought of the botulism outbreak in Texarkana. Digesting afterward over his tea, fending off stares from the move-'em-out supervisor, a plan assembled itself in Shaw's head. He was supposed to be in Malibu on Friday. Four days. Riding the rails was free, but getting off could kill you, if heatstroke hadn't done the job already. Hitchhiking was just as dangerous. There was no chance of his renting a car without a driver's license and credit card. This left only one option that he could think of: a bus. Safe, inexpensive, air-conditioned. Plenty of chance to meet his fellow Americans. All he needed was the fare. Then it struck him that his sling might turn out to come in handy if he did a spell of panhandling the next day.

He savored the sensation of ballast in his stomach when he finally got up. On his way to the door, he was halted by his own face staring at him from a display on an information table. He approached. The photo had been taken in the Rose Garden. He remembered the chartreuse dress Bianca was wearing, the negotiations needed to get Cassandra to take off her spiked choker. He recognized his Burberry blue checked tie. He was mentally climbing into the scene when a male voice said, "Used to get four goddamn meatballs. And seconds if you wanted 'em." The leather-faced man beside him glared at Shaw's photo. "This chintzy bastard doesn't even give you Cool Whip on your pie." The man farted for emphasis and ambled out the open door. Shaw sighed. Maybe it was just as well that he never read his mail.

He picked up a brochure about a shelter from a stack. Then he fished through the basket of glasses donated by the Lions Club, seeing the world through the strange eyes of a score of his citizens until finally coming on a pair of heavy black glasses that were big but which roughly matched his contacts' prescription. They slid down his nose, but looking out the doorway he felt like he'd been endowed with superhuman vision. He went into the bathroom and checked himself out. The glasses gave him the look of a down-and-out science teacher. All the better. He peeled off the ridiculous Kool Aid bandage. His beard was coming in, reddish blond and at odds with his brown crew cut, though most of his hair was under his cap. He'd never worn a beard and found he liked it. Less chance of being taken for gay and a much better disguise than the mustache, which he happily tossed in the trash. He took advantage of the toilet, then headed outside.

Dusk was falling. He walked to the shelter, a county facility four blocks away, but found that the governor had gotten there before him. It was closed. Shaw understood. The homeless didn't vote; soccer moms did. Cut high school football and you'd have riots. The homeless were trees falling in a forest without TV reporters. Why hadn't they hired lobbyists like everyone else?

He got directions to a mission two blocks further on, but found the beds long filled when he got there. Maybe he shouldn't have lingered so long at the soup kitchen. He asked for a recommendation from another man who'd been turned away, whose only advice was to stay clear of the river—illegal aliens were rumored to camp there, luring packs of teenaged boys with baseball bats. Illegal aliens didn't vote either, Shaw mused. Apparently he'd been right to promote voting all these years. There was nothing we wouldn't do to nonvoters.

He wandered up a busy street past a check-cashing business, a bar, a muffler shop, a hair salon. A burned-out building across the street stared at him through empty sockets. It was still hot, cars passing with lowered windows, dispensing what Shaw suspected was hip hop. He hadn't seen any parks, but didn't get the feeling that bedding down in one would be wise. He felt nervous and replaced his new glasses with his sunglasses, despite it being night, for psychic armor. He'd been in inner cities plenty of times, but not without a wall of Secret Service agents or the even larger UCLA linemen. He turned left at a light, hoping to exit the neighborhood. A teenaged boy fell in beside him and offered him crack, then marijuana, then sex, then shoes, determined to ring up a sale. The president ignored him, passing an empty lot where a clot of African-American men were gathered, laughing, their purpose murky. Closer to the sidewalk women were hawking socks and diapers and batteries, their inventory in milk crates. Shaw felt he was walking through a dream, his mind so absorbed with trying to come up with a sleeping plan that he barely noticed himself nearing the woman in the long boots and short black leather skirt standing by the payphone on the corner, under a streetlight.

"Ten dollars," she said as he approached.

Shaw stopped. What I wouldn't give for ten dollars, he thought. But prostitution? And yet the woman before him had stood at the same crossroads and answered yes. He stared at her, fascinated.

"Nine dollars," she said. She was African-American, short, well-rounded and sharp-chinned, her tight lavender blouse matched by her eye shadow. "Running a special tonight."

Mondays must be slower, thought the president. He appreciated her commercial instincts, but worried that her price structure was too low and was amazed at how cheaply his nation's women could be bought.

"Nine dollars isn't much," he said.

"Sure isn't."

"I mean for you."

She cocked her head, her straightened hair curving around her ears like sickles. "You want to pay me fifteen, go right ahead."

"My point was—" Shaw was uncomfortable sounding like her career counselor; she was surely reacting rationally to market forces. "Anyway. I'd like to help you out, but I'm broke. Plus it wouldn't look good. You know, if I ever, you know, ran for office or something." He tried to pass it off as a joke.

The woman gave him an off-kilter squint. "I ain't no psychic or nothing but I don't really see that in your future."

Shaw had a vengeful fantasy of sending her an autographed copy of *He Walked Among Us*. He described his search for a place to sleep and asked if there were other shelters around.

"Most homeless up here sleeping in empty buildings. But there's a shelter way down by Mandan Park you could try."

"How far's that?"

"Three or four miles."

Shaw leaned back against the payphone. His feet weren't up for another cross-city trek. "Is there a bus?"

"Sure, you could take a bus. They got one goes on Thirteenth every couple of hours."

"Hours? Are you kidding me?" Shaw shook his head in disgust. No wonder nobody used public transportation. "That system needs work, you know?"

"It needs money, what it needs."

"True. A first step." His own budget hadn't been kind to mass transit. "Of course there's less money around these days." Though the American Association of Highway Builders had enough to give him another hefty donation, he recalled. And that concrete pavers trade group.

"But what you talking about buses if you broke? Bus cost a dollar seventy-five."

"A dollar seventy-five?" The last time he'd ridden a bus, at age fifteen, before getting his driver's license, it had cost a quarter.

"And if I was you, I'd make sure they got a bed open before you bother going all that way."

Shaw flipped up the payphone's telephone book holder and found it empty. His hands flew upward. "And what is it with people stealing phone books in this country?"

The woman looked puzzled. "It ain't hard to understand. The paper's good for starting fires if you got you a barbeque. Good for filling cracks in the wall, keep out the wind. All kinds of things. Plus it works for toilet paper in a pinch. And it's free. Guess you ain't been out on the streets too long."

The president nodded. "And how long have you been on the streets?"

"Turning tricks?" The woman considered. "Five years, off and on. Ain't that bad a gig."

"No?"

"Demand's always there. You talk about recession-proof. Lets me be home for my daughter after school. Help with homework. My pimp ain't bad. That's how I got this corner. One of the best." She sounded proud as an Employee of the Month with a plum parking place. "Got different jobs in the day. I'm saving a little money. Gonna buy me a house someday, all mine. And then my daughter's, for her and her kids."

Hard work. Saving. Ownership. Family values. Shaw was astounded to hear his own platform roll off the woman's tongue. Maybe the pundits and policymakers were as clueless about the country as he'd been. Or maybe that's why so many politicians had been caught with prostitutes—a philosophical as much as a physical thing.

"Actually," she went on, "speaking of jobs, and you needing a place to sleep and all." She gave him a judicious appraisal. "My sister manages a place you could sleep, and she be paying you 'stead of the other way around. Right around the corner. If you're interested."

The idea of not having to walk another block bathed the president in endorphins. He checked the recorder in his pocket to make absolutely sure it was off.

"I'm your man," he declared.

# 15.

Shaw walked beside the woman.

"You're big. And you're white. That's a plus. You ain't crazy, like lots of 'em. 'Cept about stealing phone books."

The president wondered if he'd signed up as a gigolo. Was white flesh prized in these parts? Could there be a high-priced niche market for men wearing slings? On the one hand, he might spare himself days of panhandling, make his bus fare in one night, and get laid in the bargain. On the other, a president selling his body? Both major parties might be quick to forgive their own, but this would be in an orbit out beyond Watergate.

"You don't stink too bad. Look like you know how to use a toilet." The woman stopped in front of a laundromat. "Last one we had got his ass hauled to jail." She opened her purse and pulled out a ring of keys. "I'm Shequille."

"Scott—Matt Dawes." She'd caught him off guard. It was the first time he'd slipped.

"Scotmat? What kinda name's that?"

Shaw's eyes searched the heavens for help. "Scottish." The woman looked doubtful. His mind whirled. "It means 'man of Scotland.'"

"No shit. You from there?"

Helplessly, Shaw nodded. The woman put a key into the lock and opened the door. "Scotmat. Sounds more like some cleaning product or something."

Shaw made no move to defend his nonexistent Scottish ancestors. She-quille stepped in and flicked on the lights. The laundromat still held the aroma of drying towels. Shaw followed her to the office in the rear, largely taken up by an exhausted gray couch. "That's where you sleep."

Oatmeal-colored stuffing was boiling out of a long rip in the vinyl but the couch looked like paradise to the president. "So why's she paying me?"

"You security."

So much for his stint as a gigolo. "I am?"

"Can't pay for no guards. Who can? So we hiring people like you. Lot of businesses using homeless. Do folks like you a favor and us too. More than the damn government doing."

Shaw let the slight pass. "So what do I do?"

"Somebody try to break in, you call the cops." Shequille pointed to a wall phone. "And you having a white voice, they might actually come."

Was that really how it was? The president half hoped he'd need to call. He was Commander in Chief. They'd damn well better come. "So what's the pay?"

"You get a couch to sleep on instead of cement." Shequille took some quarters from a desk drawer and dropped them in Shaw's hand. "Free wash and dry. And breakfast delivered."

Nothing that Greyhound would accept as tender, but he'd take it.

She headed out of the office. "Oh, yeah. I'll be using that couch till two o'clock." She locked up the laundromat and left.

That could be a little awkward, Shaw thought. And it was, ten minutes later. Then half an hour after that. Then three times more over the next five hours. In between he chilled the hospital's ice pack in the office's minifridge, took two more Advil, then washed himself from the waist up over the laundry sink and soaked his aching feet in a mop bucket filled with water and Cheer. He sifted through the pile of abandoned clothing and wore a crotch-pinching pair of overalls while he washed and dried his own clothes. Taking advantage of the castoffs, he put a red bandana and an extra pair of socks into his Piggly Wiggly bag but couldn't bring himself to do the same with the clean pair of underwear in his size, bothered by their unknown biography. On a shelf he found masking tape, a piece of which he wrapped around the bridge of his glasses to keep them from sliding down. He iced his shoulder during Shequille's last assignation, sitting in one of the hard plastic chairs and flipping through *O Magazine* for the first time in his life. He turned on the fans to cover up the noise coming from the office. Before bedding down he washed the couch with a hot soapy rag.

He shot upward at the noise hours later and suddenly remembered about calling the police. A bright clatter hit his ears. Then he realized it was morning.

"How you sleep, darlin'?" A woman entered the office, arms full, wearing an airy white dress, bearing a family resemblance to Shequille but older and with more honey in her voice. "Brought you some breakfast." She flipped the switch for the fan with an elbow and set a grocery bag on the desk. The fragrance of food helped clear the president's head. "Scrambled eggs with hot sausage, home fries, and toast." She pulled a cup from a cardboard holder. "And coffee. You take cream?"

Shaw shook his head and accepted the cup. "You're like a restaurant." He'd slept without his sling and rotated his right arm experimentally. It felt better.

"That's what I am. Shantala's Café." She had a big lipsticked face, faintly freckled, hair held high with a paisley band. "Everything but the tables and chairs. And the tax on the bill."

The president sipped, staring quizzically. "What do you mean?"

"What do I mean?" She unloaded rolls of quarters from her purse, then poured herself coffee from a thermos. "You from Scotland, ain't you?"

Shaw sighed deeply and nodded.

"I cook out of my house and deliver. People a mile around eating my food right now."

The president washed two more Advil down with his coffee, then peeled the foil off his paper plate and produced Buddha's ineffable smile. Coburn, his running mate, would be eating at a $1,000-a-plate fundraiser tonight in D.C.; Shaw inhaled the scent coming off his food and felt sure he was getting the better deal.

"Plenty people round here doing business without their own building. Like Shequille using that couch four nights a week." Shantala sat in the desk chair, reached into a bag, and pulled out a cake doughnut to dunk in her coffee. "Got a woman braiding hair in here this morning. Another one doing manicures tomorrow. Tarot reader on Friday. They all get to work. They happy. Convenient for people doing their laundry. They happy. I get my slice. Police get theirs for not making any trouble. Everybody happy. Ain't no other way to survive."

Shaw picked up his plastic fork with his right hand and began to eat. "And how come you don't do things, you know, the normal way?"

"How come?" The woman stiffened, then relaxed, apparently remembering his foreign status. "Ain't no money in this neighborhood. Where's all that drug money going? Mexico. Or Germany, when the big shots buy their BMWs. Ain't going to no factories right here. All these people, but no good-paying jobs. No way to save up for down payments and rent and permits and taxes and all that. So people gotta get creative. You put your business inside somebody else's. Or you work outside. Street corners, alleys, empty lots. Those places big real estate round here. So big you gotta pay a street tax to a gang or whoever got the right to the place. My man's a mechanic, but his shop's the church parking lot. Keeps his tools behind the organ. Pastor gets his cut. Everybody surviving."

The president ate, taken aback at his country's workings. He'd heard something about underground economies but had never seen one up close. Why weren't Republicans building bridges with African-Americans, with their dislike of taxes and love of free enterprise? He had a vision of himself as the new Nixon, leading his party not into the South, but into the inner cities. He speared pyramids of potato, thinking.

"But if you're not paying taxes, you're not going to get Social Security," he said. "Then surviving's really going to get tough."

Shantala waved her free arm in a circle. "I got Social Security. My family! And my friends. I got two different girlfriends living with me now, and their kids and one of their boyfriends. Crowded as a bus station. Lost their jobs and couldn't make the rent. They ain't got money to help with mine, but they babysit, help with the cooking, deliver meals for no pay. One of 'em knows how to make different medicines out of flowers. And if I get in a bad way down the line, they know they better step up and help me out. Same with the grandkids I'm raising. World ain't just about money." She poured herself more coffee. "Half the people eating my breakfast don't pay cash. Fix a toilet instead or do my hair or advertise for me at their church. Rich folks got money. Poor folks got people. Which one gonna die all alone sitting in his shit in some nursing home?"

The president gawked. Here was the Family First Initiative in action. Families taking care of their own, the way they used to. With the billions saved in Medicare, there could be shelters galore and buses every five minutes. If only his recorder had been on...

"Actually, I'm needing some money myself." He felt sheepish saying this after the woman's speech. "Kind of thinking of panhandling."

"You and a bunch of other folks. They's thick around banks, so I guess that's a good spot. But you gonna have a lot of competition. Got to find a way to stand out."

Branding identity, thought Shaw. This woman knows her stuff. "What about all those creative jobs around here?"

"For you?" She scratched her scalp with an elaborately painted nail. "Lot of people selling stuff on the streets, but it don't look like you got anything to sell. And I don't have no delivery openings right now." She thought. "Sometimes my man hires folks to walk all around looking for cars that got flats or need other kinda work. Drumming up business."

Shaw's feet were still sore from the day before. "I'd kind of like to stay in one place."

"You picky. Beggars can't be choosers, or ain't you heard?"

Shaw lowered his eyes. "You Can't Always Get What You Want" began playing in his head. He'd heard the song a thousand times, but had never thought that the lyrics applied to him.

"You could hang out at the liquor store and buy booze for kids too young. Pick up a little change."

Surveillance camera. YouTube. Impeachment.

"Anything else?"

Shantala considered, then looked at her watch and got up. "Maybe help my cousin make fake ID's. Or you could be a lookout. No walking and it pays good."

"Looking out for what?"

"Police. While the gang's making crack. Or maybe moving stolen stuff." She opened a cabinet door, revealing a stack of car radios. "I make a little extra money in that line now and again. Temporary storage. Don't tell the owner."

Vertical diversification, thought Shaw, impressed. But working for gangs, against the police? He'd just filmed a spot with McGruff the Crime Dog. He saw problems.

"Maybe I'll stick with panhandling."

Shantala opened the laundromat to the public. Shaw finished his breakfast, washed up in the bathroom, filled his water bottle, then picked up his Piggly Wiggly bag.

"You traveling pretty light, coming all the way from Scotland."

He nodded and took Shantala's picture, allegedly to show to his mother in Edinburgh. He thanked her and walked out the door.

He'd call the Omaha chapter of his book "Bed and Breakfast." He spoke the thought into his recorder, then had another idea: an audio portrait of the neighborhood. He left the recorder on and put it in his left shirt pocket with the flap up, and at once was approached by a costume-jeweled preteen who sidled up and spoke almost directly into the device, "Suck your dick for five dollars." Maybe another neighborhood, Shaw thought. He pressed Stop and headed toward the upthrust of tall buildings to the south. Buckled sidewalks, potholed asphalt, and humans curled like grubs in garbage-filled entryways gave way to well-maintained streets and shiny exteriors. Shaw noticed that eye contact between strangers was frowned on. Likewise speech. People walked faster and seemed not to know anyone around them. Nobody offered him sex. He felt like an explorer in his own land and wondered if people thought less about sex here or whether that drive had been diverted via mental gears and pulleys into the making of money. The buildings about him were certainly phallic. Why hadn't he had these insights back in college when he needed them? It struck him that people didn't want a president with an inquiring mind. A leader like that might commit the cardinal political sin of speaking unpleasant truths. He halted. Half a block ahead across the street a motley row of panhandlers stood and sat and lay against the polished granite wall of a bank. Unpleasant truth made flesh, the kind people preferred to turn away from. Shaw prepared to take his place among them and knew that the first challenge would be to get passersby to look.

He ducked into a bus shelter and put on his sling. Who could see a sling and not feel the wearer's pain? His own had diminished, but he slowed his gait, favoring one leg, and felt he'd created a strong brand identity. Would anyone else have a sling? He crossed the street and passed before his competition. There were no other slings, or stumps, or running sores. What there was were photos of foreclosed homes, babies sleeping in arms, life histories spread over poster boards like science fair projects, timelines with snapshots of pets and vacations and ever-taller children, framed commendations, newspaper clippings about layoffs and locusts, medical bills, bowls with hard candies as Thank You's, printed donation receipts… One woman was industriously weaving on a miniature loom, proving she wasn't a passive parasite. Another plucked a small harp, lending the feeling of a medieval fair to the gathering. A grandfatherly man offered while-you-work car washing. The young couple farther down was taking a fresh batch of muffins from a solar oven. Shaw looked down at his sling and realized he was seriously underdressed.

He sat down at the end of the line. The bony, gray-ponytailed man next to him, shirtless and with a beach bum's deep tan, had fashioned a waist-high coin-catching device from an upside-down traffic cone and wood, allowing pedestrians to drop their donations without breaking stride, like toll-payers in an express lane. A businesswoman in slacks and jacket did exactly that, her handful of change ringing an ear-pleasing series of hidden bells before dropping into a brass bowl. The man glanced into the bowl, then checked out the president from head to heels. Shaw felt as if his act were being critiqued by a fellow comic at a club.

"You don't even have a can."

Chagrined, Shaw realized he was right.

"You one of those conceptual panhandlers? Commenting on begging?"

Shaw shook his head firmly in denial. His country contained conceptual panhandlers?

The man studied him further. "No can. No kids. No shtick. Nothing." Rather than criticizing, it dawned on Shaw that the man was analyzing his approach, taking it apart, perhaps to see if there was anything worth copying. "Strong. One image—a sling. Bam. Everything focused on that." He stared at Shaw, blue eyes bright as beads, an untended mustache reaching into his mouth. "Forget all the knickknacks. Too much clutter, obscuring the message. I hear you. People don't have time. It's a street, not a museum." He gave the president an appreciative nod. As with hailing from Scotland, it seemed easier for Shaw to simply nod back. "I like it," said the man. "Austere, but strong. Simple lines. Classical."

But not very successful. In the course of the morning the man's bells chimed regularly while he played back his life story for Shaw, from six-figure furniture designer to tow-truck driver for a car repossessor to cog in a gang of recyclables rustlers in Chicago, hitting the trash bins at dawn before the garbage trucks. Nowadays he was sleeping in the bed of an engineless pickup parked in his nephew's driveway, feeding and clothing himself from the twenty-five dollars a day he pulled in. Shaw's takings over three hours totaled forty-five cents. He'd have happily abandoned his classical approach, but was held back by his companion's respect for his aesthetic. When the sun swung around and reached them, the line broke up and reformed on the building's shaded side. This gave Shaw his chance. He parted ways with the man, found a scrap of cardboard in a dumpster, borrowed crayons from the mother homeschooling her daughter on the sidewalk, and wrote "Keep Nebraska Beautiful—Send Me to California," a naked theft from the sign of a dreadlocked teen who'd left the line earlier. "Original," mocked the old man now on Shaw's right, who had the squinting eyes of a rights and permissions lawyer. Shaw ignored him and gnawed on a dried apple, watching for signs of life in the masklike faces flowing past, fantasizing Warren Buffett stopping by his spot, then fearing it. They'd dined at the White House that spring. The other panhandlers' concerns were more commonplace: "Repetitive butt syndrome" from sitting on concrete, "GWTs" (Gucci-wearing tightasses), and "NPR" (No public restroom). The president was amazed the bank hadn't driven them off with fire hoses to spare its customers running the gauntlet, then found out from his neighbor that banks actually lured beggars with doughnuts; the unpleasant sight was helping to popularize online banking, letting the banks shed more employees. Shaw wondered if some of them were seated nearby.

By one o'clock he was ravenous. He'd noticed a small Italian flag in a stand beside a woman's basket of change, and remembered Omaha's large Greek community. He borrowed the crayons again and the girl's geography textbook and did his best to draw the Greek flag. Why stop there? Looking for any way to connect to passersby, he added the U.S. Army's gold and white star, a Christian fish, the breast cancer pink ribbon, and the red capital "N" of the Nebraska Cornhuskers he'd hated in college. Ten minutes later when he was addressed in Greek, he grinned and nodded energetically and simulated comprehension, to the suspicious smirking of his lawyerish neighbor. More money began dropping into his Spiderman hat. He passed the three dollar mark, folded his sign under his arm, and cashed in his winnings at a hot dog stand. He'd heard that the Greyhound station was close by and realized he'd better find out the fare to Los Angeles.

The building was low and windowless, fortified against winter. Shaw entered, made his way to an agent, and was dumbfounded by the one-way price: $158. It would take him a month to save that much. He walked out, not only despairing but disquieted. A man reading a newspaper had seemed to be looking at him. Did the Secret Service have agents watching all the bus stations? Maybe the bus wasn't the best way to travel after all.

He walked back to the bank, checked to see if he was being followed, and took his place at the end of the line, so far from the entrance that he was almost in the alley. He put out his hat and thought. Across the street, the Canaan Fellowship Church's sign read "If you don't like the way you were born, try being born again." Shaw felt he'd tried that the past week and it wasn't working out. He was still determined to finish the trip on his own, as he'd bragged he could, but not at the cost of working as a police lookout. He had no idea what to do. He took his new pair of socks from his bag, carefully folded his bandana around them, placed this improvised pillow behind his head, and was just closing his eyes when he heard running footfalls to his right. A man in a gray suit and tie wheeled around the corner from the alley. He was long-necked with a lush widow's peak of wavy black hair, indistinguishable from the thousands of office workers who'd walked past Shaw except for his maniacal smile and brown grocery sack. He braked, pulled a bundle of bills from the bag, broke the seal, tossed them into the air above the panhandlers, then dashed back into the alley. Tires squealed while the bank notes fluttered down. The president's distance from the bank entrance turned out to be an advantage, giving him fewer rivals. He plucked bills out of the air like mosquitoes, then frantically grabbed them off the ground, dueling with the blind grandmother to his left. They were hundreds. Someone shouted, "That was Pretty Boy!" Shaw's eyes lit. The police would be here any second. He snatched a last bill that had fallen atop the woman's straw hat, stuffed the money in his pocket, grabbed his own hat, and ran.

*    *    *

Three hours later, the rush-hour herd plodding nose-to-tail on Interstate 80 through Omaha contained a haggard gray 1995 Mercury Mystique that in turn contained the nation's president. The car had 228,960 miles on it—high for a U.S. car, the linebacker-built salesman had admitted, and therefore a sign, he said, of good genes. Shaw had doubts about the man's science. He'd have preferred the red Toyota Supra convertible, but sensing that the photo of him pulling into his Malibu mansion's parking circle might become iconic, he needed an American car. He also didn't need to be driving anything that looked like cop bait. Both the police and the public were on his mind.

After the robbery, with $1200 in his pockets, he'd headed toward Shantala's laundromat, where he got directions to her cousin with the fake ID sideline, who'd taken his picture against a white slab of sheetrock and charged $50 for a Nebraska driver's license. Shaw wasn't sure it would stand up to a rigorous inspection and was even less sure about buying one of her boyfriend's attractively-priced but undoubtedly-stolen vehicles. Too hazardous to his political health, he decided, and walked to a car lot instead. The Mystique was anything but mysterious: a bland, barely furnished room with hand-cranked windows, no power steering, no cupholders, but a price Shaw could afford. He'd hit the road with $315 in his pocket and a smile on his face, alternating with grimaces when his right arm had to help turn the wheel. The engine sputtered slightly, an old horse who couldn't believe it was being asked to plow again. The dashboard was cracked and faded to a sickly yellow, the driver's seat was deeply cratered by previous derrieres, but Shaw felt jubilant to be an independent agent again, able to will himself from place to place when he wanted and by whatever route. Would a fake ID be a problem for voters? He could see the apoplectic speech, or rather the song, that would come from the strumming senator from Texas, an immigration hawk who'd vilified Shaw for not taking a tougher stand on the issue. The man had posted on YouTube his self-composed "The Cheats of Laredo," describing a Latino staffer's stroll through that city, with close-ups of the four different Social Security cards he'd purchased. Then again, the country didn't need to know about Shaw's bogus license or the carjacker who'd forced him to buy it. He'd simply leave those out of the story. And since people wouldn't know his wallet had been stolen, they'd have no reason to suspect that he'd needed tainted money to pay for the car. He changed lanes abruptly, as if to escape the memory of his less-than-presidential behavior. On the way to the laundromat, knowing hundred-dollar bills would be hard to use, he'd hurriedly changed two at one bank and two more at another before news of the robbery spread. His criminal cleverness bothered him. What else was he capable of? Mixing ground glass into his wife's hummus? In his defense, he heard Shantala's voice: "Everybody surviving." He turned the blower a notch higher and finished the first of the two Big Macs he'd bought, washed two more Advil down with a slurp from his shake, then said aloud, "And survival's important."

In Lincoln he bought a pack of three white t-shirts and underwear to match, a pair of shorts, soap, a toothbrush, and a towel. Somewhere beyond Grand Island the sun set, working color changes from offstage for half an hour, Shaw watching raptly. He rolled down his window. He was in a compact car, but felt himself breathing in and joining the infinite vista around him. The Rockies were still 300 miles away, invisible but implied in the gradual upward grade. With the radio off and Venus glowing in the west, he felt the warm wind coursing over him and washing away the previous days' stresses. Driving at night through open country, alone and in no hurry, conferred peace the way hot cocoa gave warmth. He glided onward past Kearney, Gothenburg, then North Platte, pulled by the promise of mountain air and a morning swim in a lake. By Ogalalla he knew he was too tired to make it that night, then compromised with himself: he'd find a motel, someplace that wouldn't dent his wallet too deeply, and bathe in the waterfall of a shower instead. He'd certainly earned an indulgence. He hadn't showered since St. Louis; Dr. Weiss would surely approve. He veered onto I-76, felt buoyed at crossing into Colorado, got off in Julesburg, and pulled to a stop at the River View Motel.

Wagon wheels and cow skulls set a western theme, but inside the office there was the clashing smell of curry and the unexpected sound of Hindi passing between a man and woman. A meal was sizzling in a pan on a hot-plate behind the desk. A plump, mahoghany-skinned man checked him in with no request for his driver's license. It was a Tuesday, reducing the price to $55. Shaw paid in cash and five minutes later was under his room's shower, at the start of a twenty-minute session that probably put the owner in the red on Shaw's room. He dried off, ripped open his sealed t-shirts and underwear, and put on one of each. Then he ordered a pizza with six different toppings from the card by the phone and peeled back the bedspread, sitting on the pristine sheets, luxuriating in the sensation of being clean. Instead of kissing the ground in gratitude, like a returned hostage, he wanted to kiss the room's shower stall, its queen bed, its coffeemaker, its sink with water—at two different temperatures!—always available on demand. He picked up his recorder.

"Did Peter the Great have free soap? And shampoo, and conditioner? Did he have free delivery? Did he have cable? Coffee in his room? Air-conditioning? You want to know why we won the Cold War?" The shower had left him too dazed to say more. He lay back with his head on a pillow and snapped the TV to life with the remote, but felt too tired to watch. He hadn't seen the news in days but realized that he hadn't missed it. It was just after ten. A pair of local newscasters were on. Through slitted eyes, Shaw watched their perky faces replaced by the glum one of Gil Olivares, his press secretary, saying, "Our hearts go out to the victims of the earthquake in Jerusalem. I've just spoken with the president, who's been on the phone with world leaders all day and likely will be all night, monitoring the situation."

Shaw closed his eyes all the way. "That's me."

# 16.

"And try to get Bianca to put on some weight," Thorne barked into the phone.

On the opposite side of the country, pacing one of the Malibu mansion's decks, Cora rolled her eyes. It was late morning, overcast and frigid. The unseasonable chill was giving her own lean limbs goose bumps and she was anxious to get back inside.

"Slip some lard in her smoothies," said Thorne. "Whatever it takes. Women won't vote for candidates whose wives are thinner than they are. And Barry says she needs to be wearing red more. New research in on colors. Red and plump."

What did Barry Schraftstein know? He was nominally campaign manager, but like a king outgunned by the nobles, held little power except when Cora was outside Washington and couldn't put herself between Barry and Chuck. She was glad he hadn't come west yet.

"Maybe Bianca will eat the lasagna she's making," said Cora.

"You're going with lasagna?"

"I've got a promise for monster donations from Del Monte and ConAgra for using tomato sauce and fighting the whole E. coli thing."

"But lasagna's Italian. That's Fiore's territory."

"Bianca's one-sixteenth Italian, so she's entitled. Plus it's comfort food, which is what we need. Something down-to-earth that everybody loves, not some fat-free mango alfalfa-sprout compote. If Fiore doesn't like it, tough. It's a statement. We're coming after him."

"Are we ever. Too bad we don't have a candidate."

"Still nothing?"

"Nothing." Thorne sighed.

"Jesus. He could be dead and dismembered and buried by now."

"Thanks for the thought."

"Or maybe just trapped somewhere, being brainwashed."

"Much better."

Cora hung up and retreated to the kitchen, overcrowded with people holding clipboards, booms, cameras, and makeup brushes. The air was tense, portable lights blazing, the floor covered with a black spaghetti of cords. "Sorry about that." Her voice was drowned out by the hubbub. She banged a slotted spoon against a cast iron pot, a petite Napoleon twice as old as most of the others and feeling like a parent who's lost control of her toddlers. She shouted, "Are we finally ready? Let's cook or get off the pot, people!" It was hard to believe comfort food could come from such a room.

Water was boiling furiously, not in the kitchen's shiny top-of-the-line pasta pot, but in a battered kettle meant to suggest long usage on the family front lines, brought from the cooking consultant's mother's kitchen. The consultant was conferring with Heather, the First Lady's chief of staff, a scrawny blond whose body had absorbed much silicone but possibly never tasted full-fat ricotta. Bianca, in a crisp orange blouse and brown corduroys, was released by the woman in charge of her makeup. Cora banged the spoon again for attention.

"Okay!" The room quieted. "Let's set the scene. This is not a state dinner. It's a typical evening for the Shaws." Cassandra, in flannel pajamas and flip-flops, drew closer, seemingly interested in finding out how her family lived. "And this is not a cooking show, okay?"

"Sure as hell looks like one," said Cassandra.

Cora closed her eyes, asking for strength but privately wishing for a bullwhip. "But it's not." She looked at Bianca. "So no worries. Nobody's gonna ask you to bone a quail. And this isn't *Top Chef*. You're not going up against Fiore's wife. So let's everybody stay *calm*." Cora modeled breathing deeply. Heather copied and tried to pass it on to Bianca. The First Lady looked as brittle as the waiting lengths of lasagna.

"Think 'everyday occurrence,' " Cora went on, despite knowing full well that Bianca didn't cook. "And it's no problem if something goes wrong. All we're going to do is use a few key moments along the way." Cora faced Bianca. "You're calm. You're content. You're happy, because you're making one of your husband's favorite meals." She gestured upward, maintaining the illusion for Cassandra and the rest that the president was upstairs working.

"His favorite meal's actually steak."

"With Kraft Instant Sour-Cream-and-Garlic Mashed Potatoes," added Cassandra.

"Well, we're going to pretend he has a different favorite. Something his mother might have made."

"His mother put the whole family in the hospital with her turkey surprise. The cottage cheese was about a year past its—"

"Okay, okay. Not made by his mother. Made by you. With a simple salad and a California wine." Cora turned the bottle of Gallo zinfandel on the counter toward one of the two cameramen. "Make sure we see the label."

"The hell with Gallo," snapped Bianca. "Their last bottle gave me a headache." She'd been in a waspish mood for days. It had been uncomfortable sharing the house with her husband's double after he'd spurned her advances, even if he kept to her husband's office all day. Then there was the additional clutter of men impersonating the president's doctor and football carrier, and the need to keep Cassandra in the dark. She felt she was living on a movie set, with the kitchen shoot one fakery too many. "I really can't stand cooking. And I hate lasagna."

"No need to pronounce the 'g' actually," Heather mentioned deftly.

Just then, the family's golden retriever bounded into the room, immediately knocking over one of the light umbrellas on his excited way to the First Lady.

"And I can't stand dogs either! *Rolf!*" She felt ridiculous sounding like a dog herself every time she called the dog's handler. A short, silent redhead came on command and took the pet from the room, Bianca gripping the counter, eyes closed, then swatting at the dog hairs left behind on her pants. "Why don't we barbecue the goddamn dog. That's a meal I could get excited about."

Never, in a long career of crafting attack ads, had Cora conceived of such a potent campaign-killing image. Unfortunately, the campaign was her own. The White House photographer, who also thought in pictures, saw the dog's golden tail hanging over the barbecue's side, then tried out the scene with the animal on a spit. Like a discreet English butler, he was used to being an unavoidable witness to the family's private moments. Unlike an English butler, he planned to write a book about his employers and took special note of this scene.

"Lasagna's what we're making," declared Cora. "Okay?" Her yellowed teeth ground against each other like glaciers. "It's decided. Everything's ready. Margie's here to help."

The June Cleaverish cooking consultant smiled and handed Bianca a burgundy apron. "The weather's so cold that we're all going to love having something hot."

"And you don't have to even taste it if you don't want," Heather reassured her.

"About all you need to do," said Cora, "is take it out of the fricking oven and pronounce it. Now let's get the hell going!"

Outside in the house's front patio, Nathan Klotz, one of three deputy press secretaries, attempted to impose his will on a much larger crowd of journalists. The air bristled with booms, as if they were about to attack Frankenstein's castle.

"Which is why he canceled the week's campaign stops," he said. "He felt he needed to reflect on the country's challenges. To take time to think deeply about our present and our future." Nathan did some quick thinking of his own. "Not that he's been stationary all this time. Not at all." Thinking wasn't considered presidential. He searched for action. "This morning, just to give you a picture of a typical day, he swam thirty-two lengths, half a mile, before his security briefing. Then he had orange juice, fresh-squeezed for him by his daughter." Not true, but it had a nice ring. "He spoke with the Israeli prime minister again. Then he breakfasted on sliced fresh pineapple and wheat toast, no butter or margarine, only honey." Nathan's background in improv theater had come in handy but he wasn't sure how long he could keep this up. The broth he was serving was so watery that the bowls would start flying back at him any day. "I remarked to him how very fit he's looking." Just after I spoke to Elvis, he thought.

"Digressing for a moment from the president's muscle tone, what can you tell us about the earthquake?"

That it was a gift from the heavens, Nathan felt like answering. It had been just the distraction they'd needed and had given a further explanation for Shaw's confinement.

"Naturally that's been on the front burner. He's taking a major role in the very complex relief effort. Growing up in California, of course, the president has a lot of first-hand knowledge of earthquakes." He felt a soliloquy coming on and shuffled to the top of his stack of papers the outline he'd put together after interviewing Bianca about her husband. "His father's parents' home was heavily damaged by the 1933 Long Beach earthquake. The house was one-story, but brick—" Shaw's record with legislation might be paltry, but his earthquake resume was long—so long, Nathan realized as he clambered from disaster to disaster, that Shaw began to look like a marked man, someone God had repeatedly tried to kill. He decided to skip over the 1989 quake and shortened his account of Shaw's heroics in Northridge in 1994.

"Speaking of nature, what about the weather? Does he have a comment?"

That bitch in a parka from *The Huffington Post*. They were all well-bundled, actually, with Nathan himself secretly wearing long under-wear. Though it was as obvious as it was cold that the climate's behavior had gone from odd to unhinged, Nathan had his orders.

"The president's view is that the weather lies outside the three branches of government." He chuckled, hoping it might be contagious.

"So does he also think that mileage standards for cars and burning coal for electricity and solar power incentives lie outside of the government?"

Nathan fantasized rejecting reporters' questions, as his troupe used to reject audience suggestions for skits.

"Actually, energy policy is something he was working on intensely before the earthquake. I believe you may see him present some new proposals in that area to the public."

"Is his speechwriting team here?"

Nathan tried not to let the question register on his face. "They are not."

"Where are they?"

He chuckled. "That's a lot of people to account for." He sipped from his thermos of hot tea. "I believe several are on vacation at the moment."

\* \* \*

At that moment, Victor and Kyle's van was nosing through a gritty zone south of Albuquerque's downtown, the buildings heavily vined with graffiti. The motorcade's two other cars followed, on high alert for gang activity, careful not to give offense to other drivers.

"I could be lying on the beach on the Outer Banks right now," Jess told Lola.

"But wasn't this all your idea?"

"True," said Jess. "But not this part."

The van's brake lights lit. Victor's arm pointed. The van angled into a driveway and stopped in a dirt lot, the other cars turning sharply to follow. Ahead stood a hangerlike metal building with its big sliding door open. The darkness inside was lit by a sudden fountain of sparks. Jess got out and walked up to the van.

"Bingo," said Victor.

"Are we going in?"

"We'll let the telephoto do that for us."

"Yeah?"

"It's perfect. The guy's under the car. And if he comes out, he's got that Darth Vader mask on and coveralls. Nobody'll ever know it's not Shaw." He opened a case behind him and pulled out the lense, thick and long.

"I don't know."

"You don't know? Are you crazy? Nothing gives blue-collar credentials like welding. Plus you tap into a whole other thing." He attached the telephoto with a dramatic click. "Women dig it. Subconsciously." He gave Jess a "Don't you?" stare, lips curled slightly above his red goatee. She answered with her "Not really" look and walked one car back.

"He's got a point about nobody knowing it's not Shaw," said Trevor.

"And maybe the Freudian thing, too," said Hugh. "We could play some Wagner behind it."

"Or Yanni. Orgasm but no Nazism."

"Push the country's hidden buttons."

"And what if you accidentally push the button that makes people hate your candidate?" Jess asked.

Hugh sighed. "We'll cross that hidden bridge when we come to it."

"Great. I'll let you two write his welding diary."

"Already got the title. "Man of Steel."

Trevor gave Hugh a thumbs-up. "More hidden buttons."

"Right," said Jess. "Pittsburgh. Unemployment. Rust belt. Unions. Fiore."

Hugh shook his head. "How about strength. Flight. Speed. Justice. And, subconsciously, the ability to maintain an erection for a thousand years."

Jess made a face. "I'm not sure that would really be a plus. Even ten years is kind of long."

"You leave it to us."

"I feel confident," said Trevor, "that he'll look back on this day with the usual pride in his accomplishments and new lessons learned."

Hugh opened the glove compartment and pulled out the Shaw bobble-head. "I'm sure you will," he addressed it and gave it a pat, sending the head springing back and forth. The trip's second half had the bizarre feel of a journey taken for the benefit of a doll, spoken to and photographed and held up to see the sights. In this case, the adults were keeping a diary for it, describing its deep sympathy for the plight of the people of Missouri, its visit to Eisenhower's family home in Abilene, its thoughts on overcoming obstacles, inspired by the view of Colorado's Front Range, its celebration of diversity during its passage through New Mexico. Without the president or a double, they'd shot footage that Shaw might have taken himself, but they hadn't before filmed someone they'd pass off as the president.

"What if the welder guy sees it on TV and comes forward?" asked Jess.

"Probably blind from all the sparks."

"That's really not what I'd call a comprehensive strategy."

"We could crop the shot," said Trevor. "Stay below the sign." Above the doorway, in black handpainted letters, was "Padilla Machine and Welding" and the address.

"True," said Jess. "But then it's too much like stock footage. The place could be in Finland."

"No problem," said Hugh. "If the scene's after the 'Welcome to the Land of Enchantment' sign and before the 'Now Leaving the Land of Enchantment' sign, you could splice in an Eskimo whale hunt and people would swear it happened in New Mexico."

"Maybe," said Trevor, "just to make it even more real, we should get Lola to put some fake burns on Shaw's arm."

Hugh liked it. "Camera zooms in. The audience winces but Shaw shrugs it off with 'You get used to it.'"

"Hombre-in-Chief of the United States."

Jess was the one wincing. "Lola gets him ready for speeches and press conferences. I don't think she's had a lot of practice giving him fake burns and black eyes." She checked the time, then the map on her BlackBerry. "If we bust our butts we can hit the Grand Canyon in time to shoot in that great light just before sunset."

"Again with the parks," protested Hugh. "Sure, they're pretty, but what's that got to do with Shaw getting to know his people? It's off-message."

"It's a national symbol! Trumps the hell out of welding! One shot of the Grand Canyon and you're showing people strength, independence, patriotism, appreciation of God's glorious creation. It's a multivitamin of messages! Plus you get the idea of endurance over time. Instead of a piddly thousand-year hard-on, this gives 'em eternity!"

Hugh sighed. "Now that would get old."

"The other thing," said Trevor, "is that we're looking good in Arizona but New Mexico's close." He zoomed out on his GPS's map. "We should do more of the state. Go all the way down, then cut over on I-10."

Jess's green eyes flashed. "And skip the Grand Canyon? What have you got that can possibly top that?"

Trevor followed the Rio Grande south, then enlarged the area north of Las Cruces. He pointed at the screen. "Hatch, New Mexico."

"*Hatch?*" Jess realized she'd yelled. "And what wonder of the world I've never heard of is located in this town you can barely see?"

"I did some reading last night," said Trevor. "The place is famous for chiles. Big festival every Labor Day."

Hugh nodded in confirmation. He'd heard it mentioned in the hotel in Santa Fe.

"And?" Jess's jaw dropped.

Hugh took over. "Maybe you didn't pick up on it, but chile peppers are a big deal here. Super macho. That guy at the bar last night? Bragging about eating 'em raw, seeds and all? And Hatch is the capital."

"Like Mecca for a Muslim?" Jess tossed out sarcastically.

"And maybe, being the gringa you are, you don't realize the hidden buttons we could push by panning over a big luscious field of ripening phallic symbols." Hugh got a further idea. "Then we bring some to Malibu and film Shaw biting into one. Mama! Five electoral votes guaranteed! And maybe get the Hispanic vote in California."

Jess stared at the pair in awed disgust. "Is it really all about dicks?" she shouted. "They're what makes the world go around? I thought it was money!"

"If it was just about money, Ross Perot would've won." Hugh pointed his nose at the welding shop. "Victor's onto something. You need a stud on the ticket. And you gotta keep pushing those hidden buttons to prove it, with any appendage that reaches. Next stop, Hatch!"

Dazed, outvoted, and more surprisingly, partially convinced, Jess got back in her car.

\* \* \*

Four hundred and fifty miles to the north, the president was climbing a grade on I-70, guessing that Thorne and the Secret Service would expect him to head down through New Mexico and therefore avoiding it, on a course through Colorado and Utah instead. He had the window down and was feasting on the mountain air. Denver's smog lay behind him, he was among the Rockies at last, his car was wheezing only slightly, and the Eagles were on the radio. Shaw was whistling along. When he'd lunched in Arvada and seen the woman in the kitchen take a drag on her cigarette while assembling his sandwich, he'd known it for certain: he was back in the West. These were his people. He'd eaten among them at the crowded bar, his recorder running in his pocket, listening like a spy to their talk. Conversation turned out to be limited to sports, spurred by the buffet of TVs offering Olympic water polo, a replay of the 1982 Bassmaster Classic, and the Australian rules football match between Port Adelaide and Brisbane. The TVs were muted; the male patrons were not. After half an hour of auditing a Talmudic disputation on fantasy football league player-drafting rules, Shaw began to have doubts about how many feet his citizens maintained in the real world. He'd had the same thought at the rest stop that morning, where the man peeing beside him was using his free hand to play Scrabble on his iPhone with his sister in Florida, as he'd proudly explained. Studying the map outside the bathroom, Shaw had found his Spiderman hat eliciting a high-speed treatise from a woman his age on the latest Spiderman movie, leading to her thoughts on manga versions and parodies, the effect on Peter Parker of his girlfriend's death at the hands of the Green Goblin, then the woman's ranking of his enemies, from Dr. Octopus through Mysterio, Morlun, Hydro-Man, the Sinister Six...

How, Shaw wondered, did people have time for so much flight from reality? Maybe this explained the vast tent city he'd spied from the freeway: people had simply forgotten to go to work and pay their mortgages. No wonder they weren't attending school board meetings or following public affairs, unless a crisis could be dressed up as Good vs. Evil. Reagan had been onto something with "evil empire." Maybe instead of this trip, what his campaign really needed was a shot of him in a cape and tights.

He climbed beyond 10,000 feet, wrapped in a world of rock, tree, and cloud, then passed through the endless Eisenhower Tunnel, feeling like an electron in a supercollider, and emerged on the other side of the Continental Divide, descending swiftly, watching his speedometer. He couldn't afford any run-ins with police and had scrupulously obeyed all traffic signs. He seemed to be the only one in the country doing so, a teetotaler who'd wandered into a rave. Driving through Denver, he'd drawn angry honks from those disgusted by his tooth-fairyish belief in the speed limit and incomprehensible braking at yellow lights. A fine people, but willing to kill and be killed rather than not make it through an intersection. He turned on his recorder.

"It turns out that speed limits are kind of like a suggested retail price," Shaw said. His mind jumped to Texas, which had bowed to public pressure and raised the limit on sections of I-10 to 120 mph. That seemed a little high, but he'd campaigned in 2010 to give the states more leeway in setting speeds and couldn't flip-flop now, not after ridiculing his opponent as "Senator Speed Bump." Shaw searched for a silver lining of spin. "On the other hand, our desire to get places fast indicates that we're still optimistic about where we're going," he told his recorder, then was blasted by the freighterlike horn of a gigantic black SUV and swerved into the runaway truck lane so as not to unnecessarily detain the car further, strangling the wheel as he bounced over the gravel, struggling to get back to asphalt. He finally succeeded, his heart decelerating slowly. He bent and picked the recorder up off the floor. "More on this later."

He parked at Lake Dillon and marched down a trail sweet-scented by ponderosa pines, feeling like Roosevelt without Muir, joyously free of his handlers. He'd realized they'd need reassurance that he was alive and so had called his brother the day before, swearing him to secrecy and telling him to call Bianca this morning, by which time he'd be long gone from the payphone on Interstate 80 he'd called from. He returned to the car, took his own picture with the lake behind, his glasses off, and liked what he saw—his beard at that just-sprouted stage favored by actors, the scrapes on his face giving the photo the look of an action-movie poster. He drove on, passed Vail, buoyed by the landscape's roof-of-the-world feel, then was jerked back down to the world of men by the sign on the side of a trailer: "Firewood, Rodent Control, Snowshoe Repair, Jigsaw Puzzle Rental." Making a living was tough. Tourism was down, staycations were up. "Relacations"— moving into relatives' houses—were also on the rise according to the talk show he'd tuned into that morning. And then there were "Regresations"— moving back into the room you'd occupied as a child. He passed another Fiore billboard, the one in which he looked down like a beneficent god on an army of men building solar-powered, transit-served, low-cost housing, according to the ad copy. Once again, Shaw felt like the problem rather than the solution. To be an incumbent was to defend the status quo, but defending this one was a hopeless proposition.

The road joined the Colorado River, copying the route it had sawn through the mountains as if with a hacksaw. Shaw negotiated Glenwood Canyon's curves and tunnels, his shoulder complaining about the extra work. It was past five when he stopped for gas in New Castle, the high country behind him, the trees scrubby and the sky bare of clouds. He used the gas station bathroom and stared at the words of advice left in permanent marker by an earlier patron: "Please remain seeted until excrament is deposited, thank you, the managemeant." He thought of Cora, who'd floated the idea of a truck-stop bathroom campaign of anti-Fiore jokes and pro-Shaw slogans. Jokes traveled quickly and the truck-stop venue would stamp them as genuine emanations of the People, the best possible testimonial. Gazing at the misspellings on the metal door, Shaw had new doubts about posing as the People's choice. He left the stall, washed his hands but found no paper towels in the dispenser, walked out of the bathroom and saw a payphone to his left. Remembering Omaha, he looked both ways, ripped out two pages from the phonebook's yellow pages and dried his hands on them. Not bad, he thought, then walked toward the convenience store next door for a soda—and halted. Among the line of parked cars were two dusty SUVs, side by side, both with Texas plates and "Re-Elect Shaw" bumper stickers. Talk about a photo op, he thought. He got his camera out of his car and had just snapped his third picture when the owners presented themselves.

"What the hell you think you're doing?"

The man who spoke appeared to be with his wife, both stocky, silver-haired, skin tanned and creviced. Beneath the man's thick mustache, a toothpick flicked like a snake's tongue.

Shaw was at a loss. "Just, you know, taking a picture. Just, for—"

"What are you? FBI?" The man waved away a fly with his Dallas Cowboys cap. He glared at the president. "IRS?"

Seeing them coming, Shaw had discreetly turned on the recorder in his shirt pocket, but now wondered if he need have bothered.

"Or Homeland sorry-ass Security?" suggested the wife.

"Actually—" The president longed to reveal that DHS worked for him rather than the other way around. Then the woman reached for something in her leather purse. Shaw wondered if he was about to be shot. He was on the point of blurting out his presidential code name—Roughneck—when she pulled out her own camera and snapped his picture.

"We'll find out who you are," the woman promised.

"I'm just a Shaw supporter—like you!" He tried to evict the "Don't shoot" panic from his voice. "I'm working for the campaign. Just thought I'd take a picture of your bumper stickers, if you don't mind. And maybe find out a little about you. Something we could maybe use."

The couple's weathered faces relaxed slightly.

"We're voters, is who we are," said the man.

His wife rolled her eyes. "And what a job that's turned out to be."

"Yeah?"

"Farmed in Illinois most of our lives, but got tired of our votes going down the toilet every four years, thanks to the damn Electoral College. So we picked up and moved to New Mexico, where they'd count."

"Climate was better," said the woman, "but instead of snow, there was salsa. All year long, on everything. His ulcers started acting up."

"And then came 'Vote with your feet.' "

This was Wyoming's answer to those who didn't care for its restoration of public hangings. Shaw remembered well: the Gallows Channel, Fox praising the benefits of returning public humiliation to executions, Rush Limbaugh's celebration of hanging's long and noble pedigree, the embarrassment when Georgia proposed to turn the clock back even farther and return to public stoning.

"After Wyoming, New Mexico got busy passing laws. Named the burrito the state food. Then there was the Mountain Usage Tax—on Texans who came there to ski cause they didn't have mountains of their own. Then came ballots printed in Spanglish."

"That was the last straw. So we re-voted with our feet."

"Where to?"

"Montana," said the wife. "Billings."

"But so many damn Wyoming liberals had picked up and moved there that you couldn't spit in the street without seeing 'Don't Pollute—Flows to

Gulf of Mexico Eventually' stenciled next to every damn storm drain." The man spit on the asphalt dangerously close to Shaw's left foot. "Two thousand miles from the damn Gulf."

"Plus the winter was worse than Illinois."

"We'd liked what we'd heard about the new speed limits in Texas," said the husband. "So we moved down to a neighborhood in Dallas that had some problems with liberals. Thought we'd do our part."

"Till our left-wing pastor got put on the spot and would not state that illegal aliens would be barred from Heaven when the Rapture comes."

"Plus the Cowboys went to hell. Now there is a sign of the End Times." The man's face darkened. "Then I got cancer. Probably from shaking the damn pastor's hand."

"The doctors don't like what's coming. So we're heading up to Oregon. They got assisted suicide."

Shaw breathed in deeply. "Wow. That's quite a story." He didn't know if he should feel proud of his country's spectrum of offerings or dismayed at the couple's unending Goldilocksian search.

"Rubbing shoulders with all the damn Californians living there," said the man, "I got a feeling that suicide's gonna look even better." The man leaned closer to Shaw. "What's the best form of birth control for a woman?"

The president shook his head blankly, afraid of what he'd hear next.

"A California accent."

The pair smiled expectantly at Shaw. He produced a feeble grin, unaware there was such a thing as a California accent. He decided to keep his origins to himself.

The man unlocked his car. "We'll pray for good luck in November."

It sounded like a wish with little real chance, like praying for rain. Disheartened, he gave them each a limp handshake and realized he was out of practice shaking hands.

"Shaw's not the brightest bulb in the chandelier," said the woman, "but we're hoping." She got into her car.

"And praying to God."

They left. In God we trust, Shaw muttered on his way into the store. He emerged with a drink and continued west, the couple's sagging endorsement echoing in his ears. Not the brightest bulb? He'd made it this far from St. Louis, living by his wits and without a dollar most of the time. Maybe his people were best viewed from 30,000 feet after all. Maybe he ought to stop recording their idiotic chatter and focus on his own thoughts, or on photographing the ravishing land around him. He put this in action and stopped three different times to take pictures of the Colorado and the mesas and rock walls turning pink. He was in high desert country, the air as dry as in outer space, his nasal passages registering the change. It was dusk but still in the nineties when he reached Grand Junction, his entrance noted by a cop with a radar gun. The president was unused to avoiding the eyes of the police, but did so now, realizing he was tasting a little of what it felt like to be African-American or Hispanic. He cruised safely past and stopped at the Chuck Wagon Steak House, then counted his money in the car. He was filling up the car every few hours and food was costing more than he'd expected. He knew he shouldn't eat there, and also knew that he couldn't simply borrow from future generations as he'd done often as president. He ignored all that and bucked up his spirits with a porterhouse and a football-sized baked potato. Budgets had never been his strong suit. In exchange for the binge, he vowed over the pecan pie à la mode to sleep in his car in a rest stop, waddled out the back door into the overheated night, and saw his plan go up in glass and metal when a big, battered pickup truck backed powerfully into his car's rear. The truck paused, then shifted out of reverse. Shaw realized the driver was going to take off. He ran forward, waving his arms, fearing he'd be run over next, dancing in the periphery of the truck's lights and ready to throw himself out of range if needed, finally reaching the driver's open window and hanging onto the door as if to hold the truck back.

"You just crushed my car! And leaving the scene's against the law!"

Out of the lights' glare, he saw the driver was female. He glanced at his accordioned trunk and shattered rear window and knew he wouldn't be coasting into Malibu in the Mystique. "I don't need this!" he yelled at her and the universe.

"And guess what, mister? I don't either!"

My people, thought Shaw.

# 17.

"I can't believe this!" the woman yelled. She slugged her steering wheel, burst out crying, then turned toward the president. "Please don't report it! I'm begging you!"

Shaw came to his wits and realized he was as anxious for the police not to get involved as she was. The parking lot was empty but wouldn't stay that way. "Where can we talk?"

"Hop in."

Shaw circled around and climbed up, sitting on top of a welter of papers, the truck shooting forward and leaving the parking lot. The woman turned off the commercial street as quickly as possible and wove left and right like a fleeing purse-snatcher, finally stopping in a hushed residential cul-de-sac. She cut the engine.

"I'll fix your car!" she promised. "I swear." She wiped her tears with a forearm. In the light from a streetlamp, she looked to Shaw to be in her twenties, long-necked in a clingy top, a pretty face framed by waterfalls of straight black hair.

"I'm not insured, okay? But who is, you know? I missed traffic school from my last speeding ticket cause my daughter had chicken pox, so I'm totally screwed if this gets reported. I'm two months behind on the water bill, a month behind on rent, got a hundred and forty-four thousand on credit cards, mainly medical bills, which just went up to fucking thirty percent cause of not making the piddly ten-buck minimum payment on my fucking Sears card from a couch I don't even have cause I had to sell it to get the heat turned back on in February." She peered into Shaw's eyes. "I'm trying. I really am." She wiped away more tears, dragging eyeliner across her cheek. "I'm cleaning motel rooms in the morning, doing childcare for three new moms in the afternoon and taking classes at night so I can get into a nursing program. But I got two kids of my own, my ex works at the Chuck Wagon but he's flat out refusing to make his damn payments, even when you show him his name on the fucking papers"—she indicated the documents Shaw was sitting on—"which is why I was so mad I didn't even see your car."

Shaw had been focused on his own predicament, but found it washed away by the woman's flood of woes, added to by her daughter's asthma, her son's allergies, and the infestation of bedbugs courtesy of Hilton's "We Care" furniture giveaway.

"I'd declare bankruptcy but I don't have the money for a lawyer! Can you believe that? Next thing, they're not going to let you die if you can't afford a casket! They'll store you in a warehouse till you can buy your way out!"

Staring at the rips in his nation's safety net, Shaw wished he could magically sew them up for the sake of the attractive woman beside him. It was something he ought to be capable of, he thought. But what government agency dealt with bedbugs?

"The drought's killing the farmers, so stores are closing. Tourism's way down ever since that big pack of foreclosure dogs, the ones people abandon when they leave town, attacked those four golfers right there on the course—pulled the biggest guy apart limb from limb—which is why the motel just cut me back to three days."

Her name was Brandy. She was twenty-seven, a mix of Ohio, Mexico, and the Navajo Nation. Her recitation finally rolled to a halt. The president glibly encouraged her to apply herself in school, feeling like one of Job's comforters, blithely predicting the end of the drought.

"Bullshit," Brandy replied.

Shaw felt slapped. She was probably right. He was a peddler of bullshit, and was tired of it. He put that thought aside and returned to his own problems.

"About my car—"

"I'll get it fixed! I swear I will!"

Given the length of her To Do list, Shaw had trouble imagining this taking place in anything less than two decades. Unfortunately, he needed to be in Malibu on Friday.

"It was totally my fault! My goddamn ex—"

"I'm not really interested in your ex. All I care about is finishing my trip."

"You don't live here?"

Shaw didn't think he could pull off his "I'm from here" pretense. He was about to say he lived in Alexandria, VA, where the fictional Matt Dawes lived, then suddenly remembered Matt's Nebraska driver's license in his pocket. "I'm from far away," he said vaguely.

"Yeah?"

The president saw Brandy stare at him warily, as if he might not be an earthling. At that moment, Washington, D.C. did indeed feel like a distant planet. "I'm on a pretty long trip."

"How come?"

Shaw had never had to explain himself before. "Just curious."

"Yeah? About what?"

"Finding out, you know, how people really live."

Brandy gave him a quizzical look. "But you're a person. You walk on two feet. You know how people live."

"Not all that much. And not in places like Grand Junction."

The woman cocked her head at him. "And then the mothership picks you up and you show the captain his very first taquito and then you show him how to put on the hot sauce and he bites into it and he's totally blown away?"

"Not quite that extreme." He felt he'd told her too much. "The important thing is I need to be in L.A. on Friday."

"I'll drive you."

Behind his black glasses, Shaw's eyebrows hopped upward. "You will?"

"If you won't report the accident. Or sue me."

The idea appealed to Shaw. More fun than driving alone. Getting to know his constituents. And the woman wasn't exactly a burden to look at.

"Fine by me." He scanned the truck. It was a bruiser with an eight-foot bed, old, no Air Force One, but it would do. "My other problem is a room. I'm kind of short on—"

"Stay at my place. If you don't mind the sofa bed in the living room."

Better than his car's back seat, where he'd planned on sleeping. "You sure?"

"Sure I'm sure." She paused to think. "I'll need to make some calls. Line up child care. It's eleven hours to L.A. Tomorrow's Thursday. I'll get you there a whole day early, in time for dinner."

"Sounds good."

Brandy thought some more. "We'd need to leave early. Like six. That way I can get back here for work on Friday."

"When are you going to sleep?"

"You let me worry about that."

"Deal," said the president. They shook hands. Her fingers, slender and rough, sent a wave of protectiveness through him.

She looked into his eyes. "And I'm gonna call up a friend about fixing your—"

"Don't worry about it. Not important." Shaw enjoyed speaking the line, glossy with his former immunity to mundane worries.

"Are you bullshitting me?"

The president shook his head. Brandy seemed to want to smile but feared to do so or to rock the boat with more questions.

"I just need to get some things out of it," Shaw said.

They drove back to the Chuck Wagon. The president waited until the parking lot was empty, threw his clothes and toothbrush and towel in his Piggly Wiggly bag and grabbed his water bottle.

"You travel really light," said Brandy. Shaw shrugged off her puzzled look, wondering what she'd think if she found out he didn't even have a wallet. Only aliens and serial killers didn't carry wallets.

They continued down streets and through neighborhoods he didn't know, Shaw reminded of being driven in his limousine, content after so much scrambling on his own to return to having someone else move him around. They ended at an apartment complex and got out, Brandy turning out to be tall and leggy, in a short ruffled black skirt he'd been unaware of. Behind her, he climbed a stairway whose wobbly metal banister wouldn't pass muster with OSHA, then walked down a stifling hallway perfumed by a litter box placed outside a door like a room-service tray. Shaw had visited Americans in their workplaces, in schools, at volunteering events, had met with voters in fastidiously cleaned dens in Iowa and New Hampshire, but had never entered one of his citizens' homes unannounced, like a busybody mother on a surprise visit. He followed Brandy through the door to 2-F, into a toy-strewn living room that was air-conditioned to Arctic standards. A kindergarten-aged boy was jumping up and down on the couch, preparing it for Shaw's night of rest, imitating the Olympic trampoline competition on the big-screen TV across the room. A guinea pig clung to the center cushion like a shipwreck survivor in rough seas. On the far cushion sat Brandy's busty daughter, Jade, deaf to her introduction and ignoring the president's outstretched hand, her own thumbs busy twitching over her cellphone's keys. Shaw was introduced as a friend but felt more like a ghost.

"She's eleven," Brandy excused her. "They're like that."

Eleven? The girl was already a c-cup and climbing. Maybe growth hormones in meat really were a problem after all, thought Shaw. He made a note to check his own chest in the morning in the wake of the sixteen-ounce steak he'd just eaten. He trailed Brandy into the cramped kitchen-dining room and sat, glimpsing a different portion of her ancestry in her face each time he saw it from a new angle. Tattoos peeked out from under every article of her clothing. Before the trip he'd never known how many of his citizens felt compelled to decorate their skins. He wondered if a study group should be convened on the topic.

"Beer? Wine?" She opened a high cupboard. "Tequila. Smirnoff. Johnny Walker. I make a good White Russian." She seemed anxious to show him a good time and make sure their deal didn't dissolve. "Weed? Speed? My neighbor sells Ecstasy." She looked at Shaw. "Or do you want something stronger?"

There were sufficient ingredients at hand, he saw, for derailing dozens of political careers. He settled for a beer and listened unavoidably to her phone messages, hearing for the first time in his life the deep-voiced delivery of collection agency callers, their messages curt, projecting a Mafia menace. Brandy cut them short with airy unconcern, listened in full to the message about her overdue tax penalty payment, and joined Shaw at the wooden cable-spool table with a beer.

"Goddamn IRS. I paid my damn tax but they say they never got it, probably from people stealing the mail, which is keeping half of Colorado alive since AFDC ended thanks to goddamn welfare reform." She unfurled her dispute in detail, the president thinking guiltily of the charge that his administration was hard on the low-income bracket but too soft on white-collar tax fraud, recalling the whistleblower videos showing waitress service and chair massages for corporations' tax lawyers at the IRS's Platinum Resolution Center in the Poconos. Shaw finished his beer, resolving to be her knight, not her enemy. He couldn't change any laws on the spot, but could surely help her out somehow. He scanned the room for a quest, didn't feel up to remounting the precariously hanging hood over the stove, then gazed at the sticking liquor-cabinet doors Brandy had fought with earlier. She was delighted by the offer. He asked if she had a file or a plane, stood on a chair with a cheese grater instead, reaching high to scrape the wood, and was making progress when he gave a yelp at the bolt of pain in his right shoulder.

"Separated it a few days ago," he explained and climbed down. "It was getting better—"

"I know just the thing!" Brandy left the room, then burst back in. "Someday I'm gonna be a nurse, but until then—" She opened a booklet. The president spied what looked like the logo of the Department of Health and Human Services. "We're gonna fix you right up." She pulled her chair around in front of Shaw, who was amazed to realize she was holding one of the Family First Initiative's *We Can Handle It!* pamphlets.

"Okay," she said. "First thing. Assess the problem."

Shaw's eyes expanded. "But those have all been recalled!"

Brandy looked up. "What have?"

"Those booklets. After that lady tried to fix her husband's collapsed lung and sued the hell out of—" He excised the word "us." "Sued the government."

Brandy regarded the booklet, then looked back at Shaw. "Are you kidding me? These are great! Especially when you've got kids who are always getting sick or hurt and you can't afford a doctor. They're the one good thing the government's ever done." She returned to hurriedly flipping pages and scanning text. "Okay. Here we are. 'Manipulating a dislocated shoulder back into place isn't brain surgery—and it isn't hard either. If you've already read Volume 4, *Knocking 'em Dead and Other Secrets of Anesthesia*'—which I have, a bunch of times—"

"Hold on!" Shaw grabbed his shoulder protectively. "It's separated, not dislocated. I don't need anesthesia. It's a Type One separation. The mildest."

Brandy looked up at him. "Are you sure?"

"Positive. Trust me. All I need is an anti-inflammatory and some ice."

The woman seemed disappointed. "Whatever." She put down the booklet and entered the bathroom around the corner. "I've got ibuprofen, Naproxen, Tylenol, Tylenol PM. Or, even better"—she poked her head back into the kitchen—"I've got some Percocet left over from my back surgery." She gave the president a Special Offer smile. "And man, I'm telling you, you and your shoulder are both—"

Shaw appreciated the thought. He took two ibuprofen, put ice cubes in a baggie, and joined Brandy and her kids in the living room for the end of the pet-swapping reality TV show *Bad Dog!*, then *The Throne Room Chronicles*, ABC's fairy-tailish bathroom makeover hit, then *Mops*, the mysteriously popular look into the real lives of maids and janitors. Brandy held the remote in one hand and her cellphone in the other, serving a finely sliced visual chiffonade during commercials and hunting down a babysitter for the next day. She told her children about the Los Angeles trip, parried their moans, sent them to their room, and made up the sofa bed with Shaw's help. This joint domestic activity, centered on a bed, gave him a pleasing thrill. Her collection of bracelets slid up and down her arm, providing a tambourinelike accompaniment. She was twenty years younger, with a naturalness that his guest-list-conscious, calorie-counting, couture-crazed wife lacked. He had a feeling that the car accident merited a visit to Brandy's own bed. Then again, her kids were a room away. They wouldn't be tomorrow, however, when he had a free night in L.A. Then the post-reptilian part of his brain reminded him that he was president. In reply to that, he wondered if he could pass it off as part of Operation Compassion. A struggling single mother, in need of confidence in herself...

Alone in the living room, he waited for the bathroom to become free—a novel experience—through Brandy's son's oatmeal bath for a sudden case of hives and her daughter's endless shower and 128-step grooming regimen, peering into family photos, scanning shelves, kicking guinea pig feces under the furniture, then listening with interest to Brandy's own shower. He decided to let the next day unfold as it would.

\* \* \*

By eight the next morning they were in Green River, Utah, filling their bellies with coffee, huevos rancheros, and hash browns with fry sauce, then driving the big blue truck three blocks farther and entering a Safeway to fill up on supplies for the following hundred miles that offered no services. Brandy was a black-haired ghost, in white embroidered blouse and white shorts, hair up, ready for the heat to come. The store was new. Shaw had claimed to be a grammar-school P.E. teacher in Omaha, fitting his build but not his fascination with the man dumping a Mason jar of change into the Coinstar machine, his ignorance of Red Box video rentals, and his foreigner's stumbling through the self-check process. He prayed that Brandy hadn't noticed his cultural clumsiness, or that she wouldn't tell once his identity became known. A hundred-roll carton of toilet paper, a gift card to the emergency room in Grand Junction, and a bottle of José Cuervo would probably keep her quiet, he calculated.

They climbed through rock canyons, Shaw feeling as if he were in a kaleidoscope of ochers and oranges. Above, the cloud formations echoed the solidity and fantastical shapes of the land below. He'd never felt air so dry or seen sky so blue. While Brandy drove, he had her last semester's chemistry textbook open on his lap, reviewing her on covalent and ionic bonds, acids and bases, and other matters he knew nothing about but that clearly were the stuff of the world out the window. He felt he was in touch with the universe's elemental workings, always active but only obvious on those rare occasions when nothing human was scribbled over the landscape. Why had he never studied chemistry before? Why hadn't he built a science museum in the bottom of the Grand Canyon instead of fighting to let McDonald's and Banana Republic go in?

The president switched to biology in Salina, getting Brandy ready for her upcoming semester, impressed with her work ethic, ears open when she traced the E. coli outbreak to raising cows on a grain fast-track instead of the grass they'd evolved to eat.

"Not that you'll ever hear that from the FDA," she added.

"How come?"

"Cause that would mean our limp dick of a president would actually have to care more about our health than the beef industry's." She gave a bitter cackle. Shaw waited for the words to disperse and vanish. He tried to convince himself the exchange had never taken place, closed the book at the end of the chapter on metabolism, and escaped into the *Serenity Through Stoicism* CD Brandy popped into her player.

"Remind yourself, as Marcus Aurelius advised," spoke a plummy male voice, "that outward things cannot touch you. Nor outward people who tell lies, are abusive, or use violence. They're ignorant of what is good, and of the brotherhood of man. Remember that they can do you no real harm, for they cannot make you pursue evil with them."

Shaw listened. When the burble of a mountain brook signaled a new track, he paused the CD.

"So you get something out of this?"

Brandy squinted at him. "Are you kidding? Why do you think I wasn't afraid to let you into my apartment? A built guy like you could break me in half." The line removed the thorn of "limp dick" from Shaw's ego. "Why else would I let in somebody with no luggage? Who's apparently never shopped in a grocery store before? Who's got a degree in physical education but doesn't know squat about biology? Who keeps his cash loose in a pocket instead of in a wallet? And weirdest of all, who's from Omaha but roots for UCLA instead of the Cornhuskers? That's why I'm into stoicism!" She took her eyes off the road to give Shaw a potent look. "I don't know what your game is. But I do know that I smashed into your car, and driving you to L.A. is the one thing I can do to help make things right."

The president felt himself one of the lying evildoers and longed to come clean.

"Stoicism's about virtue. And evenness. Avoiding destructive emotions and reactions."

Shaw thought contritely of the airstrike he'd launched against Honduras in a fit of pique.

"Not that I'm too good at that," Brandy admitted. "That's how I backed into you." She gazed at the cliffs ahead. "But I'm working on it. Learning to find happiness inside, no matter what happens outside. And with so much shit falling out of the sky, no wonder people are going back to the Stoics."

Shaw felt some responsibility for the nation's mindset and listened to the rest of the CD in silence, watching the Sevier Valley flow by. The day was scorching: 95° in Cove Fort, where they turned south on I-15, 98° in Beaver, and rising three degrees higher while they ate their lunch in Cedar City. Dropping down toward the Mojave Desert, the temperature climbed past 110°—and then they both had a chance to practice emotional detachment when steam began pouring out from under the truck's hood. Shaw was driving.

"Jesus Christ!" shouted Brandy.

Shaw noticed she wasn't calling to Marcus Aurelius. He was having trouble seeing the road through the steam. He stole a glance at the temperature gauge. "It says we're fine."

"The gauge is broken!"

"What do you want me to do?"

They were passing through St. George. "We need to get off!" Brandy gestured him toward the exit directly in front of them. Shaw cut off a sports car, drawing an angry squawk, and wrestled the truck onto the ramp and up to a traffic light beside a KFC. Diners pointed. Shaw had gotten used to avoiding the public eye and didn't like feeling stared at. He waited through the interminable light, then pulled in at the first gas station he came to, where the affectless teenager at the till told him without a scintilla of concern that there was no mechanic on duty. No mechanic at a gas station? What was going on with this country? He drove seven more blocks through his private fog, the focus of all eyes as if leading a parade, and turned at last into Royster's Auto Repair. They bailed out, Shaw running into the first bay and halting before a man with his head deep in a Mazda's engine.

"We need help!" He sounded as if Brandy were about to deliver a child. The grizzled, grease-smudged mechanic slowly withdrew his head, straightened his long back, took in Shaw, then Brandy swearing at her truck.

"Running a little hot?"

He'd clearly seen the scene often. That he was experienced was a comfort, but the nonchalance that came as a by-product nettled the president.

"We really need to get back on the road."

"Too hot to handle right now. Be patient, young man."

Shaw was unused to hearing the imperative mood. He felt like a chastened child and joined Brandy, resisting putting an arm around her shoulder, leading her into the pocket-sized waiting room and buying her a cold drink from the vending machine. She sat and flapped her shirt and blouse to move some air around her, allowing her tattooed menagerie of Gila monsters, hawks, scorpions, and angels wrapped in barbed wire to look out and see where they were.

" 'Man is disturbed not by things, but by the views he takes of them.' " she quoted and looked at Shaw. "Epictetus."

"Guess he had a lot of chariot problems."

"Gotta align yourself with what's happening." Brandy noticed Shaw scratching his forearm, dotted with a neat row of red marks. "Like those bedbug bites."

The president's eyes widened. "Are you kidding me?"

"Sorry about that. They're a drag. Don't I know it. Hydrocortisone cream helps." She put her drink to her cheek. "Remember—it's all about reactions."

Shaw struggled not to scratch. They waited half an hour. Then the mechanic lifted the hood, did a quick exam, and moved the truck into the last bay. Shaw sat with Brandy, as if in a hospital waiting room, melting in the unairconditioned air, the president distracting himself with an article in the latest *People* about his wife's lifelong campaign for a cure for irritable bowel syndrome, unknown to him. Thorne had been busy. Shaw supposed that all the more-appealing medical slots had been taken by other politicians and celebrities. The mechanic entered.

"Head gasket's blown."

Neither of his listeners knew what a head gasket was, but his manner told them that the patient was in peril.

"Not to mention your radiator, pump, hoses, a bunch of stuff. I could start on it on Monday."

"Monday?" said the president.

"That's right."

"How much?" asked Brandy.

"Might bring it in under seven hundred dollars. If I'm lucky."

"Jesus Christ in a fucking wheelbarrow."

The mechanic flinched. "I'm going to ask you to clean up your language, ma'am. Then you come see me." He left. Brandy began crying.

"I knew I should have fixed that damn temperature gauge, after the last time. Should have had the whole cooling system gone over. But who has money for that?" She stood up and paced, then seemed to make up her mind. "That's it. We're done. Damn car's not worth it even if I did have the money. Got it free anyway, from my uncle."

Shaw looked gloomily into her face. "Easy come, easy go."

"The fucking way of the world. The world I'm trying to align myself with. Problem is, that leaves me with no car."

Shaw's brain began to turn. "This guy would probably give you something for it."

"Probably not much."

"Who knows," said the president. "I'll take the bus to L.A. You take the bus to Grand Junction. Then you use what he gives you to fix my car."

"And how are you gonna get it back?"

"I won't. You can keep it."

Brandy's eyes were uncomprehending. "Are you crazy?"

"Brotherhood of man," Shaw replied.

"You don't need it?"

He shook his head. "A long story. Maybe another time."

* * *

An hour later, they were sitting in St. George's tiny bus station, their belongings in plastic bags at their feet. Holding a pencil from Brandy's glove compartment and using her chemistry book as a desk, the president wrote out a bill of sale, copying the VIN number off the documents he'd signed for the Omaha car dealer. He listed the price as one dollar, wrote "Received, cash," then the date, but insisted she keep all of the $650 the mechanic had given her. Shaw stared at the stubby pencil in his hand. There were no souvenir pens or flashing cameras at this signing. He gave her the piece of lined notebook paper he'd written on.

"Maybe the Mystique's not in too bad shape," he said.

Brandy tried to smile. "Maybe so." She read through the bill, then put her hand on his. "You're a good man."

Shaw savored the words as much as the feel of her fingers. He'd miss holing up with a her in a hotel for a few hours, but the universe had apparently realized what an astoundingly poor idea that was for a president running for reelection and had intervened. Shaw was still working on aligning himself.

Brandy's bus pulled in at three in the afternoon. She wrote down her contact info for him; in reply, he improvised a lurching explanation, contradicting various earlier statements, of why he had no address and phone to give her in return. He took her picture, gave her a hug, and saw her off, waving as the bus disappeared, then gave in to the urge to scratch his arm. He stared at his bites. We'll always have Grand Junction.

His own bus wouldn't come until eight. "Improve public transportation," he wrote with Brandy's pencil on the back of a bus schedule, then spent five minutes of his remaining five hours drawing an ever-enlarging star above the words. He took out his ticket to Los Angeles, photographed it, then remembered Adlai Stevenson's sole-with-a-hole photo and took several shots of his weary-looking shoes, to the bafflement of the mother and twin girls scrutinizing him from across the room. Stevenson's shoe photo should have made him a man of the people, but he'd lost, and twice at that. Shaw hoped his handlers knew what they were doing. He counted his cash, thinking back to the bank robbery and hearing the Nebraska governor's pet phrase, "I'm using your money." Truer in this case, he mused, than anyone would ever know. After buying the car, the gas and meals on the drive, and paying $53 for his bus ticket, he had $17 left. He spent half of that on an enchilada dinner around the corner, picked up a *Sports Illustrated* at the grocery down the block and was disbelieving when the clerk asked for $5.95. He put it back in a huff, then remembered how much more time he had to wait and gave in. The Sprite he bought two hours later left him with $2.85 to his name. He was thirsty again an hour later, but filled his bottle from the station's tepid water fountain.

His bus was late, without explanation or apology. He took a seat, watched St. George recede and night come on, looked behind him up the aisle, waited, and finally realized there'd be no stewardesses passing out snacks and drinks. If I'd known that, he thought, I'd have saved my money and never bought the damn magazine. He closed his eyes for most of the two hours, then opened them when they approached Las Vegas, where he'd need to transfer. He knew that the city had been hit harder than most, but wasn't prepared for the dogs and swirling dirt and tumbleweeds in the streets where Hummer stretch-limos, like dinosaurs, had once ruled. He had an hour to kill and walked out of the station and into the Plaza Hotel across the street. Only a few heads were visible in the casino, the room producing just a whisper of the usual factorylike clunking and ratcheting and jingling. In a corner, he confided to his voice recorder the good news that fewer of his citizens were trusting to luck to solve their money problems, though privately he knew that they hadn't gotten smarter but simply couldn't afford the trip. He returned to the bus station, taking one of the hard plastic seats, scanning the dark skins and old skins around him. This was how the other half traveled, he realized: eating mysterious meals from tin foil, sleeping against each other like puppies, staring at nothing. Shaw turned off his camera's flash and surreptitiously took a few pictures.

His bus boarded at 11:05. Shaw took a seat next to a man with flowing white hair and beard to match, who was reading a book by flashlight. The transmission grumbled below, the door closed, the overhead lights went out, and they were off. Shaw looked behind him up the aisle, then at his neighbor.

"No stewardess on this one either?"

The man lowered his book and gave an amused snort. "Another CEO?"

The president shook his head in denial. "It's just been a while."

The man's bulbous nose twitched. "Let me break it to you. No stewardess. No linen napkin. No Chardonnay. No dinner. No hot towels. No reading light. No bathroom—"

"No bathroom?" Shaw hadn't needed one on his first bus and hadn't noticed its absence.

"The bus companies found out they could get two more seats in."

"You're kidding."

The man released a sigh. "It's a wonderful system, capitalism. Funny thing is I don't remember voting for it."

Shaw sighed. His bladder felt instantly weightier. He leaned close to the man. "So what do people do?"

"They squeeze everything out in the station." Shaw had neglected to do so. The man reached into his threadbare coat's pocket. "Then some people use these." He held a quart-sized opaque bottle. Shaw now noticed the tree-shaped air-fresheners dangling from above each pair of seats. "Women have their own arrangements."

The president feared to ask more. There were limits to what he wanted to know about his people. "How long till the next stop?"

"Barstow. Three hours. Assuming you've got a buck twenty-five in quarters."

Shaw gawked.

"It's a pay toilet. All about income streams."

The president was disbelieving. "And what if you don't—"

"The one in Victorville's free. That's another hour. Then there's San Bernardino. Voluntary donation at that one." The man returned to reading. "Best not to think about it."

Shaw added this to not thinking about his bites, the Category 4 snoring coming from behind him, and the scent of urine rising from the upholstery. He drifted to sleep, dreaming of Air Force One's plush bed. He jerked awake in Barstow, used the pay toilet, bringing his balance down to $1.60, then slept and woke several times, gazing out at the distant towns glowing like galaxies in the blackness, and found his neighbor gone when he opened his eyes as the bus braked and turned into the downtown Los Angeles terminal just after sunrise. He could hardly believe he'd arrived.

Passengers unfolded, stood, and stretched like plants breaking ground. Shaw clumped down the steps with the others, surprised at the wintry air outside the bus. He cleaned himself up in the bathroom, then followed his nose to the Starbucks inside the station, peering at the pastries like a child at a toy-store window. He ordered a coffee and a thick slab of coffee cake, then found out the prices were so high that he couldn't afford either. "Coffee price-gouging!" he spoke into his recorder as he walked outside. He found $1.25 coffee at a greasy spoon down the block and got it to go, feeling his spirits lift with the first sip. He hailed a cab, threw his plastic bag in before him, and sat down for the last leg of his trip.

"Malibu," he announced proudly.

"Yes, sir." His driver had an African accent. The cab zigzagged four blocks, then accelerated up a freeway ramp. Moments later Shaw heard popping.

"What was that?"

"Just a little gunfire, sir."

"Gunfire?"

Shaw whirled his head, looking for the source. The driver pointed ahead with a bony hand. "Fortunately, the bullets seem to have ricocheted off the truck delivering the Miller beer."

The president craned his neck to see. "What's going on? Road rage? Gangs?"

The driver shrugged his shoulders. "It's Friday, sir. And it's rush hour. So people are rather in a hurry to get to their jobs. Or perhaps they are quite excited to make an early start on their weekend vacation."

Shaw had grown up in Los Angeles, but didn't recall family trips starting in a hail of gunfire. More shots were heard.

"Ah," the driver said. "I see the problem. The gentleman in the BMW has apparently given some offense to the gentleman in the red Ford pickup truck." The man produced a giggle. "Unfortunately for him, the BMW is on his lefthand side, and he appears to be right-handed, requiring that he reach across his body while shooting and driving. And it's this that explains his very poor aim."

Shaw was torn between watching the festivities and throwing himself to the floor, where the Secret Service would have him. He reclined across the seat, head low, like Cleopatra in her barge, as a compromise.

"Kind of exciting," he said. "Hardly need my coffee to wake up."

"Yes, sir."

"Where are you from?"

"Ethiopia, sir."

"No kidding." The president sipped, then turned on his recorder. "And what do you make of Americans?"

The driver considered. "Despite what we have just seen, I would say they are much more polite than the drivers in my country." The man thought further. "Beyond that, I would say to you what your president has often said, that the Americans are a fine people."

"Really?" More gunfire erupted. Shaw wondered if the taxi driver was out of his mind.

"And you, sir? Where are you coming from?"

Truthfully, for the first time in weeks, Shaw spoke the words, "I'm from here."

The driver gave him a big, snaggletoothed smile in the rearview mirror. "Welcome home, sir."

Shaw failed to return his smile. The hills to his right, the cluster of skyscrapers ahead in Westwood, the movie billboards and palms and red-tiled roofs and bougainvillea—all was familiar to him, but his country no longer felt like a place he knew. They reached Santa Monica, headed up Pacific Coast Highway, turned inland half an hour later, winding their way up a narrow canyon, and finally stopped at the guarded gate to the Shaw family compound. The president got out, leaned toward the uniformed guard's ear, and whispered "Roughneck." The man took him in and beamed. Shaw retrieved his bag from the taxi.

"That will be ninety-six dollars and forty cents," said the driver.

The president had only a quarter and dime in his pocket, then watched one of the Secret Service agents step forward to take care of the matter. He was back in his former life.

A car drove him the eighth of a mile to his house. Shaw flipped down the visor to see the mirror, smoothed his quarter-inch reddish beard, straightened his black glasses and Spiderman cap, picked up his Piggly Wiggly bag, and got out. He walked unrecognized past a trio of reporters, was admitted by the agent at the door, who'd been alerted, stood a moment in the dark-tiled entry, inhaled deeply, smelled breakfast, turned right down the hallway, and was passed in the other direction without acknowledgment by his daughter, wearing flannel pajamas and holding a bowl of cereal.

"Mom!" he heard he her call behind him. "The plumber dude's here."

# 18.

"A flop," said the president. "First your plan, then mine."

Jess felt her heart fall.

"And if I might ask," Chuck Thorne's gravelly voice inquired, "what exactly was your plan?"

He and everyone else in the house's conference room—Hugh, Jess, Cora, Victor, Trevor, Barry Schraftstein, the press secretary, speechwriters— peered in at Shaw. He'd had breakfast, made calls to his vice president, to Archibald at Secret Service headquarters, checked in with his National Security Advisor. Though he'd showered, been given a thorough physical by the horrified Dr. Weiss, changed into clean corduroys and a Pendleton shirt, he looked disturbingly distant from his inauguration portrait on the wall. His beard and black glasses were still in place and his dyed brown hair was showing blond roots and beginning to bend into waves.

"My plan? After the St. Louis foul-up? To ditch everybody. Turn my back on the pros and give the country the real me. Pure undiluted honesty."

Hugh sipped and swirled the notion about his brain. "Frightening. But interesting. You know, as a concept."

Barry, the heavyset campaign manager wondered aloud, "Maybe we could do something with it."

"My guess," snapped Cora, "is there's a reason it hasn't caught on."

The president scratched his bedbug bites under his sleeves, avoiding the shot site where Weiss had immediately injected him with antibiotics.

"I also thought I'd get a more honest view of things." From his pants pocket Shaw produced his camera and recorder and laid them on the glossy table.

"And?" asked Thorne.

"And I did.  And guess what.  The country's a wreck.  Top to bottom.  Pure and simple." He turned on the camera and backtracked through his photos, smiles and winces flickering over his features, stopping at the Omaha homeless shelter's "This Facility Has Been Closed" sign. He put the camera down and faced Hugh. "Don't give me the old lines to say, cause I really can't say 'em anymore."

Mouths sagged. Jess closed her eyes. The rest of the group stared as if he'd just ordered an end to life-support.

"It's like the weather," said Shaw. "This is supposed to be the dog days of summer, but it's not." He gestured out the window at the frigid overcast.  From the basement came the sound of the men working on the heating system, which had broken down the evening before, putting sweatshirts and sweaters on the group around the table.  "It's crazy pretending things are normal.  Or that they're getting better.  They're not.  And the 'fine people' of the United States?  When they're not holding you up at gunpoint or blasting at each other's cars, they're scraping their knuckles raw trying to beat the system and survive." He surveyed the ring of gloom around him.  "And I'm part of the problem. We all are. So maybe if I lose, things will actually get better.  Which is good, cause from what I saw, that's sure as hell where the election's heading."

The uniformed stewards who entered with trays of hot chevre cro-quettes seemed suddenly part of the problem as well. Shaw's words floated among the chandelier's crystal prisms.

"You're tired," said Cora.  "You had a lousy sleep on a crowded bus.  You're worn down from not eating—"

"I'm fine," Shaw replied.

"Then it's time to get back on the horse," said Thorne. "We need to tape tomorrow's radio address. We've got the press conference set up for nine tomorrow morning. And we've got to get going on the convention. The speech, the film—"

"Your diary," said Barry.

"I'm not ready."

"Well, we need you to be ready real quick." Thorne rubbed a hand over his gray crew cut. "We've got everything in place. The country's waiting for you to jump out of the cake."

The president's features solidified. Jess gazed at his scratched glasses and beard and scabbed forehead. She'd turned him into a different man, and now they couldn't get the old one back. She sympathized and found herself with no energy for the effort to tie Shaw back in the saddle. Beside her, one of the press secretary's assistants spoke up.

"It's not all a wasteland." He looked around, trying to round up votes. "My mother, for instance. She's had a good life. A nice apartment in Seattle. A little arthritis, but otherwise I'd say she's reasonably satisfied."

"Fascinating," said Barry.

"You've lost your confidence," Thorne told Shaw. "It happens. But it's temporary. You'll bounce back."

"And hold the malaise," said Hugh. "Carter tried that. It bombed."

"People prefer fairy tales," said Trevor. "They need you to be bigger than life."

Hugh nodded. "Which is why Victor filmed every goddamn national park in seven goddamn states."

Victor, in watch cap and fisherman's sweater, leveled his blue eyes on the president. "You are," he intoned solemnly, "the land."

This pronouncement made no impression on the room. Another silence descended. Jess broke it.

"Frankly, I think the President's onto something."

\* \* \*

Gil Olivares, the press secretary, postponed the press conference. Shaw's campaign appearances for the following week were put on hold. Cassandra was sworn to secrecy, her parents clutching her cellphone privileges as collateral. That afternoon, the president gave a detailed account of his trip to the inner circle in the house, with his photos and clips projected on a screen in the family room and his audio recordings crackling through speakers. As the media hadn't recognized Shaw and knew nothing of his trip, the president's advisors had time. Gil and his assistants cobbled together a radio address from earlier speeches, drawing on plagiarizing skills honed in college, sprinkling in just enough new material to deflect suspicions. Shaw recorded it in the nick of time, late Friday night. The weekend was spent in further debriefing and debating, a free-for-all between the hired consultants, campaign manager, White House staff, the First Lady, and the president himself, arguments circling endlessly around the pool and over meals, with figures crossing swords on balconies and giving soliloquies on stair landings as if in a play. On Sunday, the Olympics finally ended. The country would wake hungry for fresh diversion, Gil knew. Like zookeepers tending lions, the media would need fresh meat. Monday morning, he provided it.

What had begun as a press conference became something more. Gil sent word ricocheting through his address book, alerting both the national and foreign press. The venue was changed from the Malibu house to the Omni Hotel to its final location, an unused, potholed parking lot two blocks down 7th Street from the Greyhound station where Shaw had disembarked. Gil had given out no details, promising the invitees only that they'd be present at the journalistic event of the century. The century was young, but the parking lot held a throng of reporters, photographers, bloggers, and local news crews at ten, when the proceedings were supposed to begin. Gil had brought in power and rented a small stage. Putting everyone through the Secret Service's metal detectors slowed things down, which was fine with the press secretary; frustration would raise the crowd's childlike desire to unwrap their present. He delayed their gratification further by vamping about the economic leading indicators trending upward, the South Dakota woman who'd confessed that her video of locust swarms had been faked, a new public works program starting up in Michigan to repair infrastructure, and other uplifting stories, building suspense for an additional ten minutes. He then described the president's two weeks of relaxation and reflection in sunny Malibu. While he spoke, a bearded man in dirty jeans, scuffed shoes, sweat-stained khaki work shirt, and Spiderman cap approached the lot from the direction of the bus station, passed through a metal detector, and silently made his way through the crowd. He reached the rope line running across the lot in front of the stage, stood watching Gil for a time, then ducked under the rope and slowly climbed the four stairs leading up to the stage. The press secretary stopped talking and seemed to notice him for the first time. The two men faced each other as if strangers. Traffic passed to the rear, but the lot had grown silent with the fear of a prank or violence. Half a head taller, Shaw stepped forward toward the podium and grabbed hold of the microphone stand, shouldering Gil aside. The surprised press secretary backed away, looking for help but receiving none. The president tapped the mic with his thumb, too loudly, the amplified boom straightening the crowd's already erect spines. He cleared his throat.

"You all are from the press." He disguised his voice behind a rasping mumble. "So you want to know the facts, right?"

No one answered.

"So let me give you some facts. And if say anything untrue—" He turned toward Gil. "You raise your hand. How 'bout that?"

Looking helpless as a hostage, Gil nodded.

"First off, leading indicators aren't going up."

The press secretary's arms, in his suit's gray sleeves, remained at his sides.

"There's no public works program in Michigan for fixing infrastructure."

Shaw turned toward Gil, who hung his head contritely.

"Locust swarms are real."

Gil munched on his lips.

"The weather in Malibu the past two weeks has been colder than it's been since people started keeping records."

The press secretary stared at his shoe tops.

"And the president?" Shaw turned toward his audience. "You all think he's been there for the past two weeks. But let me give you the facts." He faced Gil again. "He hasn't, has he?"

Gil's head shook slowly left to right. A tremolo of murmurs rose from the crowd.

"In fact, for a lot of that time, you didn't actually know where he was, did you?"

Another head shake.

"Or who he was with. Or what he was doing. Or if he was even alive. Did you?"

As if a colony of bats had descended, the air grew louder with clicking of cameras.

"And the Secret Service—they were just as clueless, weren't they?"

Gil nodded.

"Nobody knew what was going on. Cause something happened, didn't it? Something you were afraid to tell the country about."

Shaw looked out and saw fear in many faces. It was satisfying to find they were worried about him. He waited, letting them suffer. He'd never liked journalists.

"How do I know all this about the president?" Another pause. "Well, because we're pretty close, him and me." Shaw slowly removed his glasses. "Known each other a long time." He took off his cap. He ruffled his short brown hair. He flashed his trademark grin. Then he cast off his mumble and heartily declared, "A real long time."

There were screams of surprise. Talk and shutter-clicks filled the air. The president stepped down and walked the rope line, giving the jostling crowd a chance to see for themselves, greeting those he recognized by name.

"My god, it's him!"

Shaw's slow progress down the line was followed by a wave of such exclamations. The uproar lasted a full ten minutes. When the president finally returned to the podium, Gil had moved off the stage and there was a party atmosphere in the air, a mix of relief that the president was safe and the expectation that what he'd been doing the past weeks was about to be revealed. It was, complete with his disgust with his handlers, his intentional evasion of the Secret Service, the carjacking, the prostitute, the fake driver's license, the country's contempt for his leadership. He'd been prevailed on to cut out the bank robbery windfall—using stolen money was a crime—and claimed to have bought the Mystique with the $1000 the Secret Service had hidden in the sole of his shoe for just such an emergency. Fortunately, the old woman scooping up money beside him that day had been blind. He left her and the whole panhandling scene out, placing himself in another quadrant of Omaha. Jess and the rest had won other concessions that could give him a better chance in November, but he'd insisted on describing the country as it really stood, which he proceeded to do, though without the photos and films he promised to unfurl to the nation at the convention. Against the wishes of all his advisors save Jess, he closed with his most shocking truth-telling.

"Heads of state sometimes use stand-ins, for security reasons. This fall a book's going to be published, written by my own stand-in. And in that book he states that it was he, and not me, up in a helicopter surveying the damage from Hurricane Holly three years ago."

A fresh murmur rippled through the crowd.

"That man is telling the truth."

The throng collectively flinched. There was another burst of clicking, the cameras licking up the moment. Shaw faced not only the multitude of journalists before him but the millions of readers and viewers behind them. He stood stolidly, taking his punishment, defenseless, no wife or family at his side for distraction and support. Finally, he took off his black glasses and held them before him.

"I picked these out of a basket of donations in Omaha. They used to belong to somebody else. They're out of style, they're scratched up, but I gotta tell you, I can see better through these than through my old contacts." He leaned in toward the cameras. "That's right. My eyes are really brown, not blue." Another wave of astonishment swept the gathering. "It's not every day that you actually get the chance to walk in someone else's shoes." He put the glasses back on. "Or see the world through someone else's eyes. But I got that chance. And it's amazing what I can see that I couldn't before. Like the laziness and the lack of concern that led me to skip that helicopter ride."

He paused for another blame-taking photo op.

"My advisors recommended a cover-up. I said no. In fact, I recommend that people buy the book when it comes out. Read it. I'm sure you'll find out a lot." His hands reset, grasping the sides of the podium more firmly. "But I hope you've found out something even bigger today. That the trip I just finished taught me a ton more than I would have learned on that flyover. That I'm a changed man, and not just in my appearance. Because, believe me, after feeling real hunger, and thirst, and fear, I wouldn't dream of missing a chance to comfort my people when they need it. And they need it now."

Applause rose up from a group accustomed to using their hands for note-taking and shutter-pressing.

"And that's why I'm seeking a second term."

The long breaking wave of applause confirmed for Shaw that he'd made the right choice. Off to the side, where they could observe both the president and the crowd, Thorne and Hugh had sweated through their jackets. Jess had her hands covering her mouth, as drained by the public purging she'd orchestrated as Shaw was. He waved to the crowd—left, center, right, took no questions, descended the steps, and floated over the asphalt, feeling reborn.

* * *

The president's campaign schedule was reinstated, but with a new program: the brotherhood of man, respect for nature, honesty, and a host of planks, from tighter gun laws to support for mass transit, that had been pried up from Fiore's platform. His appearance was different as well. Instead of suits, he wore the same clothing he'd worn on his trip. He dropped the Spiderman hat after complaints of product placement but kept his old black glasses. He left his hair dark, his blond roots increasingly obvious, and let his beard and mustache grow.

"It's too weird," Hugh complained to Jess about Shaw's fast-growing whiskers a week after his press conference. "It's gone beyond the fashion-model look. He's starting to look like a bum. Plus there's the Benjamin Harrison thing. The last president with a beard. A Republican. Also ran for reelection, and lost."

"Persuasive," said Jess. "He was also warm-blooded and had a four-chambered heart." After ten days in the East and Midwest, they were back in California, riding Shaw's campaign bus up the Central Valley on a tour of the Foreclosure Belt.

"I don't know." Hugh poured more Veuve Clicquot into his plastic cup. "There hasn't even been a mustache on a president since Taft. I looked it up. Another one-term Republican."

"You're just spooked. Facial hair goes through cycles. This could be the start of a new one. Maybe Shaw's onto something."

"We're coming into the Age of Aquarius, again?"

"Nope—Modesto. But check this out." Jess handed him the newspaper she'd bought in Merced. The page-two story about Shaw, "Perilous Journey Required Trains, Public Buses, Even Walking" was continued onto a later page, across from the church listings. "Is that Shaw or what?"

Beside a worship schedule was an image of a flock of sheep following Jesus down a road, his body long, his beard short and light-colored.

"Talk about pressing the country's hidden buttons," she said. "We need to get Shaw out walking more."

"And herding more." Hugh finished his champagne. "Lucky for us Jesus always looks Nordic. This one looks like a Swedish high-jumper."

"It's the movies. Charleton Heston playing Moses."

"Should have been Danny DeVito. C'mon. People were all four-foot-three back then. Not enough Cocoa Crispies in their diet." Hugh studied the drawing further. "Nice California tan. Same broad shoulders. All Shaw needs is the shepherd's crook. Or the button that pushes the shepherd crook button."

"I don't think the country has that."

"Sure it does. A cane." Hugh thought. "Which we explain with his fall from the train."

"He's not into lying, remember?"

Hugh rolled his eyes. "This whole honesty thing's a bitch." He sighed at his oppressive working conditions. "All right. No cane. Maybe give the family a lamb."

"A lamb?" Jess considered. "The beef industry wouldn't—"

"They're not going to eat it! It's a pet."

"Right. So then when a million people get lambs as pets for their kids and abandon them six days later and the SPCA—"

"Okay, okay. Even better. A border collie. You see one, you

automatically see a flock of sheep even though they're not there. No bleating. No maintenance. Perfect."

"Not perfect. Bianca's not ready for more pets. Real or imaginary. I think she's made all the adjustments she can make."

There was truth to this. A photo of her at a children's hospital a week before in a carmine dress and caged pearl earrings had been shown on Jay Leno next to her husband's attire the same day, with a zoom in on his shirt's carefully preserved armpit stains and the dirt patted into his pants before each appearance. Since then, Bianca had been forced ever farther down the sartorial low road: first a gingham monstrosity from Macy's new line of Shaker Classics, then a soul-crushing visit to T. J. Maxx, then the clip released by the campaign, after twenty-six takes, of her delight at finding a pair of jeans in her size at a Goodwill in Chattanooga. While Thorne labored to fatten her up, Cora lobbied to confine her lipstick to a narrow band of muted shades, with chapped lips her ultimate if unreachable goal. All jewelry was banned. Taking after her daughter, Bianca had her navel pierced, then repeated the procedure, the area becoming a lush hidden oasis of diamonds and sapphires, her private protest. Jess had watched the first night of the Democratic convention on TV with her in the White House and had seen her gaping at the sight of Melissa Dabney, the candidate's wife, in a jade satin Dior off-the-shoulder creation, jewelry glinting from every possible perch. No wonder the Democrats were such a nonfactor, thought Jess. The Your Party convention the following week had been much more sartorially restrained, with Joe Fiore accepting the nomination in jeans, Bianca hooting at his flabby wife's matching denim skirt.

"They look like a couple of hicks," she announced.

Jess held off revealing what was in store for her.

At the Republican convention shortly after in Kansas City, Bianca was the first night's featured speaker. As with Shaw in the past, her speech was sketched, written, and revised by others and simply handed to her, a homework assignment too important to be left to a child. Her wardrobe was similarly dictated: a white blouse under a dreary gray wool skirt and matching jacket which she offhandedly mentioned having sewn herself. She was not a natural liar, stumbled slightly on the words, but was rescued by the thunderous standing ovation that greeted this statement. "As I was tying the knot on the last button—" Another ovation saluted this crucial labor. "—I thought that perhaps I'd alter it—" More applause, showing respect for a difficult task. "—so that Cassandra could wear it one day." Another half-minute of clapping filled the hall. The reference to Cassandra led Bianca smoothly into mother-daughter cooking, then the brief clip of her making lasagna, heavily padded with lingering shots of waiting ingredients and boiling water, leading in turn to the Family First Initiative and the campaign's core theme of compassion. After she closed, Cassandra, bribed with a trip to Paris without her parents along, shuffled miserably onstage toward her mother in an identical outfit, gave the required hug of not less than three-seconds, approached the microphone, indicated her clothes, and stated in an expressionless monotone, "I guess I beat you to it, Mom." The ovation went on long enough to outlast the commercial break that TV stations finally inserted.

Coburn, Shaw's imposing vice president, came out swinging two nights later, black hair slicked back like a porcupine's quills. He relished his assigned role of bad cop, picking apart Fiore's biography, from his Calabrian forebears' "apparent" lack of criminal activity to his grammar school report cards—his B in citizenship received prolonged exegesis—to the telling nicknames he and his college roommate acquired for their anarchic behavior: Sacco and Vanzetti. This was followed by a ghastly slog through seventy years of villainy committed by the United Auto Workers to which Fiore had belonged for twelve weeks, a glum review of a Senate career notable only for its failures, a worried reading of his medical file, and a curled-lip mention of his enjoyment of wine—insinuating alcoholism, snobbery, an allegiance to Europe, or any combination of the above at listeners' discretion. Boos rattled off the rafters.

The next morning Shaw held a rally in Wichita, then rode Greyhound 200 miles to Kansas City, wearing his working man's outfit but accompanied this time by hulking Agent Lindblatt and a full complement of protectors on the bus and in cars ahead and behind, with a helicopter escort above. Despite that, passengers entered and exited in El Dorado and Emporia and Owatonna and Ottawa, the president speaking to one and all, taking their photos and recording their thoughts. He descended the bus's steps five hours later into fall sunshine and the arms of a clamoring crowd. After shaking hands, he duplicated his trip to Malibu by hailing a taxi, exiting two blocks before his hotel, and making the trip's last leg on foot accompanied by a throng of the faithful. When he entered the arena at seven that night, wearing the same outfit as if he'd never stopped walking, and formally accepted his party's nomination, the air horns and whistling and sign-shaking and spirit-possessed dancing-in-place threatened to go on all night. Shaw stilled the waters with his outstretched hands. Reluctantly, the 18,000 attendees sat down.

"I thank you for your warm welcome this evening," he began. There was a move in the audience to stand and applaud this bold statement; Shaw quashed it. "I wish it was true that the news I bring you tonight was the sort that's usually met with such joy. But it isn't."

High above in their suite, Thorne and Hugh and Trevor watched the lights lower and the vast screen behind the president come to life, showing the Maryland countryside Victor had filmed out his moving window. The home-movie feel was supported by Shaw's seemingly unscripted annotations of a story that was well-known by this point. A sprightly fiddle and banjo came through the sound system. A parade of Pittsburgh scenes marched across the screen, then footage of Shaw washing dishes.

"I'll never forget my new friend Marco at Stan's Place," he reminisced. "They say it's better not to see how your food is made. Maybe this is why."

The score became more ominous, possibly lifted from *Jaws*, Hugh thought. An eyepatch-wearing cook appeared on the screen, then turned from the camera and began operating a meat-slicer.

"How did Marco lose his eye? Let me give you a few possibilities. Faulty equipment. Out-of-code wiring. Lack of safety inspections. Fatigue from not being allowed to take mandatory breaks." Shaw paused. "I was lucky. I only worked there one day. But I promise you, what I saw there will stay with me a lifetime."

Hugh flicked a consoling glance at Trevor, who'd written Shaw's earlier excoriations of regulation. "It'll pass. Be patient."

The travelogue made stops at Pittsburgh's overmatched job retraining center, the trash that had been dumped in the Ohio, the swarm of locusts, then the music returned from minor to major when Shaw was seen eating a strawberry for the camera and wiping the juice on his sleeve. He held his right forearm out toward the convention audience. "You can still see a little of that juice right there." A zoomed-in image of his sleeve filled the screen, the audience cooing as if he'd held up a puppy. Shaw was then shown reading a Gideon Bible before bed, drying a Jaguar at the carwash in Columbus, mashing potatoes at the Cincinnati soup kitchen, then attempting to converse in Spanish with his fellow sprinkler-installers.

"I've given the impression in the past that I speak Spanish. I don't. But I'm trying. Forty-five minutes every night. And let me tell you something— it's not easy. When I meet someone now who can speak more than one language, I'm truly impressed. And I take my hat off to 'em, with real respect."

The screen showed him doing exactly that with a pair of laughing Mexican-American teenaged sisters on that morning's bus ride. Then the mood darkened again: a recording of running feet and squealing tires sounded behind Shaw's description of getting separated from his team in St. Louis. He told the tale of being robbed of his van and wallet, explaining that he'd decided not to use the money in his shoe but to live like the poor, hitchhiking and begging his meals until he'd realized he was falling behind schedule and bought a car. He spoke of freedom, of John Muir and Teddy Roosevelt. Photos of cider-making at the hobo camp were shown, followed by Shaw's stark assessment of the nation's food and exercise habits. Then its gun laws. Its crumbling roads. Its woeful public transportation. Its neglect of the homeless, its starved schools and libraries, the abandoned inner cities, the shameful healthcare system. Heckling broke out among the Texas and Idaho delegations and others who felt abandoned by Shaw, but was quickly smothered in the name of unity. Appropriately, the screen showed a photo of a church sign in Denver: "Forgive Your Enemies—It Messes With Their Heads." The image remained there.

"There's plenty of blame to go around," spoke the president. "Our country's in dire straits, by our own hands for the most part. Our. That means your hands. And Democrats' hands. The Your Party's. Everybody's. And especially mine." A pause. "An incumbent's message is always 'Everything's great.' But not this incumbent. Because everything's not great. Not even close. And the first step to improvement is acknowledging that." Shaw hung his head, silent for several seconds, then pointed a finger at the screen. "The next step is to forgive, others and ourselves." Another pause. "The third step is to do something about it. Because, despite our troubles, we're a heckuva country." A barrage of applause was followed by the recording of his Ethiopian taxi-driver: "Beyond that, I would say to you what your president has often said, that the Americans are a fine people."

Another ovation. The fiddle and banjo returned behind shots of Nebraska wheat, the Platte River, Rocky Mountain peaks, and every national park the Southwest had to offer.

"We're a great country not just for our landscape, but because of the freedom we offer. The opportunities we offer. The pursuit of happiness we offer."

Standing in the rear of the arena like a theater director, Victor listened to the music change to a pulsing piece by Yanni and his orchestra, climbing toward a delirious crescendo.

"I don't know if I can put into words for you," Shaw declared grandly, "the glories of one of my own pursuits of happiness—the overpowering, visceral thrill... of welding."

This section of his speech was the price he paid for telling so many other truths elsewhere. Victor had convinced Thorne and the rest of the team of the power of this image and now grinned like a child at the shower of sparks exploding on the screen. The camera pulled back to show a masked figure holding a blazing torch under a car.

"My friend Ernesto in Albuquerque took this clip while I helped him out one morning, brushing up my skills." The president paused, looking at the screen. "It's like reaching into the earth's core and harnessing those incredible forces. What an amazing feeling..." He trailed off. Snapshots of the Rio Grande followed. "Later that day, I was lucky enough to spend a few hours in Hatch, tasting some of the chile crop."

The screen showed a field accented with chartreuse chile peppers, then a clip of Shaw biting into one, the stuccoed wall of the Malibu house behind him providing no identifying details. His lips buzzed, watching the scene; his sense of taste was only just returning to normal. To square his visit to Hatch with his appearance 500 miles north in Grand Junction, he rerouted his trip up through the Grand Canyon, stock photos of which flowed over the screen, followed by one allowed to linger, of a Navajo man leading a flock of sheep, wearing jeans and a shirt not unlike Shaw's and carrying a long stick in hand. The night spent in Brandy's apartment was seen as a possible problem, leading the president to move briskly through their twenty-four hours together and to hurry himself home to Los Angeles, closing with the photograph he'd taken of his scourged, haggard-looking, dust-covered shoes. The lights came up. And so did the crowd.

In her Georgetown apartment, Jess climbed forward on her bed to sit closer to her TV. It was a full five minutes before the crowd felt it had thanked Shaw sufficiently for his travails.

"My eyes were opened to a lot of things these past weeks. Not just about the country, but about our political system." Onto the screen came the portrait of a seated Abraham Lincoln that hung in the White House. Shaw communed with it a moment. "That man there didn't have a communications director," he said. "Or a press secretary to speak his thoughts for him. Or a deputy press secretary to remind the press secretary what to say." Laughter. "He got along fine without a stable of speechwriters and media analysts and consultants and pollsters and hair stylists." More laughter. "He wrote the Gettysburg Address straight from his heart, with a pen and ink on lined paper." The president paused. "I do something similar." A camera zoomed in on the yellow legal pad before him on the podium, beaming the image to the screen, showing his speech written out in longhand. Applause and awe greeted this revelation. Jess played nervously with a strand of brown hair.

"I took off on my own not only to find out about my country, but to escape my advisors. I've had it with all that. Maybe you have, too." An ovation. "I've therefore severed my campaign's relationship with the consulting firm of Zucker, Cardozo, Dalrymple, and Girard. My speechwriters will have to find someone else to write for. The words you hear me speaking will be honest words, even when honesty hurts. But they'll be my words, just as Lincoln's were his." The president's right hand went to his chin. Jess copied the gesture and spoke the words with him. "We've even both got beards, come to think of it." Laughter and applause. "If you like my style, no matter what party you belong to, I hope you'll give me your vote." The photo of the pair of cars from Texas sporting Shaw bumper stickers leapt onto the screen, triggering another ovation. "But right now, I need to leave you." Shaw rolled up his shirt sleeves. "Because there's a whole lot of work to be done. Thank you."

There was no family gathering onstage. Shaw picked up his pad, tucked it under an arm, waved to the euphoric crowd for only half a minute, and strode into the wings, anxious to start fixing the nation.

*    *    *

"Not exactly a hundred percent honest," said Trevor over breakfast the next day, "but close."

"It's a gradual thing," said Hugh. "Like quitting smoking. Ten lies a day, then seven, then five..." He was in a merry mood at the exiling of Jess and Cora, even if it was just for show. Jess's vision had shaped both the press conference and convention speech, to Hugh's disgust. Shaw had indeed vowed to write his own speeches, but Hugh and Trevor were anything but idle. Their handiwork turned up in many places over the next months: "The Shame of Our Nation's Bathroom-Free Buses: President Shaw's Bold Plan" in *Parade*; uncredited work on Bianca's memoir *I'm Irritable As Hell: My Twisty-Turny Quest for a Cure for IBS*; in "The Heckuva Country Tour" t-shirts sold at rallies that listed all the stops on Shaw's trip, and the matching "He's Been There" bumper stickers. It was Hugh who was behind the headline "First Lady Balloons to 128 Pounds!" in the *Enquirer* and the slogan "Honest Till it Hurts." Trevor reached out to the all-important freshwater fishing community by releasing the photo of Shaw in a country store next to the sign reading "Please Don't Put Minnow Buckets on Counter." Hugh did the same with the needleworkers, gathering a team of women to post in Bianca's name on websites for seamstresses, darners, knitters, and cross-stitchers.

Cassandra's blog was restored, gladdening Fiore supporters' hearts, but, as part of her Paris bargain, omitted politics, instead covering in breathless detail her relationship with a drummer she'd met in Malibu. In October, *Double Trouble* by Shaw's former stand-in hit the stores and immediately cost the president eight points in the polls. He tried to contain the damage by holding his own autographings for the book, taking public repentance to a new level. A week later, his campaign tried to wash the memory of Hurricane Holly out of the public's mind with a tidal wave of publicity for *He Walked Among Us*, released with accompanying DVD and wall map, available in separate editions for children, teens, and speakers of Spanish, Vietnamese, and Tagalog. The campaign's final debate took place a week after that. Three-way verbal ping-pong wasn't Shaw's sport; he was slow with a quip and heavy on his feet, but he scored points when he graded the nation like a schoolteacher.

"Housing—D. Medical care—D. Environment—D. Employment— F." He glowered. "I'm a tough grader. Even tougher than my opponents. But then, I've been there."

There was a noisy migration of voting blocs. Republicans repelled by Shaw had no time to front a new candidate and cast their lot with the free-market Free Party or camped angrily on the sidelines. Their places were taken by Latino voters attracted by Shaw's fumbling ad in Spanish and his frank admission of difficulties with the past tense. The Fiore campaign lost more votes when his receipt for a meal in Chicago in 2002 surfaced with a charge of $800 for a bottle of burgundy. The backbreaker was Shaw's "Let's get to work on America" ad, shot in an empty factory and ending with him lowering his welder's mask, lighting his torch with a dramatic pop, then spelling "Shaw" with the flame in the blackness. On the morning of November 5th, he awoke reelected to a second term. Other than the District of Columbia and Maryland, he carried every state his trip had taken him through.

\* \* \*

Six days later, Hugh invited Jess to lunch. He chose a mom-and-pop diner on 14th Street in keeping with the new administration's sumptuary and dietary guidelines: no entrée exceeding $15, no alcohol, mandatory salad with lunches and dinners, no cheesecake. The sidewalks were slippery from a freak ice storm, but senior staff were expected to model for the country and submit monthly exercise reports, so Hugh walked it, keeping his center of gravity low, not hard with his physique. Jess, with her cross-country skier's build, was waiting by the door, green-sweatered and red-cheeked. They picked a booth in the back where they wouldn't be heard. A waitress brought them menus but Hugh had something more important on his mind than ordering.

"You're a twerp," he said. "You could still be a high school cheerleader. And because you're kind of wet behind the ears I was sure the trip idea had to be crazy and would blow up in our faces and I gave you a ton of crap about it. And I apologize. Cause it turns out you were right about just about everything." He raised his water glass to her. "You did good."

Jess smiled. They clinked glasses. "Thanks." She unwrapped her scarf, face bracketed by lengths of oak-brown hair. "Confession and honesty's really catching on."

"I mean it," said Hugh. "I owe you, big time. I thought I'd be out on my ass right now. I still can't believe it. Honesty sells?"

"Disturbing, isn't it."

"It's always challengers bashing the country, not incumbents."

"A mistake," said Jess.

"I'm twenty years older. How come I didn't see that?"

"Incumbents are like movie sequels—always a letdown. They need to keep that fire in the belly."

"Must have been all that welding Shaw did. Kept his viscera hot."

"That and the fact that we managed to tie him to John Muir, Teddy Roosevelt, Lincoln, Jesus, and Spiderman."

"Not a bad team." Hugh considered. "Leaving out Peter the Great was a good move. No coattails on that guy."

They ordered their food, Hugh making clear he was paying.

"That trip sure had some coattails, though," Jess said. "Victor's going to Burma."

"Is that a step up? A better class of dictator?"

"I hear he'll have his own elephant."

"Whoa. Burmese for Rolls Royce, I guess."

"And Lola's retiring. Doesn't need to work after selling the blond hair she shaved off Shaw before the trip."

"Yeah? What did she get?"

"Nine-hundred thirty-two thousand on eBay."

"You're kidding! My god." Hugh thought. "He's got dandruff. Maybe I should start collecting it. In case my mutual funds never bounce back."

"So what do you think of Shaw's new hires?"

Hugh's right hand waggled in answer. "Danforth's okay. Never thought I'd have a hobo for a deputy, but the guy was in advertising so he knows how to sell." He sipped his water. "The Omaha woman, Shantala, in Commerce? A stretch, but I hear she interviewed well. Then there's Brandy." Hugh's eyes rolled. "Secretary of Health and Human Services? Give me a break! Someone's gotta talk him out of it. The woman's still working on her GED! What's on her resume?"

"School of life, I guess." Jess nervously swirled the ice in her glass. "And then there's Chuck."

Hugh stared at her. Thorne was taking a vacation as far as he knew. "What about him?"

Jess gave back the same baffled look. "I thought that's why we're here."

"We're here cause I invited you. What don't I know?"

"Shaw called me this morning. Chuck's retiring."

"You're kidding."

"He's been sitting on the fence. You knew that."

"Yeah, sure. But—"

"He's seventy-three. We pulled this one out. He's had enough. Who can blame him?"

Hugh looked dazed. He ran his fingers through his curls.

"Shaw wants me to take his place," said Jess. "And I said yes."

Hugh gaped. "Chief of staff?" He was stunned. Not that he wanted the job. If his wife thought he was too busy now, that promotion would be a death sentence for their marriage. But he wouldn't have minded being asked. Jealousy spread through him like dye.

"Wow. My god. What do you know about that." He blinked his eyes, trying to adjust to the news. "Congratulations. And why am I surprised? Cream rises. You're young, you've got great instincts, and you saved Shaw's life. There's a resume." He raised his glass her way again. "I had a feeling you'd go far."

"Maybe too far." Jess sighed. She looked troubled.

A couple took the booth behind Hugh. He leaned forward toward Jess and lowered his voice. "What's the problem?"

"We've created a monster, that's the problem." She gave a long exhale. "I rewrote his platform cause I thought it might sell. And it did. But c'mon. The rich looking out for the poor? Getting the corporations to stop heating up the planet? People canning their own food? Hiring the homeless? Mass transit so good that we'll give up owning cars? It's impossible. Obviously. You know that. I know that. But Shaw doesn't know it. And he wants me to make it happen."

Hugh saw her problem. "Kind of a tall order, I admit."

Their salads came. Hugh dug in.

"He knows football," Jess whispered. "And how to swing a golf club. Not how to bring the Kingdom of Heaven to earth. And guess what? Neither do I."

Hugh chewed. That Jess was in over her head was not a displeasing thought. This time, unlike last time, she couldn't possibly succeed. Meteorites burning up on their trip through the atmosphere made a pretty sight; her own downfall would make for excellent viewing. He felt suddenly better about the coming four years.

"Shaw's got faith in you and so do I," he said.

"That's the problem."

"You'll come up with something." Hugh speared a cucumber slice. "If there's anything I can do to help, just ask," he offered. "I mean it. Honestly."

**THE END**